MW00988003

THE FORGOTTEN FIVE

THE INVISIBLE SPY

Also by Lisa McMann

Clarice the Brave

The Forgotten Five Series

Map of Flames

The Unwanteds Series

The Unwanteds

Island of Silence

Island of Fire

Island of Legends

Island of Shipwrecks

Island of Graves

Island of Dragons

Going Wild Series

Going Wild

Predator vs. Prey

Clash of Beasts

The Unwanteds Quests

Dragon Captives

Dragon Bones

Dragon Ghosts

Dragon Curse

Dragon Fire

Dragon Slayers

Dragon Fury

The Visions Trilogy

Crash

Bang

Gasp

The Wake Trilogy

Wake

Fade

Gone

THE FORGOTTEN FIVE

THE INVISIBLE SPY

LISA McMANN

putnam

G. P. Putnam's Sons

G. P. PUTNAM'S SONS
An imprint of Penguin Random House LLC, New York

First published in the United States of America by G. P. Putnam's Sons,
an imprint of Penguin Random House LLC, 2022

Visit us online at penguinrandomhouse.com

Library of Congress Cataloging-in-Publication Data
Names: McMann, Lisa, author.
Title: The invisible spy / Lisa McMann.
Description: New York: G. P. Putnam's Sons, [2022] | Series: The forgotten five; book 2
Summary: "The Forgotten Five become spies to uncover the corrupt President's schemes and bring the world one step closer to justice for all supernaturals"—Provided by publisher.
Identifiers: LCCN 2022006912 (print) | LCCN 2022006913 (ebook)
ISBN 9780593325438 (hardcover) | ISBN 9780593325452 (epub)
Subjects: CYAC: Supernatural—Fiction. | Spies—Fiction. | Ability—Fiction. | LCGFT: Spy fiction. | Novels.
Classification: LCC PZ7.M478757 In 2022 (print) | LCC PZ7.M478757 (ebook) | DDC [Fic]—dc23
LC record available at https://lccn.loc.gov/2022006912
LC ebook record available at https://lccn.loc.gov/2022006913

Book manufactured in Canada

ISBN 9780593325438 (hardcover)
10 9 8 7 6 5 4 3 2 1

ISBN 9780593616055 (international edition)
10 9 8 7 6 5 4 3 2 1

FRI

Design by Cindy De la Cruz | Text set in Arno Pro

To teachers and librarians: Thank you for all you do for readers everywhere . . . and for me.

AN ANGRY MAN

President Daniel Fuerte sat at his cluttered desk in the presidential office on the top floor of the Magdalia Palace. The morning sunshine reflected off the gold frame of a recently stolen painting on the wall. The glare gave him a mild headache after the long night. His face was haggard and his jaw unshaven, but his shiny black hair edged with gray at his temples appeared freshly groomed. He'd dozed on the plane ride back from Estero's neighboring country, but he hadn't slept enough, and he was ready to retire to his room for a few hours. When his desk phone rang, he sighed and picked it up. "Fuerte."

A panicked voice greeted him. "Dad, I'm down in the dungeon. There's been a break-in overnight."

"What?" Fuerte's eyes widened. His daughter, Sabine, ran his secret Supernatural Locator and Recruitment Operation in the palace control room. She also managed the guards—and their captive, Elena Golden.

"The place is trashed, and they took Elena."

"*What*? No. She's *gone*?" Fuerte leaned back in his leather-and-mahogany chair, his jaw clenching and unclenching. He pumped his fist against his forehead a couple times, then slammed it on the desk. "How?" he demanded. "We've got guards everywhere! There's an iron fence surrounding us, for crying out loud!" He muttered some unsavory words under his breath.

"Security and staff are being questioned," Sabine went on. "After Elena was freed, they locked the on-duty officer inside the cell. He says it was done by . . . children. And something about a pig? I'm waiting to hear more about that."

Fuerte's face darkened. "Didn't you take care of those two kids the other night?"

Sabine hesitated. "Well, we tried. But the operation was interrupted in the wheat tunnel, and . . . we lost them. We thought we scared them off for good. Nobody knew they were capable of this."

"*I* knew." The president shook his head in disgust. "Find out if those two were working alone or if they had help. And figure out who they are and where they came from. Maybe we can . . ." He didn't finish the thought. "Never mind. I'll be right there." He set the phone down hard in its cradle and muttered an oath, then pressed both palms on the desk and stood up. He chugged the dregs of his coffee and grimaced at its lukewarm temperature. Then he grabbed his suit jacket and started for the elevator, slipping it on as he stepped inside. He straightened and tightened his necktie as the elevator descended.

The door opened onto the main floor, and he headed for the

door that led to the dungeon stairway. As he strode down the grand hall, lined with relics and priceless artifacts, he stopped short. A precious vase near the entrance to the dining room was missing. Had the intruders made off with that, too? Anger boiled up. But before he could process the implications of the theft, his cell phone rang. He pulled it from his pocket and studied the caller's information with narrowed eyes. It was his journalist contact, Emil Blanco at *Estero City News*. Had he heard about the break-in already? A mere two minutes after the president was informed? Whoever tipped off Emil would have to be fired immediately. He touched the screen to answer.

"Emil!" Fuerte exclaimed with fake enthusiasm. He wondered how much the journalist knew about the break-in. "What's making news today?"

"Supernatural people are, apparently. How are you, sir?"

"I'm fine." He hesitated, and his thick eyebrows met in concern. "What do you mean, supernatural people are making news?"

"I've received a tip," Emil said. "Apparently one of the supernatural criminals was picked up by the police about thirty minutes ago after being seen leaving the palace grounds. Are you aware of this?"

"I know nothing about it," said Fuerte, trying to sound shocked. It was a blatant lie. Jack and Greta Stone had just left the palace after returning from the overnight mission. "Which one was it?"

"Jack Stone."

The president closed his eyes briefly and let out a silent sigh. "Glad the police are keeping an eye out," he said lightly. But he knew he'd have to make a call to get Jack out of hot water.

"Any idea why he'd be hanging around the palace?" Emil asked.

"No, but it sounds alarming," said the president. "I have a meeting now, but let me know if you find out anything else." He hung up the phone and dialed another number.

"Commander Collazo speaking."

"It's Daniel."

"I know, sir," she said.

"Listen. You're going to release Jack Stone. The statute of limitations on his thefts fifteen years ago is almost up—just a couple of weeks away. And you've got no evidence he's done anything since then. Tell your department to let him go."

Commander Collazo sighed. "Just because the statute of limitations has nearly been reached doesn't mean my squad won't pick up people like him. You tightened the laws on supernatural people to an unbearable level—even for the ones who *haven't* done anything wrong. Jack Stone loitering around the palace before daylight is a crime merely because he's supernatural. You make the rules. I just enforce them."

Fuerte pinched the bridge of his nose, as if that would ease his growing headache. But then his eyes flew open as an idea came to him. "All right, fair enough. Let Jack go. I'll be making some changes to the law. Soon."

"It's not that easy," the commander insisted. "The people of Estero will hear about this, and they're not going to like it. You've spent years turning everyone against supernatural people. Now you're changing your policy? It's going to be tricky. You've . . . conditioned them to hate supers. And believe me, they do."

"Don't worry about it. Just do what I tell you, and we'll get along, like always. You like our arrangement, don't you, Commander?"

There was a long, heavy pause on the other end of the line.

"Commander Collazo?" the president prompted.

"Yes. All right," she said with finality. "I'll let him go."

The phone beeped in the president's ear. With a smug smile, he proceeded to the dungeon to see about the *other* mess.

A MOMENT OF CALM

Cabot Stone sat on the floor near The Librarian's biggest apartment window, using the early-morning light seeping between the curtains to see as she paged through a book from one of the stacks. The others were still asleep, wrapped in The Librarian's blankets or their own parachute ones, and using their backpacks as pillows. Elena Golden, enjoying her first night out of prison in three years, was curled up on the sofa with Brix. Birdie slept on the floor next to them.

The Librarian emerged from her bedroom, freshly dressed for the day in a casual khaki-colored jumpsuit and white sneakers. She held a pair of binoculars. She went to the window near Cabot and smiled warmly in a silent greeting, then put the binoculars to her eyes and peered out.

"What are you looking for?" Cabot whispered, her green eyes glinting. She flipped onto her knees and ran her fingers through her hair. Her white-blond buzz cut was starting to get annoyingly long—so long that it wanted to flop to one side. She wished she'd brought her homemade haircutting tool, but she hadn't thought to grab it in their haste to leave the hideout. Surely people here in Estero had something similar—The Librarian's hair was evidence of that. She'd be on the lookout.

"I'm looking for drones," said The Librarian. Her super-short coiled Afro shone where the sunlight hit it. "Also wondering if the president's guards or Estero police are milling around."

"What's a drone?"

"It's a mechanical flying device that contains a video camera, which can be used to spy on people. Some of them look like birds, insects, or toy airplanes."

Cabot's eyes bugged out at the description. *A video camera that looks like a bird?* She didn't fully understand how video worked, but her mind leaped to the problems and solutions it could create. Pro: easier to spy on others. Con: easier to be spied on.

The Librarian continued, "I'm concerned the palace will use everything they have to try to track us down. And if they do, it's my fault. I woke up in the middle of the night and realized I . . . well, I made a mistake. A big one."

Cabot's brow furrowed. The Librarian made mistakes? Cabot's impression that The Librarian was nearly perfect began crumbling. "What mistake?" she asked hesitantly, hoping it wasn't too bad.

Someone stirred on the floor nearby. The Librarian beckoned Cabot closer so she could talk more quietly. "I wiped all the palace workers' short-term memories, but I forgot about the dungeon security guard. And he saw some of the other kids. That means he can potentially identify them."

"Here's hoping for a concussion," said Lada wryly from the shadowy living room. She lay on her back and gingerly pulled one knee toward her chest in a stretch, grimacing as she did so. She was really sore after last night's activity.

The Librarian glanced at her and smiled grimly. "That's a possibility."

"Do they know where we are?" asked Cabot. "They couldn't have followed us."

"My mistake last night has me questioning all the other moves I've made recently. I'm starting to wonder if they've been tailing Lada and me, in addition to Tenner and Birdie. Probably not, because we've been extremely careful, but . . ." The Librarian put the binoculars down. "Out of an abundance of caution, we're not taking any chances." Her expression was stern, like she was disappointed with herself, which made Cabot empathize with her even more. The Librarian moved to the nearby desk and opened the lid of a small, thin computer. She entered a password, clicked the touch pad a few times, and started skimming the news headlines.

Cabot had crawled forward to watch the keystrokes. Fascinated, she memorized them—even The Librarian's password. Then she got up and peered over the woman's shoulder, trying to figure out how she was pulling up the various news pages and making the headlines scroll on the screen. Her eyes darted from The Librarian's fingertips tapping the keys and brushing the touch pad to the page on the screen refreshing to something totally different. "How do you know where the letters are without looking at them?" Cabot asked. "Do you have a photographic memory, too?"

The Librarian glanced up. "All keyboards are the same—just like the one on Lada's cell phone you were looking at yesterday. With practice, everyone can type without looking. It becomes automatic." She typed the words *learn how to type* in the search bar and selected a video from the results that came up. Then she told Cabot to fetch the small black case from her bedside table. Cabot located it, then took a moment to admire the crisp white comforter and colorful pillows on the bed, and the towering stack of books in the corner of the room. She returned and put the earbuds in, and The Librarian showed her how to pair them with the computer. Then The Librarian got up from the chair. "Have a seat, Cabot. Watch and listen to this video. Then play around with the keys and click on things. You'll figure it out."

Cabot pressed her pink lips together. "Thank you," she said fervently. She sat down, then startled when the video sound played in her ears. She pulled one earbud out to make sure it wasn't blasting through the room, because it seemed like it had to be. But all was silent in the apartment, just like the night before when they were all using the earpieces to communicate during the dungeon break-in. Cabot focused on the screen, then followed the tutorial, placing her fingers on the keys in the proper alignment.

"I'll be back in a few minutes," The Librarian said. Cabot nodded, mesmerized. The Librarian took the binoculars and her keys from the kitchen counter and left the apartment, closing the door softly behind her.

Others stirred. Seven got up and trudged to the bathroom.

Tenner awoke, feeling a new sense of purpose after their decision to stay in Estero. The Librarian and Lada were determined to end oppression of people like them, and he wanted to be part of it. As he blinked at the ceiling, thinking about his dead father, he couldn't help but feel a bit of relief that one of the worst criminals was out of the picture. Troy Cordoba had been a terrible dad, and an incredible asset to the criminals because of his X-ray vision. Him working with President Fuerte would have made the fight even harder for the good guys.

Tenner sat up and looked around at the people he was with. He realized he cared about them all, and they cared about him. It was comforting. He was glad they were all together again. He slithered out of his blanket and went to see what Cabot was doing with The Librarian's computer. Seven exited the bathroom and joined them, while Lada, who'd finished stretching and gotten to her feet, used her forearm crutches to make her way to the bathroom. Soon Birdie, Brix, and Elena were waking up, too.

All of them were anxious about what the day would hold. The

night before, they'd learned from Elena that President Fuerte had recruited the other living supernatural criminal parents to help him steal precious artifacts from other countries, and that he had a desire to meet more supernatural people—which seemed extremely odd based on how he'd been oppressing supers in Estero for years. They'd agreed to help fight against the oppression . . . and stop their awful parents from assisting the hate-filled leader.

As the kids moved about the tiny apartment, they had brief conversations. Would the palace break-in make it into the newspapers? Were they finally going to go after the hidden stash using the flaming map? Where were their parents living, and could they find them? How long would they stay in The Librarian's apartment . . . and was there anywhere else to go?

"It would be nice to be somewhere with more bathrooms," Birdie remarked, legs crossed as she waited her turn. Puerco, her tiny pig, snuffled and snorted near her feet, looking for something to eat. "Do you think we'll be able to move to a bigger place once we cash out the stash and the diamonds Troy stole?"

"A place with beds for everyone," Brix added, rubbing his sore neck.

"That would be my preference," said Elena. "Once we find the stash, we'll have plenty of money to fund our operation and give The Librarian her space back."

Cabot finished her typing lesson. Having fully memorized the keyboard, she put the earbuds in their case and returned them to The Librarian's bedside table. Then she turned her attention toward the others as Brix beat out Birdie in a race to the open bathroom.

"Sunrise Foster Home has available rooms and multiple bathrooms," Lada offered with a laugh.

Elena cringed. "I don't want to go back there."

"I won't be going back, either," said Lada.

"Good," Tenner said sharply. "The man running it seemed awful."

"He was," Birdie said, nodding vigorously. She remembered the threatening way he'd acted toward her when she'd peered in the window.

"LaDuca is the worst," Lada agreed, but she didn't seem to be overly bothered. "He hates me." She leaned on one of her forearm crutches to keep balance as she fluffed her light brown hair and smoothed down the flyaways. Then she started cleaning her glasses on her shirt. When she replaced them, she noticed one of the tools that had been specially retrofitted into her crutches was loose, so she clicked it securely into place.

"Won't they consider you missing and go to the police?" Elena asked.

"They can't tell the police about me," said Lada. "They're not supposed to be giving shelter to a supernatural person. They'll be relieved if I never return—it would make life a lot easier for them."

"And you're . . . not sad?" asked Brix. He tried to imagine

what it would be like if the people he lived with didn't like him. The thought made his chest hurt.

"No. I'm thrilled. I hope I never see that place again. With all of you here in Estero now, I feel kind of like my long-lost cousins came to adopt me." Her cheeks flooded with color.

Elena gave her an understanding smile. "I remember wanting something miraculous to happen to me when I lived there," she said. "Even though the staff was supportive of supers back then, I still wanted a regular, accepting family after mine dumped me there and told me never to come back." She'd never had anyone want to take her out of the foster home—none of the criminals had. Maybe her life would have turned out differently if that had been the case. "But Sunrise is where I met Louis, and I wouldn't trade that for anything. Still, let's hope this is a life-changing pivot for you, Lada."

Before anyone else could respond, they heard the key in the lock, and then the door flew open. The Librarian stepped inside and closed it behind her. She flipped the dead bolt. "There are palace security guards surrounding the building," she said, breathing hard. "Pack up everything you own. We need to run."

ON THE RUN

The group of children stared at The Librarian, trying to comprehend what she was saying. Then they sprang into action. They rolled up their blankets and put their belongings in their backpacks. Elena, who had nothing but the clothes she wore, went straight to the kitchen to see if there was anything useful worth taking with them. She found a cloth shopping bag and began to fill it with snacks, then added a box of matches and a couple of sharp knives . . . just in case.

"I'm loading up on toilet paper," Tenner announced, stuffing extra rolls from the bathroom into his bag. "This stuff is amazing."

The Librarian disappeared into her bedroom, quickly packed a bag of essentials, then returned to the living area and grabbed her binoculars as well as her computer and phone and the charging cords that went with them. Seven set Puerco gently inside his backpack while Lada stashed her crutches in their carrier bag and sat down in her wheelchair, then put her belongings on her lap. She wheeled herself to the kitchen, hoisted herself up to collect a water bottle from the cupboard, and filled it. Then she got one for Elena and The Librarian, too. Soon the other five children were filling their canteens. Lada wheeled over to the door, ready to go.

"How bad is it?" Birdie asked, breathless, as The Librarian put one eye to the peephole to check the hallway. "Are they inside the building? Coming after us?"

"No, the hallway is empty. They're outside, casing the place. I recognized one of the palace goons by the intersection in front of the building, and a few more at the corner—including the guy who was tailing Birdie and Tenner the other day after they went to the penitentiary. And there were two suspicious-looking people hanging around at the entrance of the parking garage, as well. I don't know how they found us here. Maybe they've got guards stationed throughout the city." She put her finger to her lips and quietly opened the door and peered out. "We're clear. But . . ." She glanced over her shoulder at Seven. "You have climbing gear, right?"

"Y-yes," said Seven cautiously.

Lada looked up in alarm. "Why do we need climbing gear? Do you think we'll have to climb out the window or something?" Unexpected situations caused anxiety—Lada was constantly faced with challenges others without disabilities wouldn't have to think about. *How will I . . . ? Where will I . . . ? What if . . . ?* It could make her muscles tighten up even more.

The Librarian had learned this about Lada. She put her hand

on Lada's shoulder to reassure her. "I'm just taking stock of our belongings. You can teleport out of here if anyone comes after us. Or—"

"But where are we going?" asked Lada. "To the library?"

The Librarian frowned. "I don't want to endanger anyone there. We might have to leave Estero. At least for a short time until they take their focus off us." She looked pained, as if realizing what a logistical nightmare it would be to flee the country with a car full of super kids. "I don't know where else to hide eight people." Then she turned sharply to Elena. "You're not tethered, too, are you?"

"No," Elena said. "I never left Fuerte's prison once he got ahold of me, so there was no need."

Cabot nudged Seven. "What about the lower tunnels?"

"The what?" Lada looked curiously at them.

Seven shifted his backpack as Puerco moved around inside it. "The ancient underground tunnels."

"Underground?" Lada asked. "You mean aboveground? The ones with etchings outside the doors? People travel through them all the time. They wouldn't be good hiding places."

"No," said Cabot. "We know about those. But there are some underground, too."

"But we don't know where any entrances are," Birdie said. "My dad wrote about the lower tunnels in his journal. He found one entrance right before they left Estero, but he didn't say where it was." She looked suspiciously at Cabot. "Or did you snoop for that information, too?"

Cabot raised a disdainful eyebrow.

"Well, we *did* find out where an entrance is," Seven admitted. He glanced at Elena, who was nodding as if she remembered Louis telling her about it. "We brought all of Louis's journals with us. You can have them if you'd like them, Elena."

Elena smiled warmly, and her eyes shone. "I would. Thank you."

"And yes, Birdie," said Cabot, now that Seven had admitted to snooping. "I looked again because clearly I *have* to now. But Brix and Seven were there when I found it. It was after you and Tenner left."

"As if that makes it okay," Birdie muttered. But it was true Cabot's hurried research before coming to Estero had given them more clues than what Birdie and Tenner had found. She flashed Cabot a reluctant grin. "I guess it's a good thing this time."

The Librarian remained paused with her hand on the doorknob. "I've heard rumors of the lower tunnels but have never been able to find any details about the entrance locations," she said, her interest piqued. "I searched all the books I could find." She opened the door again and glanced around the hallway uneasily. "Which is good for us, because if *I* can't find information about those entrances, it doesn't exist for the general public."

"The one my dad found is in the park," Brix offered.

"Don't say any more," The Librarian whispered, then waved everyone outside into the hallway.

"Do you think your apartment is bugged?" Elena asked, her voice barely audible.

The Librarian closed the door and locked it before speaking normally. "I don't think so. We've been a step ahead of Fuerte's thugs the whole time. But I'm being extra cautious." She peered out the window at the end of the hallway. "Hmm. More guards on the next block. So they're not just surrounding our building. I'm sure they hope to find Elena, if not catch the ones who broke into the palace and freed her." She shared her mistake of not wiping the dungeon guard's memory and explained that by now, everyone on palace detail might have descriptions of a few of them, like Lada and Brix, who'd interacted the most with the guard. "Let's travel in smaller groups so we'll be less obvious. Lada, how does taking the service elevator sound? Bring one other person with you. Go out the exit into the back alley. I doubt they'll have any guards stationed there—the ones I've seen so far are on the major street corners."

"Got it," said Lada.

The Librarian continued, "The rest of us will split up and take the two different stairwells to the ground floor so we go out through opposite side-street exits. We'll meet at the park across from Sunrise. Make sure you're with someone who knows how to get there."

"I can find it," Cabot said. She had the map memorized.

"I know how to get there, too," said Birdie, and Tenner nodded.

"As do I," said Elena.

"And me," Lada said. Her eyes narrowed, as if she was calculating who she wanted on her team. "Seven, will you come with me?"

Seven shifted uneasily. "What if someone sees me? Shouldn't I be hiding in a group?" It was broad daylight, and he was a camo boy. He had his scarf wrapped around his camouflaged face and his gloves and sunglasses on. Anyone looking for someone unusual would notice his strange attire.

"Trust me," Lada said wryly, "if you're pushing me in a wheelchair, I guarantee most people will be glancing side-eyed at me, not studying you. It's the perfect way to get you out of here safely."

"We don't want them looking at you if the security guard gave them your description," Seven reminded her.

"The guard would have described me as using crutches. I'll be in my wheelchair. We'll be totally fine—I'm not worried. Maybe you can wear The Librarian's sun hat, too." She looked up at the woman.

"Clever," The Librarian said. "I like it." She unlocked the apartment door and went inside. A moment later she emerged carrying a straw hat with a wide, floppy brim and an orange ribbon around the crown. She handed it to Seven, and he put it on his head and pulled the brim down so it shaded his face. "Perfect," she said. "You two can get moving while we sort out our groups."

Seven and Lada went to the service elevator. Brix clung to Elena, not wanting to let her out of his sight after having lost her for three years, and he tugged at Birdie to come with them. Cabot moved toward The Librarian, leaving Tenner shifting uncomfortably in the hallway, not sure which group he was supposed to go with. Would he be intruding on Birdie and Brix's time with their mom? And he was still a little bit intimidated by The Librarian. Plus, he'd been feeling out of sorts since he'd learned of his dad's death. It was hard to make a decision.

Birdie looked at Tenner, then shook her hand loose from Brix's grasp. She'd become used to having Tenner with her all the time now. "Come with me, T," she said, more kindly than she'd ever said anything back home when he'd been acting uncertain about his place in the group. "You and I will stick together like usual." She'd recognized his old familiar hesitation and self-consciousness resurfacing. Instead of being annoyed by it, which would make him feel even less sure of himself, she realized she could help him through it.

"Yes, you two should be a team," said The Librarian. "I want Brix with me in case his bouncing gives us trouble. And Elena because she's the most recognizable. And Cabot, in case we need to think fast."

Cabot beamed from her spot next to The Librarian.

Tenner flashed Birdie a grateful smile. Now that everyone was together again, he'd been worried that Birdie would resume treating him with annoyance, like she'd sometimes done at the hideout. But she'd changed. And so had he. "I know a good route," he offered.

"Lead the way," Birdie said.

THE THREE TEAMS made it to the ground floor and went their separate ways. Lada directed Seven through alleys and down quiet streets to avoid the president's people as much as possible, and they reached the park first. They settled out of sight near the tree Seven had first hidden behind when he, Cabot, and Brix had confronted Birdie and Tenner. While Lada kept a lookout through the bushes from her wheelchair, Seven let Puerco out of his backpack to get a drink at the fountain and root around in the grass for snacks.

Birdie and Tenner arrived next, and the raven that Birdie had befriended during her time in Estero landed on a tree branch overhead. "No one is following us," Tenner reported as he swept his gaze through the neighborhood before slipping into the shady, sheltered area where Lada, Seven, and Puerco had settled. "I saw a security vehicle like the ones in the palace garage last night. But we hid behind a car until it went past. Two guards in the front seat were looking up and down the street like they were searching for us."

"We were super stealthy," Birdie said. "Even crawled on our hands and knees." Her bare knees had grass stains on them. The red dress with white dots, which had once been her mother's, was sticking to the sweat on her back in the warm morning. "I wonder where the others are."

"I hope they're okay," Lada said quietly.

Tenner squinted and aimed his extra-large pupils down the street. "I think . . . they're . . . coming?" He didn't seem sure. "I can see Cabot and The Librarian, anyway. And they're pulling something big and green."

"Pulling something?" Birdie joined him and peered around some branches to look, too. After a few moments, The Librarian and Cabot came into view for Birdie, who had average eyesight. When she didn't see her mother or Brix, her heart began to pound. "Did they split up? What the heck is that big green thing for?"

"What's going on?" Lada muttered, unable to see anything. Most of the time she found it charming that the newcomers didn't know what ordinary things were, but under these tense circumstances, it was more stressful than quaint. She twisted to remove her crutches from the pouch behind her back, then locked the wheelchair wheels in place and carefully maneuvered to the edge of the seat. With a steadying breath, she planted the crutches firmly and pulled herself up to her feet. Once she had her balance, she joined the others, staying mostly hidden behind Birdie. She could hear a familiar rattling sound . . . like a large receptacle on wheels being pulled to the curb on collection day. Lada stared, then adjusted her glasses. "That, my friends, is a yard waste recycling bin."

"Where are my mother and brother?" Birdie asked. She clutched and unclutched her dress.

"I mean, I can guess," Lada said with a slow smile spreading on her face. But she didn't offer the guess.

The Librarian and Cabot acted like they didn't see the others. When they drew near, the two glanced in all directions, making sure no one was tailing them.

"The nearest guard is two blocks that way," Tenner murmured to them, pointing. He went to help pull the bin out of sight behind the trees, next to Lada's empty wheelchair. "Were you followed? Are the others still coming? Or . . ." He looked at the bin.

After The Librarian took one last cautious look around, she opened the lid. "Okay, you two," she said into the container. Sweat shone on her bare, muscular arms from the effort. "We made it."

Elena and Brix stood up straight. Brix wrinkled his nose. "It was a fun ride," he said. "But a little smelly and hot. And I've had a stick poking into my right butt cheek for ten minutes." He rubbed the sore spot.

"We had to dodge guards a few times," The Librarian

explained to the others. "I knew they'd recognize Elena if they saw her. And I was worried they'd be suspicious about Brix with his bounce, since the guard saw him bouncing everywhere last night. So we snagged this from in front of a house. Cabot's great idea."

Cabot shrugged. Her cheeks were red from exertion after pulling the container so far, and they grew a little redder from the praise. As Brix climbed out, Cabot glanced over her shoulder, past the foster home, to a small sign that had caught her eye. It had her name on it: CABOT INDUSTRIAL SERVICES. Birdie had told her about it at the library and had mentioned she'd gone inside and found it empty except for some workstations and equipment. The name was probably a coincidence.

"Nobody stopped to ask why you were pulling the bin down the sidewalk?" asked Birdie, helping her mom out once Brix was on the ground.

"Nobody gave us a second glance," said The Librarian. "You wouldn't believe the weird stuff people do in broad daylight around here."

Elena motioned for everyone to follow, and she guided them deeper into the thick trees. "Man, everything is so overgrown compared to how I remember it. Your dad and I used to come here after dark and kiss."

"Gross!" Brix exclaimed.

"Mom!" said Birdie, turning bright red.

"Slick move," Seven said appreciatively.

Tenner laughed nervously and exchanged shrugs with Lada, while Cabot charged forward, annoyed and wanting to get on with the task.

Unabashed, Elena parted the branches and stepped carefully into the overgrowth. "Watch your step here. It's somewhere in this area," she said. At Lada's request, Seven folded the wheelchair and hoisted it up, giving it to Birdie to carry. Then Tenner assisted Lada in navigating the uneven terrain. The rest followed and spread out, searching the ground.

"What are we looking for, exactly?" Birdie asked. She balanced the folded wheelchair against a tree and kicked at a root, then winced in pain. Her mom's old sneakers, fastened with paper clips, were worn thin.

Seven stopped to pull out Louis's journal with the drawing. "There should be a door in the ground," he said as he opened the journal and searched for the entry.

Cabot nodded. "Hopefully one that hasn't been opened in fifteen years."

THE ANCIENT LOWER TUNNELS

"According to Louis's sketch," Seven said as he passed the journal around so all could see, "the door is in a level area between two groups of large trees." He located a space that looked like Louis's drawing. "This appears to be the spot, only the trees seem bigger and the ground is much more overgrown. But that makes sense because it's been fifteen years since Louis was here." As he spoke, he took a grappling hook from his backpack and used it to dig. After sinking the sharp point into the earth in several different places, he heard a muted clinking noise. "There's something under here," he said in a low voice, and sent the hook into the ground again, producing the same *clink*, as if it had struck stone.

Birdie knelt next to him, and the raven took to the trees overhead and cawed. Birdie glanced up as the bird sent a protective message to her. "It's keeping watch," she told the others. Once Seven loosened a section of earth, Birdie helped pull back a layer of sod. Puerco grunted and bounded over to snuffle through the loose dirt.

Seven continued striking the ground with the grappling hook, moving methodically in a large square. They heard repeated clunking sounds of the hook hitting something hard beneath the moss. "I'm sure this is it," he said, glancing down at the journal, then squinting to eyeball the distance to the surrounding trees. He sat back on his haunches, breathing hard from exertion. Birdie, Tenner, Cabot, and Brix started raking the clods out of the way with their fingers.

"I wonder what ancient doors are made of," Cabot murmured, wiping her dirty hands on her parachute pants.

"This probably isn't the original door from thousands of years ago," The Librarian said. "From my studies, the lower tunnels were used regularly as recently as two hundred years ago, so improvements would have been made over time."

Birdie dug her hands into the tilled earth and swept it aside, then started feeling around, looking for something to grab on to. She cleared a spot and rapped on the ground. "It might be solid stone."

"Heavy, if true," Lada said skeptically. "Too heavy to be useful."

"A thin slice of slate wouldn't be too heavy," said Cabot. "And it would make more sense than wood, which would rot." Seven stood back to wipe the sweat off his brow and let the others clear the remaining dirt and moss.

"Here!" said Brix, whose hands were plunged in deep. "I found something." He started tugging. "It feels like a metal ring." He stood up for leverage and pulled. Silt danced on the door, but it didn't open.

"Keep digging, everyone," said Birdie. "We need to clear the corners."

Soon they had scraped off the entire square trapdoor. Seven tried pulling the ring, and this time, the door lifted a few inches. "It's pretty heavy," he said. Tenner came to help him, and the two wrested the door from the earth's grip until it creaked and stood upright on its own.

A blast of stale air whooshed out. Birdie and Cabot wrinkled their noses, then leaned over the hole and peered into the darkness. "I can't see anything," Birdie said.

Tenner, who actually *could* see in the dark, tried to get a view between the girls. He cleared his throat. "Maybe I could have a look?"

"Oh," said Birdie. She caught his eye and gave him an embarrassed smile. "I mean, if you really think you've got something over *us*." She and Cabot slid aside.

Tenner leaned over the hole in the ground. "There's a ladder," he said as his eyes adjusted. "Hard-packed dirt walls and floor. And I can hear water running."

The Librarian rummaged around in her bag and pulled out her phone, then turned on the flashlight. She shined it into the hole, illuminating an iron ladder with unevenly spaced rungs going down. She aimed the light at the bottom, revealing the smooth floor of the tunnel. There were unlit lanterns attached to the walls. A clay trough ran the length of the tunnel wall.

Lada leaned forward on her forearm crutches and peered down. "Great," she said, eyeing the ladder. A fresh knot of anxiety grew in the pit of her stomach. "I've been wondering how this part was going to work. Will my chair even fit through the door?" She frowned as she measured the opening with her eyes.

Birdie hefted the folded wheelchair from where she'd set it against the tree trunk and held it above the square hole in the ground. She turned it diagonally and dipped it in. It barely cleared.

"Thanks," Lada said. "That fixes one issue. But there's still the getting-Lada-down-there part that I've got to figure out." She was constantly on high alert, calculating how she would need to adapt.

"Can you teleport?" asked Brix.

"I *can,*" said Lada. "But what fun is that?"

"Everything seems fun about teleporting," said Brix.

"It's lonely," said Lada. "I like to go places *with* people, not by myself." She clenched and unclenched her fists, testing how strong her hands were feeling. "Go ahead, everyone," she said. "I think I can do this."

Tenner started down the ladder. "Sixteen rungs," he called up. Brix went next, skipping the rungs completely and bouncing at the bottom. Then Birdie, Elena, and Cabot climbed down.

"I'll go last," Seven said to The Librarian and Lada, "so I can close the door."

Lada turned to The Librarian. "You go before me and take the chair from Seven. Then stay at the bottom and catch me if I fall."

"Got it." The woman descended partway. Seven grunted as he lowered the folded wheelchair through the opening, tilting it to fit. The Librarian took it and continued down. She returned for Lada's crutches, then waited at the bottom.

Lada looked at Seven. "I'll need the most help getting safely onto the ladder. Once I'm there, I think I can go down it all right. So if you can help me stabilize at the top, I should be able to do the rest alone. My arms are strong, but my hands are always a little stiff, so my grip sometimes gives out." She looked up, trying to see through Seven's amber-tinted sunglasses. "You should see me rule the monkey bars, though."

"I'll bet." Seven smiled through his scarf. He would ask her what monkey bars were later, though he could guess. "Whenever you're ready," he said. He held his gloved hands out.

Lada instructed him on how she planned to move and what she needed him to do. Soon she was gripping the ladder and cautiously descending, concentrating to control the constant movement in her legs and adjust her foot placement. Sometimes it felt like her brain spoke a language that her other body parts didn't understand, so getting her mind and her feet to communicate successfully with each other was a challenge.

When she was almost at the bottom, Seven collected Puerco into his backpack and climbed down a couple of rungs. He remembered the raven and looked up. "You coming?"

The raven stayed in the tree.

"I don't blame you," said Seven. "Underground is no place for a bird." He found another ring on the inside of the heavy door and pulled it, easing the door closed behind him until it clicked into place with a dull thud. He could only hope no one else would decide to brave the mosquito-infested overgrowth and stumble over their dig site.

In the tunnel, Elena used the matches she'd brought to light the lanterns. They moved about cautiously to take in their surroundings. The air was pleasantly cool and unspoiled by the city pollution, but the earthy smell was musty and stale. Despite the low ceiling, they could all stand up straight with a few feet of clearance overhead. The floor of the tunnel was hard, flat, and smooth, so the wheelchair could move along it without too much effort. Lada sank into the chair, her muscles aching and contracting involuntarily from the ladder exertion.

Seven let Puerco out again to roam, and they all heard some sort of critter scurrying away. Birdie shuddered. She tried to talk to it through her mind but got no response. "Bats?" she wondered aloud. "Or a rat." She shuddered.

"Let's pretend that wasn't a rat," The Librarian said firmly.

"I'm sure whatever it was, it's more scared of us than we are of it."

"This is where the water sound is coming from," Tenner said, kneeling by the clay trough that ran the length of the tunnel for as far as he could see. The trough was about a foot wide, built into the floor where it met the wall. It looked like it had once been painted or decorated, but most of the design had faded to an earthy brownish gray now. A stream of clear water ran through it, deep enough to be able to fill their canteens. "This is amazing," Tenner said. "How did they do this?"

"Whoever built these tunnels put a lot of thought into them," said The Librarian. "Either the ground is at a slight incline, or the trough is angled to allow the water to flow downhill."

Cabot's mind whirled, thinking about inclines and gravity. She was envious of whoever had had the idea to incorporate a water source into the intricate underground maze. It could allow people to live for days or weeks down here without having to surface. Had they ever used the space for that purpose, perhaps during war? She went to the water trough and used her hand to measure the depth of it. Then she ran up the tunnel and measured there, too. "It's too close to tell," she called back to the group.

"If it helps," Lada said, "my chair is gently nudging me backward, toward the ladder, which is the same direction the water is running."

"Maybe it's a combination of the two," Cabot mused, measuring again. If these tunnels went on for miles under the city, how tall would the trough have to be to keep the water moving? If the floors were slanted too, that would mean the trough's incline wouldn't have to be as big.

"I've got a book on aqueducts at the library," said The Librarian. "Next time I venture out, I'll pick it up for you if it's safe for me to sneak in there. I need to stop by, anyway, to get a few of my personal belongings."

Lada looked sharply at the woman. "Don't you have to work today?"

"I was scheduled to," The Librarian said. She pressed her lips together. "But I'm afraid it's not safe for me to be there, at least for a while. I called in to let them know."

"Oh," said Lada, looking troubled. "But how . . ."

"Don't worry," The Librarian said, as if she knew her concern. "I have a little savings left that we can use for food."

Lada turned to explain to the others. "The Librarian used most of her savings to design and add tools to my crutches, in preparation for me having to do some . . . *interesting* work. So money has been tight, as I have none, and I'm assuming you all don't have any, either."

"Don't forget we have the thirteen diamonds to sell," Cabot said. "You still have them, don't you, Librarian?" The night before, Cabot had given her the precious stones that she, Brix, and Seven had found inside the skeleton's backpack on their journey to Estero. They'd figured out that the skeleton had to be Tenner's dad, Troy Cordoba, since he'd been the one hiding the diamonds.

"I have the pouch," The Librarian assured her. "Is everyone all right with me selling them? That should provide enough money for me to get some urgent supplies and to keep us afloat for a while. At least until we can get to the stash."

"Where are you going to sell them?" Elena asked, concerned. "I don't think it's safe to bring them to a local jewelry store. They'd be suspicious. The diamonds are large and recognizable—they were chosen for Sabine Fuerte, the president's daughter. He wanted them for her future wedding, even though she was still in school back then. We lifted them from the biggest jewelry shop in Old Town before Fuerte could pick them up. The jewelers wouldn't have forgotten what they look like, even this many years later. I'm sure they alerted the other shops in Estero, too. It was big news."

"Don't worry," The Librarian said, brushing off her concerns. "I won't be visiting any jewelry stores."

"More mysterious sources?" Birdie said, raising an eyebrow.

The Librarian gave a secretive smile. "Let's just say one can meet a lot of interesting people at the library."

FINDING THEIR WAY

The group of eight ventured deeper into the lower tunnels. Soon they came upon a chamber that would serve well as a temporary camp. It was small enough to feel cozy, yet large enough for them to each have space to spread out. And it wasn't far from the tunnel exit. Ancient-looking oil lanterns hung on the uneven rock walls, which appeared as though they'd been chiseled by hand. Elena lit a few, finding most still held oil. There was nothing else inside the cavern—not a single gem, jewel, or sign of treasure, which, according to Louis Golden, was what the ancient tunnels were once known to hold in centuries past. The place had been cleaned out.

The Librarian set down her things. "Okay," she said briskly. "Home sweet home. It might not be much to look at, but we're safe down here." She unpacked a few things, then took her phone, wallet, and the pouch of diamonds. "I'm going to do some errands while you explore. Seven, may I please borrow your disguise?"

"Sure," said Seven, happy to be removing his various coverings. "Be careful out there."

"I won't be gone long." The Librarian retrieved the floppy hat and took Seven's sunglasses, too.

Once the six children were unpacked, they lifted one of the lit lanterns from its hook on the wall and left Elena to rest and have a private look at Louis's journals. The kids set off down the main tunnel, which had the water trough running along it and was wider than the ones that branched off it. They began looking for other exits. Whenever they strayed from the main tunnel, they were careful to note which way they were turning so they could find their way back in the maze. But they didn't have to worry too much about getting lost, because Cabot was memorizing their journey.

Most of the tunnels were wide enough to fit a few children comfortably side by side. Lada, who knew the city best and had at least a faint idea of what part of it was above them, wheeled herself between Tenner and Birdie, who held the lantern. Seven, Brix, and Cabot followed with a second lantern.

They peered into other small chambers similar to the one they'd settled in and checked the floor for anything that might sparkle in the light, but there were no forgotten treasures in those, either. "I figured there wouldn't be giant piles of gold coins, or anything major like that," Seven said, mildly disappointed, "but it would be cool to find *something* that was left behind."

They arrived at an intersection. The hallway to the left was narrow, and it came to a dead end. "There's a ladder disappearing into a hole in the ceiling," Tenner said, spying it in the darkness. He ran ahead, and the others followed swiftly. They looked up—*way* up, for the surface of the ground was apparently much farther above them here than at the other entrance, though the ceiling height in the tunnel had remained the same. At the top of the ladder was a door similar to the one they'd come through, only this one was rectangular in shape instead of square.

"Shall we try it?" Lada asked.

"It depends," said Birdie, tapping her lips. "Where do you suppose we are? I don't want it to open up near the police station or right under the noses of guards who are looking for us."

"I know we're going in the direction of the library," said Lada. "Have we traveled that far, though, Cabot? It's about half a mile from the park." She frowned, thinking. "If we're short of that, we might be beneath the old national cemetery, where all the soldiers from a big war three hundred years ago are buried."

Cabot narrowed her eyes and glanced back the way they had come as she calculated the distance they'd traveled. "I don't think we've gone half a mile," she said.

"I bet the door has been covered up by something, like the one we went through," Seven mused. "They all must, or people would know about them and use them." He went up the ladder and squinted at the door. It was speckled stone, stained with age and water that had seeped through. Tentatively, he pushed on it. It didn't budge. He went up another step and bent forward so that his shoulder pressed against the door. He took a deep breath and put his weight into it. This time it shifted slightly. Silt rained down, and they quickly covered or closed their eyes to protect them. Seven glanced down at the others. "If I really put my back into it, and if someone comes up here to help, maybe we can get it open. I'm game to risk it."

Cabot piped up. "I say we do it. A cemetery seems safe. I doubt anyone will be around grieving people who've been dead three hundred years."

Lada shrugged. "We might scare a jogger or two, but I'm okay with that."

"Let's get to it," Birdie said agreeably.

Tenner, who was tallest, carefully climbed the ladder and stood on the rung below Seven. While Seven used his shoulder, Tenner put his hands on the door. On the count of three, they both pushed as hard as they could.

One corner of the stone door rose, sending more dirt raining down. "Push!" Seven directed, and they went at it again. Sunlight streamed in, and the stuck parts cracked and gave way. The door creaked open and came to a rest standing straight up, like the first door had done, as if hinges stopped it from thudding to the ground. Seven shook the dirt out of his hair to keep his head from being visible, then proceeded up the last few rungs and looked around. "Holy expletive," he said, his voice hushed but excited. "It's a cemetery, all right. And this door is a fake headstone."

EXPLORATION UNDERGROUND

Is it safe for me to have a look?" Tenner asked. He and Seven awkwardly traded places at the top of the ladder. As Seven descended, Tenner poked his head out of the opening. They were in a section of the cemetery where all the grave markers were flat gray stones, flush with the ground. The one they'd lifted was larger than the others around it, but it blended in.

In the distance Tenner could see an area where the gravestones were tall and grand. In another direction was a street. Across it, he recognized the monastery—the church-like building marked on the map of flames where he and Birdie had stopped to listen to the bells ringing. That building, plus a number of others and lots of huge old shade trees, made up a whole compound that was surrounded by a high wall. Tenner and Birdie had walked all the way around it, noting the etched designs marking entrances to a couple of the upper tunnels.

Tenner's eyes landed on the people outside the monastery wall. Men and women in black suits stood alert at the corners of the intersection near the gated entrance. Tenner narrowed his gaze and focused on them, trying to make out their features so he could recognize them in the future. The guards peered down different streets, looking for *them*. It made Tenner's chest tighten. How long would the president's people keep up the search? After what they'd done, he didn't think they'd give up easily.

Tenner blew out a breath to steady his anxiety, then stepped down a rung and took a closer look at the underside of the gravestone trapdoor. The stone was only about an inch thick and was reinforced with iron, perhaps to keep the stone from cracking and the door from breaking into pieces. No wonder they'd been able to lift it. He noticed a handhold carved into the stone along one of the non-hinged edges, which must be the spot to grab if you were on the outside trying to open it.

He heard a faint clip-clopping noise and turned sharply. Entering the cemetery far away were some police on horseback, like the ones he and Birdie had seen in the park. He ducked into the tunnel and quickly pulled the stone door closed, trying to soften its landing so it wouldn't make noise and so the old hinges wouldn't break. "We're across the street from the monastery," Tenner told the others. "There are guards standing on the corners looking for us, and I just saw some police on horseback starting to search the cemetery."

That sobered the mood. Tenner went down the extra-long ladder and joined the rest of them.

"I hope The Librarian is okay out there," Lada said as she

turned her wheelchair around and started back toward the main tunnel. She sounded worried. "I'm sure she's fine. She's probably back by now—she said she wouldn't be gone long."

"So . . ." Cabot said, thinking aloud about something else entirely. "If these lower tunnels are thousands of years old, and the cemetery up there is hundreds of years old, that means someone intentionally disguised this entrance to the tunnels when they decided to put a cemetery up there."

"Sneaky," said Brix. He bounded through the passage and ran up the wall, then slapped the ceiling and bounced down to the floor. "Hey, wait," he said, stopping. "So there are dead bodies right above us? That's creepy. Like all those bones we found."

Tenner recoiled.

Birdie shot Brix a look, and his face fell. "Sorry, everyone," he said, glancing at Tenner. Those bones probably belonged to dead parents.

Tenner reached back to pat Brix's shoulder. "It's okay. We're deep enough that the caskets won't fall through the ceiling. That's why the ladder went up into the ceiling for a ways—there's no grave in that space."

"I think the ceiling must've been reinforced back when they formed the tunnels," Cabot said, rapping on the hard wall with her knuckles. "Otherwise they would have all caved in by now."

They turned down the main hallway in the direction of the monastery to continue exploring and eventually came upon a third ladder leading to a door that seemed like it could be somewhere below the monastery compound. But, try as they might, this one wouldn't budge.

"There's probably an entire church built on top of this door," Seven grumbled as he came down the ladder with a sore shoulder from trying to open it. They continued on, never straying far from the main tunnel so they wouldn't get lost.

"Hey," said Lada, rolling to a stop. "I totally forgot I have GPS. We'll be able to tell exactly where we are. Why didn't I think of that before?" She took out her phone, leaving the five wondering what GPS was. Swiftly she tapped her phone screen with her thumbs as Cabot migrated over to watch the keystrokes. "Nothing's working. There's no signal down here." Lada sounded disappointed. She looked up at the quizzical, lamplit faces and explained what she was doing, and why it didn't work. "The signal towers are aboveground, and they might not penetrate all the way down here."

After discovering one more ladder leading to another unopenable door, they stopped to refill their canteens in the trough, then headed back to the stone chamber. During their absence Elena had gathered two more lanterns and hooked them to the wall to light the room, making it look much more inviting. She'd set out the snacks she'd taken from The Librarian's cupboards, and when the kids returned, Elena was sitting on the floor near a lantern, reading one of the journals. Puerco sat on her lap, munching on a cracker.

"Where's The Librarian?" Lada asked as she rolled into the chamber.

"Not back yet," said Elena. "I'm starting to worry. Can you text her? Or call?"

"Not from down here," Lada told her. "No service. I'm worried, too." She gripped her armrests and frowned. "I'm going aboveground to get a cell signal."

"I'll go with you," said Birdie.

"Me too," said Cabot.

"I want to go!" Brix said.

Elena shook her head. "No, you're too recognizable and suspiciously bouncy. Girls, stay hidden in the trees, please."

"Yes, be careful," Tenner said, sort of wanting to go with them but eyeing the crackers and other snacks Elena had set out. "Can you open the door?" Seven had already settled in and started eating.

"I'm sure I can manage," Birdie said.

The three girls set off down the hallway. "I'll teleport this time," Lada said when they reached the ladder. Her muscles would be sore enough that night without wrestling with the ladder again.

While Birdie and Cabot started up, Lada pulled her forearm crutches from the bag behind her and got out of the wheelchair. Before the other two could get the trapdoor open, Lada was gone.

Outside the trapdoor, Lada planted her crutches on the

uneven ground, trying to stabilize so she wouldn't fall. She pulled her cell phone out as Birdie and Cabot joined her. While they peered between the trees to see if The Librarian was anywhere nearby, Lada texted her: **Are you coming back soon? I'm starting to worry.**

"There are two security people coming up the sidewalk," Cabot reported. "They're checking out the park, but not coming into it."

Birdie scanned the area, then ventured a little farther, trying to see around the other group of trees where the yard waste recycling bin still stood. When the two security guards were out of sight, Birdie crept forward.

"Your mom said to stay hidden," Cabot said worriedly. She took a step toward Birdie.

"I can't see anything from back there," Birdie replied. "I'm just going to these other trees over here. So technically . . ." The raven hopped to a branch above her, then soared down in an arc and landed on Birdie's shoulder. "Hello, Raven," Birdie said, pleased the bird had continued to stay nearby. In her mind, Birdie asked, *Can you find The Librarian?*

The raven flitted to a low-hanging branch and moved with it as it bounced. It had known where the library was, but recognizing individuals seemed much more complicated than identifying a place that had an awesome bird feeder. Plus the raven hadn't had any direct interaction with The Librarian yet and probably didn't know how to identify human names, other than maybe Tenner by now, since Birdie had called him that a number of times in front of the raven. But maybe it knew.

The bird hopped to the ground, pecked at the grass, then moved to a tree closer to the street.

Birdie followed stealthily, repeating her request. While she waited for the raven to continue, a different familiar animal spoke in her mind. She closed her eyes and concentrated but couldn't recognize its voice. Was it one of the Rottweilers from the palace last night? She turned her head slowly, trying to determine which direction it was coming from. As she did so, she took a few more steps into the grassy part of the park and looked up as the raven moved again, this time to the sidewalk. It turned its head to look back.

Then came a faint clip-clopping sound. While Birdie focused on it, Cabot and Lada tuned it out as ordinary city noise. Lada checked her phone.

"Any response?" Cabot asked her.

"No. I'm going to call." Lada put the phone to her ear while Cabot watched anxiously. One part of her mind raced, trying to understand how telephones worked. The other part focused on Lada's expression, which was growing more concerned. After a long moment, Lada lowered the phone. "No answer. It went to voicemail."

"Voice . . . mail?" Cabot asked.

"Yes. You can leave a voice message for the person you call if they don't answer. They can listen to it later."

"Unbelievable," Cabot murmured. "Why didn't you leave a message?"

"Because she'll get a notification that I tried calling—" Lada stopped abruptly as Birdie darted out toward the sidewalk. "Birdie!" she whispered harshly. "Get back here!"

The clip-clopping grew louder. The raven flew across the street and looked back, as if beckoning Birdie to follow. All of a sudden, three police officers on huge brown horses emerged from the sidewalk behind the trees, just feet away from where Birdie was hiding.

Birdie stopped in her tracks, aware now of who she was communicating with—it was the police horse she'd talked to before, back when she and Tenner had seen Lada for the first time outside the foster home. Torn, she looked from the horse to the raven across the street.

"Birdie!" Cabot whispered. But the older girl was too far away to hear.

An officer turned sharply to look at Birdie. "Hey, it's the girl who puked in my car," he said to the others.

"Birdie?" said another officer. She narrowed her eyes and lifted the brim of her hat.

Birdie froze, then slowly looked up. It was Commander Collazo.

REBEL MONKS

Birdie stared up at the commander on her horse as the raven returned and landed on her shoulder again. Commander Collazo stared harder. Birdie panicked and shooed the bird off her as she tried to decide how to escape. If she ran back to the trees by Cabot and Lada, she'd lead the police to their hiding place. If she ran somewhere else, she'd be putting herself in danger with all the palace security guards milling around. So she spoke to the horses. *Run!* she screamed in her head. *Go! Run away as fast as you can!*

The first horse, who knew Birdie, neighed and reared up, startling the other two. Then it took off at a wild gallop, nearly unseating its rider. The other two went after it, racing through the park. Birdie heard Lada shriek and ran for the trees. As she neared the entrance to the lower tunnels, Cabot reached out and grabbed Birdie by the arm, yanking her into their hiding space.

"What do you think you're doing?" Cabot yelled in a whisper, her green eyes sparking with anger. "You just about messed this up for everyone!"

Birdie covered her face with her hands. "I know, I know," she moaned. "There were a lot of animals talking to me. The raven seemed like it knew where The Librarian was, and then this horse I'd spoken to before came out of nowhere . . . I messed up. I'm sorry." She glanced around. "Where's Lada?"

"She disappeared," Cabot muttered. "We both freaked out—you really scared us."

Birdie hung her head. "Thanks for waiting for me."

Cabot frowned hard. She was still really mad, but Birdie had owned her mistake. "It's not like I was going to leave you," she said in an almost growl.

Birdie felt the hint of warmth in her voice. "I hope Lada is okay," she said, looking around anxiously. "Do you think she went into the tunnel? Or should we search the park?"

"She can't teleport far," Cabot said, "so she'll be around here somewhere."

Before they could start searching, Lada reappeared, looking scared and disheveled and only carrying one crutch. She teetered and stabbed the crutch into the overgrowth, trying to get her balance, but the ground was uneven and she tumbled onto her bum . . . which was still sore from the night before. "Dang it!" she muttered, struggling to get up, then falling back again, looking annoyed. "Can you give me a hand, please?"

Birdie and Cabot rushed over and helped Lada to her feet. Cabot stayed beside her so Lada could use her arm to get her balance.

"I'm so sorry," Birdie said, her voice filled with remorse. She explained what had happened and apologized again as the raven returned to the branches above them.

"It's fine," Lada said, but she still sounded grumpy. "My teleportation kicked in without me telling it to—it does that sometimes when I'm in danger. I ended up in the tunnel, and I must have dropped my crutch on my way back. I *really* hope it's down there and not lost somewhere in nowhere-land. It has my best tools in it." She blew out a steadying breath. Her legs trembled, feeling stiff and like noodles at the same time.

"Nowhere-land?" asked Cabot. "Does that happen often?"

"I lost a cupcake once mid-teleport," Lada muttered. "I really wanted it, too."

Cabot's eyes widened as she tried to imagine what a cupcake was. "And you think it's, like, floating around in nowhere-land forever?"

Lada shrugged. "I might have just dropped it on the ground when I disappeared."

Birdie, who'd scrambled to the secret tunnel door, peered down. "I see your crutch!" She wrinkled up her nose as her eyes adjusted to the dim lantern light. "I'll go down and have it ready for when you arrive," she said meekly.

"I'm not going anywhere until I hear back from The Librarian," Lada said, pulling her phone out of her pocket again. She glanced at it. "Oh! She responded to my text. She says, 'Are you in danger?' " Lada typed and sent a reply, saying they were fine, just worried about her and waiting in the trees.

The Librarian's response came quickly this time: **I'm on my way back. Was in the middle of something when you called. Go back to home base, please.**

The three obeyed. Soon they were safely underground with the others.

As they started to tell Elena and the boys about what had happened, they heard The Librarian returning and calling for assistance with her packages. Birdie and Tenner jumped up to help her get them down the ladder and bring them to their living space.

"How did your shopping go?" Birdie asked her, eager to stop talking about her mistake. "And your, um, dealings with your contacts?"

"I sold a few diamonds," The Librarian said. "We got more money for them than I expected, so I'll hold on to the rest for now." She started unpacking a bag. "I picked up cell phones for everyone. And some other stuff."

"Too bad the phones won't work down here," Lada said. "Plus we can't charge them. No electricity."

"So it's kind of like we're back home," Seven whispered to Birdie.

Birdie laughed softly. "Pretty much."

"I thought of that, Lada," The Librarian said. "So I bought a

Wi-Fi extender that I'll attach to the trapdoor—we should be able to pick up the city Wi-Fi that way. And I've got rechargeable batteries for it and for the phones, which I can power up at the library or at my apartment when I go out next—if the coast is clear, of course. We'll be fine until we find a more permanent place to stay . . . which I think I've already done." She flashed a smug smile.

"You found a place?" asked Elena, leaning forward. "Already?"

"She's got connections," Lada reminded everyone, though they didn't need to be told. "Where are we going? We're staying in Estero, right? We'll need to, if we're planning to keep an eye on the president and the bad supers." Suddenly her eyes widened, and she looked at the five other kids apologetically. "I'm sorry. That's what we called your parents before we knew they had cool kids."

"That's what we call them, too," Tenner said smoothly. "No worries." He'd had enough pitying glances and didn't want to start that up again.

Cabot frowned but didn't add her thoughts. She didn't like that her parents were now lumped in with the awful ones. It was still hard for her to understand why they had given in to the president's offer three years ago . . . and why they hadn't tried to come back for her—surely they'd made enough money by now. She kept feeling like there had to be something else going on. Or maybe her parents really were bad, and they had been hiding their true selves from her. It was heartbreaking to think about. But Jack and Greta Stone were leaving Cabot with few other options to consider.

The Librarian unpacked another bag. "So, about housing—I've got some new friends at the monastery. On a whim, I snuck in through a back way over there and spoke to the head monk, Amanthi. She said their guest cottage on the property isn't being used right now, and we're welcome to come and live there. It's not fancy, but it's big enough, and set up like a boardinghouse. She didn't want to charge us anything, but we might need to stay there for a while, and I didn't want to take advantage of her kindness. So I made a donation. We'll attempt to sneak into the property as soon as the palace guards leave. Right now I can confirm they're everywhere. The city is crawling with them." She let out a consternated breath. "We need to stay hidden for the moment."

"The monks will risk housing people like us?" Elena asked. She seemed skeptical. "Did you tell her that we're supers? I don't remember anybody at the monastery making efforts to help us back when I was younger."

"Things have changed," The Librarian said. "The mind-your-own-business order of monks that was there for decades moved on a few years back. A new group has taken over—made up of mostly women of the order of Saint Guinevere. When President Fuerte doubled down on oppressing supernatural people, these monks had no trouble using their voices and protesting outside the palace. Several of them have been arrested, and have served time at the city jail for it. Even though protesting is not a crime, President Fuerte demanded the police take the monks in to teach them a lesson. I think he and the police commander have a cozy little arrangement, if you know what I mean."

"Are you talking about Commander Collazo?" Birdie asked. She and Tenner exchanged a glance. "She's the one who talked to Tenner and me at the police station." She didn't mention their brief meeting moments before.

"Yes," said The Librarian. "She's a complicated person, and I can't quite figure her out. Anyway, you can guess how the monks feel about our country's leadership. They will help anyone in need, especially those who are being treated unfairly. It's their way."

"That's a good way to be," Birdie said quietly. But she was confused. She didn't trust Commander Collazo, but she also hadn't felt like the woman was out to get supernatural people.

The Librarian nodded and started emptying the next bag, which was full of cell phones. She handed them out. "Rebel monks," she said. "They'll take good care of us."

ALSO KNOWN AS

The group spent the night underground and awoke the next morning to confirmation that the palace security guards were still combing Estero for signs of Elena and the ones who'd freed her.

"We might be here a few days," The Librarian told them. "But we have plenty to do."

While they waited, Lada gave the newcomers a crash course in phones, computers, and general information about living in a big city. She taught them how public transportation worked, like buses, trains, and electric bikes and scooters. And she explained Estero's government system—how President Fuerte had been elected by the people multiple times, and how an election was coming up the following year. "But nobody will run against him," Lada said. "No one ever does. He's got way too much support—all the people he convinced to hate supers think he's amazing. It's disgusting."

"Do they not understand that he's working with supers?"

Tenner asked, annoyed. "Sneaking around with them at night? Read the newspaper, people."

The Librarian went out and returned with as many library books as she could carry about all kinds of subjects, which Cabot raced through while waiting for the others to pick up on easy functions like how to send text messages and emails, or how to search for topics of interest online. The books included instruction in martial arts, wrestling and boxing guides, and spy novels and biographies. There were tips on creating distractions and step-by-step guides on how to use everyday items to spy on people, pick locks, and make things explode. Cabot couldn't get enough of it.

The Librarian had also picked up the latest copy of *Estero City News,* fresh off the presses. "Listen to this," she said, flipping the newspaper open with a loud flourish, then paraphrasing as she skimmed. "President Fuerte has announced a rollback on laws pertaining to supernatural people. If caught, they will no longer be deported because of their supernatural status. And police need to have a legitimate reason for arresting them—not just because they look supernatural." She looked at the group with shiny eyes. "Supers are no longer banned from Estero."

Brix's eyes lit up, and Seven sat up straighter. "That's good, right?" said Brix.

"On the surface it is," said The Librarian. Her tone turned uneasy. "It seems suspicious, though, doesn't it? The timing of it, I mean."

Lada nodded. "Sounds to me like they're trying to make us feel more comfortable so we'll come out of hiding."

"Maybe," said Elena. "I'm not convinced this is aimed at us, though, because you could still get arrested for breaking into—and me for breaking out of—the palace, as well as for my past misdeeds. So why would he change this law now? Is something else prompting it? Something to do with his nighttime trips to other countries?"

They could only speculate. And wait. And learn how to spy, and use a cell phone, and protect themselves in a fight.

ANOTHER DAY PASSED. Tenner and Birdie laid out all the newspaper clippings they'd collected since their arrival in Estero so the others could read them and understand everything that was going on.

Brix picked up the article with the photos of their parents, and he and Lada read it together. Brix had only been seven years old when the parents left, so he had fewer strong memories of them than the others. He studied the photos of the criminals—they'd all been in their twenties when the pictures were taken.

"You look like Birdie, Mom," he said.

"She looks like me, you mean," Elena teased. She was reading articles, too, curious what the newspapers had to say about them. She hadn't had access to news in her dungeon cell. She'd only picked up bits and pieces from the occasional chitchat between guards, but Sabine Fuerte had instructed them not to talk in front of the prisoner, so they rarely gave her anything good to stew over.

"I guess," said Brix. He touched Louis's photo, and his sight grew blurry. It was great having his mom again . . . but his heart still ached as much as ever for his dad. Sometimes he imagined Louis waiting back at the hideout, taking care of things until they could come home. He blinked his tears away and glanced at the other photos, then turned to the tiny print in the caption below, where he noticed the parents' names were listed. But his eyes fell on some unfamiliar ones. "Hey, look at this." He turned to Lada and pointed to the caption. "The first four names are right—Jack Stone, Greta Stone, Louis Golden, Elena Golden—but the other four are wrong. Max Peres and Madeleine Peres? Trent Sonoma and Lola Sonoma? Who are they? Is this a mistake?"

"Wow." Elena looked up. "That's a blast from the past." She shook her head slowly, remembering. "Those are their real names. Max and Madeleine are Seven's parents. Trent and Lola are Tenner's parents. They decided to change their names after we fled to the hideout, so we've called them Martim and Magdalia Palacio, and Troy and Lucy Cordoba, ever since."

Tenner's mouth fell open. "You're saying my parents' real names *aren't* Troy and Lucy?" he asked. "And my last name is just made up?" He gestured as if his head were exploding with this weird news—something he'd learned from Lada.

He reached for the article so he could see for himself. "I never noticed the caption before—I think Bird and I were too busy looking at their photos."

"My parents never told me they'd changed their names," Seven said. It made them seem even more distant. Like he never really knew them. Like they'd just been lying to him all this time. His chest felt hollow at the thought.

"They did that to protect you," Elena said. "That way, if police ever showed up looking for us, you couldn't accidentally give their old identities away."

"Why did they want to change them in the first place?" asked Seven.

"Oh, something about having an extra layer of protection in case we were ever discovered," Elena said. "Louis and I discussed doing it, too, but in the end we decided a name change wasn't going to help Louis—one look at his charcoal fingertips and the police would know who he was. And I just didn't see the need after all we went through to find the perfect hideout."

"So the palace and museum aren't named after them," Brix said slowly. "They're named after the palace and museum. Why would anybody do that? It doesn't seem very creative."

Cabot looked up sharply from her spy book. She'd been half listening while reading, but now she tuned in fully to the conversation. "Who's not creative?"

"Our parents," Tenner said, pointing to himself and Seven.

"Well," Cabot said with a smirk, "we already knew that."

Elena tried to hide her own grin. "They said they picked those names because they wanted to remember something, but they wouldn't say what." Her smile turned to a frown. "They didn't want to share it. Which was totally fine. We all had our secrets."

"Like Louis," Seven said.

"Yes." Then Elena's expression changed. "Oh," she exclaimed, moving to sit on her knees. "I just realized why Louis was so insistent on naming our kids Birdie and Brix. I'll bet you're named after the upper-tunnel symbol by our old apartment, where Louis hid the stash! It's a dove etched into the bricks. That makes me even more certain of where he hid it."

"I actually figured out that name connection already," said Birdie. "Dad drew a picture of the symbol in the journal I have. But I didn't know that it marked the spot where the stash would be. That makes a lot more sense than him just feeling sentimental about your old apartment. It was a clue."

"You parents," Brix said, shaking his head. "So sneaky."

"I prefer *cunning,*" said Elena with a devilish look at her son. "I've been thinking about the stash. As soon as Fuerte's people stop scouring the city for us, we should be able to go after it."

"So the new location of the stash is your old home?" The Librarian asked.

"Yes. The spot Louis marked on the map is our old apartment. The tiny third floor of an old triplex—it was where Louis and I lived before we left Estero."

"Wouldn't someone else be living there now, though?" asked Lada. "How are you going to get to it?"

"I'm sure someone lives there," said Elena. "That's why it's going to be tricky. Especially if we have to go inside."

Lada and The Librarian raised eyebrows at each other. "You don't think the new residents would have found it?" Lada asked.

Elena chuckled under her breath, but her face wore a faraway expression. She tucked a lock of hair behind her ear. "Louis would have hidden it well. My guess is that he put it inside a wall or the ceiling, which was our group's signature hiding place for things. Or perhaps in the attic—I seem to remember an attic access door in the ceiling above our bed. He knew I'd figure out a way to get to it."

"So you're just going to break into someone else's house?" Brix asked, incredulous. "Do you know how to do that?"

"That's what our parents *do*," Birdie told him.

"I know it's what they *did*," said Brix, "but it seems weird to have your mom talk about breaking into someone's house."

Elena lifted one shoulder in a half-hearted shrug. A small smile continued to play on her lips. "We're not going to take anything that belongs to the current residents," she said. "Just what belongs to us."

A flicker crossed Birdie's face, and she glanced at Seven, who, like usual, did the same to her, though she could only catch the movement of his pupils. Something was unsettling about the situation. Like Brix had said, it felt different to have Mom talk about doing criminal acts in the present, rather than in the past. There were things that didn't seem right, but Birdie couldn't put her finger on what bothered her.

She shook it off. They needed that money if they were going to stop the president and the bad parents from whatever they were up to.

The Librarian's phone buzzed. She read a text message, then frowned and stood up. "Sounds like the president's goon squad is still out there, stationed all around the monastery. I'm going to check the situation and get dinner for us. They're not giving up easily."

"Neither are we," said Birdie.

The Librarian left, and the rest of the crew settled into their spaces, faced with the prospect of staring at the bare walls for even more time. But Birdie had something in mind. She turned to Lada. "You know a lot about us now," she said. "But we don't know much about you. What's your story?"

LADA

My story?" Lada fluffed her bangs, then brought the longer loose brown curls back and secured them into a ponytail. "Hm. Nobody's ever asked me that before."

She shifted in her wheelchair and rolled a few inches forward, then back, then forward again, then impressively balanced on her back wheels for a few seconds, thinking about what parts of her life she wanted to share. She'd had to keep secrets from almost everyone in her life for years now, so telling anything that made her feel vulnerable seemed risky. But she knew that she could trust these friends who all had to hide who they were, too. They were *her* people now. A warm feeling grew under her skin: She had people.

"I guess I'll start from the beginning," Lada began slowly. She hesitated a moment longer, then dove in. "Thirteen years ago, a 'grandfatherly type' man dropped me off at Sunrise Foster Home. He told the caretakers that I was four days old, and no one could take care of me. He wouldn't give his name or any information about who my parents were. Just said he'd come back for me one day . . . if he could."

"Sounds vaguely familiar," Cabot muttered. "Let me guess. He never came back."

Brix's eyes widened. "Did he, Lada?"

Lada shook her head. "No." She dropped her gaze as something inside nudged her. She'd always felt a little unsettled about being born to someone who couldn't take care of her, even though it wasn't her fault. The foster home manager, Mr. LaDuca, had made her feel like he was doing her a huge favor by taking care of her. And his attitude toward her had gotten exponentially worse once her ability developed. After that happened, LaDuca told her he'd tried to track down the man who'd brought her to Sunrise so he could come and pick her up, because they didn't want her there. But LaDuca couldn't find the grandfatherly guy. Lada lifted her head and put on a brave smile. "Maybe he just . . . couldn't."

Birdie smiled warmly at her. "Or maybe he was terrible, and you're better off with us."

"Entirely possible." Lada laughed appreciatively. Joking about it actually made her feel better. These kids had been through some things, too. They were remarkably similar in the abandonment category, and that made the tough stuff easier to talk about. This group didn't see her as a liability because of her supernatural ability or her wheelchair and crutches. In fact, they seemed to look to her for guidance, like she was a leader, which was cool—she'd rarely had that with her peers, especially after they'd found out she was a super.

Lada glanced around the room at all the interested faces looking back at her, and her eyes brimmed. They seemed eager to know more about her, and they understood her—at least parts of her. She trusted them and their one cool parent.

She tapped her fingernails on the wheelchair armrest as she thought about how to continue, because the rest of the story made her feel even more vulnerable. Then she blew out a breath and looked up. "When I was six months old, the people at the foster home noticed I wasn't moving the same way as other babies. Another year went by, and I couldn't balance or walk—I just scooted around on my bum. By the time I was three, doctors gave a diagnosis. I have cerebral palsy." She studied the kids' faces to see if they understood the term, since she wasn't sure what things they knew about and what they didn't.

"Cerebral palsy," said Cabot slowly. "I remember an entry in the *Encyclopedia Minorica* about that. So something is going on with your brain?"

"Yes," said Lada. "Cerebral palsy is a birth injury to the brain. It can happen from being born prematurely or lacking oxygen. It can affect people in different ways. Mine is called spastic diplegic CP, and—"

"Hang on, hang on," Cabot said, typing painstakingly into her phone. "How do you spell that?"

Lada grinned and spelled it for her. "My legs are affected. My hands are a little bit stiff, too, which makes it hard to do things like sew a rip in my clothes or work with other tiny things. Mostly, though, it's the muscles in my legs that are stretched incredibly tight. Sometimes, because of this, they spasm or shift in unpredictable ways. I'm sure you've seen me make some pretty random movements."

"So that's the 'spastic' part?" Cabot asked, looking up from her phone. "*Spastic* comes from *spasm*."

"Exactly," said Lada. "And *diplegic* means both sides of the body, not just one—that is, both of my legs are affected by this form of paralysis. That's why I have to concentrate so much to keep my balance, and really focus to get my feet to go where I want them to." She pushed her glasses up on her nose. "The muscles in my legs are so tight they pull on all the bones they're attached to. They make my feet turn inward, and I can't rotate my ankles. I had surgery a few years ago, which was . . . wow. Traumatic. Tough recovery, and I don't really want to talk about that part. But in the end, it helped make it easier for me to stand on my own and use crutches to move around."

"Does it hurt?" asked Seven. "Like, not just the surgery, but ordinary life?"

"Yes," said Lada truthfully. "And I get tired more quickly than you might. Especially after doing something difficult, like, you know, fighting security guards." She grinned. "A hot bath and a massage help, though. And I do physical therapy. Or . . . at least I did. I'm not sure how I'll be able to manage those things now. There aren't any bathtubs or therapists down here."

"We'll figure it out," Elena assured her.

"I can help you stretch if you want," Tenner offered.

"That would be great," Lada said. Tenner came over to her chair, and Lada showed him how to push the pad of her foot toward her chest to stretch out her calf muscles. She gritted her teeth as he did it—it helped, but it also hurt.

"Maybe the monastery will have a bathtub you can use," said Brix. "We've never been in one, have we, Birdie?"

"The only bathtub I've ever seen was in The Librarian's apartment," Birdie said. "Our bathtub was the ocean."

"So, wait," said Cabot. "How does the water in the bathtub get hot? Is there some sort of fire . . . or . . . sunlight . . ." She blushed as she realized the question might seem silly to a civilized person. And she also realized she'd just derailed Lada's story.

But Lada didn't laugh, and she didn't seem to mind. "Electricity can heat things, too—not just charge cell phones and make lights turn on. And there are certain types of natural gas you can burn safely inside your house, I guess. I don't really know very much about that, but The Librarian's stove burners turn on with a spark and make a flame for cooking."

Cabot nodded her thanks. "Sorry for interrupting your story," she whispered. With pursed lips, she went searching for more information on her phone again.

Seven leaned in. "How did you find out you were supernatural if you didn't know who your parents were, or have any information about them being supernatural? Did something happen?"

Lada laughed, and her expression took on the slightly dreamy look of someone thinking back on a fond memory. "Something did happen," she said. "I'd known a little bit about supernatural people because of the history of Sunrise Foster Home, and how it used to be a place where people sent their supernatural children if they couldn't take care of them. And I also knew that supernatural people were no longer welcome in Estero—that got pounded into us at school. So when my teleporting ability showed up, while it was a complete shock, at least I had some context."

"What happened?" asked Tenner. "Did you just teleport one day, and that was that?"

"Not quite," said Lada. "I first started feeling slightly . . . off. Like, whenever I would go to bed, right before I drifted off to sleep, I'd feel myself do one of those nap jerks—you know what I mean? When you dream that you're falling and you wake up startled?"

They all nodded.

"But instead of waking up in my bed, I'd be on the floor next to the bed. But not injured, like I'd fallen out and landed hard. Just like I'd disappeared from the bed and reappeared on the floor in an instant. After that happened a few times, I found myself in the hallway. And then the bathroom. I tried to make it happen when I was awake, but I couldn't figure out what to do.

I finally realized that it was happening only when my body was in its most relaxed state. So . . . I knew something was up, and I thought it might be supernatural, which—let me tell you—made me feel so bad for a while." Her face clouded.

"I can't imagine going through that and not having support from people who understood, people who loved you no matter what," said Seven. "At least the five of us had each other and Louis, if not our other parents."

"Four," Cabot said without looking up from her phone, reminding them all that she wasn't supernatural, and that she wasn't pleased about it.

Birdie gave her a soft look that went unnoticed.

Lada dropped her gaze, remembering. "The teleporting didn't scare me for long. The only thing I cared about was someone finding out. I couldn't ask anyone about it at the foster home. So I went to the Estero Public Library and started searching for information about supernatural abilities."

"And that's how you met The Librarian?" Tenner asked.

"She's sneaky like that, figuring us kids out." Lada paused, thinking. "She really saved my life in a way, you know?" she said tenderly. Her eyes grew moist. "I was struggling at the foster home as it was, and then things became almost unbearable. Once I started being able to control my teleporting and use it to escape from the director, Mr. LaDuca, he obviously figured out I was a super. Things spiraled after that. Suddenly the other kids weren't allowed to play with me, not that they wanted to once they heard the news. And LaDuca—he was so afraid the home would get shut down because of me. So he was pretty awful." She stopped and pursed her lips.

"What did they do to you?" Birdie asked gently.

"They tried to get me to stay inside and never leave. Like they were going to hide me away until I was old enough to be kicked out. They wanted to pretend I didn't exist." Lada's face reddened, and her eyes overflowed. "There was a shop clerk around the corner from Sunrise who saw me teleport away from LaDuca once. I thought she was going to report me, but instead she hid me in the back room of the shop until LaDuca returned to his office. But he chased me around a lot." She took off her glasses and pressed her fingertips to the inner corners of her eyes, trying to stop the tears. But still they dripped down.

Seven stood up in alarm, unsure what to do for their new friend. Birdie quickly went to Lada's side. "That's terrible. Do you want a hug?"

Lada nodded. Birdie knelt next to the wheelchair and wrapped her arms around the girl. After a moment Lada sniffled and let go, and Birdie pulled away.

"Thanks," said Lada. "I'm okay. I guess . . . I guess that's why it means so much to me to have found you. I'll never go back to that place."

"We'll be your family," Brix said. "Do you want that?"

Lada sniffed and squelched a grin at the boy's earnestness. "Yes. I think I do. Thank you."

Elena fished a clean towel from the bag of kitchen items she'd brought from The Librarian's apartment and handed it to Lada so she could wipe her tears away. "The best thing we can do now as we face some unknown dangers is stick together," Elena said. "The stronger our team of good supers can bond, the better we'll be."

Cabot, who had started giving her full attention to Lada's story and the touching scene, nodded along with the others. Sure, she wasn't supernatural like them. But sticking together sounded good. Especially since she was torn apart over her parents joining President Fuerte. Why couldn't they have held out, like Elena did? Were they gone from her life forever?

Cabot felt like she was being pulled in multiple directions. Earlier Tenner had talked like all the criminal parents were bad, as if it were a simple fact . . . but were they full-on evil? All of them? Was it that simple: There were bad supernatural people and good supernatural people, and you just sort of declared which of the two you were? You had to choose one? Wasn't it a little more complicated than that?

From Cabot's perspective, it was. Her heart was breaking because her parents had chosen the wrong side, even though they'd once been considered good parents. But what, exactly, was wrong about their choice? And what was right about the side Cabot was on? They didn't really know what was going on. There was still so much to uncover. And before Cabot could fully write off her parents as being against her and the others, she had to find out more about what they were actually doing.

THE LIBRARIAN

"Tell us how you two got to know each other," Elena said to Lada as The Librarian returned with bags of takeout food from a nearby restaurant—and confirmation that the palace security detail was still staked out around the city.

Lada shot a questioning glance at The Librarian. "It feels strange to talk about it, since we've been covert for so long," she said.

"Tell them anything about me that you think is important," The Librarian assured her. "They need to know what we're capable of. And that they can trust us to be honest with them." She handed out food containers. "Though there will always be times when I have to keep a secret from all of you—even Lada. That's just the nature of my relationships with the contacts I have. I can't betray my promises to them, or else we'd be cut off from important things we need access to."

That sounded ominous to Seven, but he trusted The Librarian. And the best news was that Cabot did, too. She had the strongest intuition of all of them and had been the one to question Birdie's motives for leaving the hideout. So what Cabot thought mattered.

Cabot was enthralled with The Librarian, so that was a good sign.

"My first meeting with The Librarian was a lot like Tenner and Birdie's," Lada said. "I showed up at the library, and The Librarian's 'super' radar went off, I guess. She had me figured out before I had myself figured out."

"You all make it so obvious, going straight for the supernatural shelf," The Librarian said. "Birdie and Tenner said they wanted to learn about the history of Estero and the currency change, which is code for 'what the heck did the supernatural criminals do?' Honestly, I don't need radar. But you need to learn to be sneakier. That's why I brought you the spy books to read. We're going to have a crash course in covert ops before we make any moves."

"Covert operations," Cabot said before the others could ask. "Secret missions."

"Can I tell them what you used to do?" Lada asked The Librarian.

The woman granted permission with a stiff nod.

"The Librarian was a military ranger," Lada told the others. "And a spy for Estero. She's been all over the world. In some really dangerous situations. She's got, like, medals and stuff."

Everyone in the underground room stopped what they were doing and turned to look at The Librarian.

"What?" The Librarian said casually. She handed out utensils and napkins, then daintily opened her meal. "Being able to wipe people's short-term memories helped."

"Did the military know about that?" Seven asked.

"No. I couldn't tell them, or they would have kicked me out."

"They'd kick you out for your ability even though it gave them an advantage?" Seven said, shaking his head. "Everything about that seems backward."

"And now you're a librarian," Tenner said, eyeing her bulging biceps.

"It's my dream job," she said. "My work in the military paid for my education. Plus I needed to find people like you. What better place is there? Instead of me having to search for you, you came right to me. And I got paid for it." She took a bite of food, then chewed thoughtfully and swallowed. "I got a tingly feeling that you were supers from the moment you stopped in front of the entry turnstile and didn't know to push it. Like you were extra special—not from here, not familiar with Estero. And it turns out I was right. Little did I know you weren't familiar with *civilization*."

Birdie and Tenner laughed, remembering. Not much time had passed since then, but they felt like they'd already learned so much about what life was like in Estero. "Just look at us now," Tenner said. "We've come a long way."

"And speaking of that day," The Librarian continued, pointing at Tenner with her fork, "you must give me those humongous shorts you were wearing so I can find a man three times your size who needs them. I'll go out tomorrow to buy clothing for everyone. We'll need you to blend in with the crowds, not stand out."

Birdie's face flickered as she looked down at her parachute top. "You said this was fashion-forward."

"And I meant it," The Librarian said carefully. "You can probably still wear that . . . under a sweatshirt. But your mom might like her dress back—the red-and-white one. The shape isn't quite right for you yet."

"She means your chest," Brix helpfully pointed out.

Birdie shot him a dirty look. "Aw, man," she muttered. "I liked that one."

"Do you trust me to pick out new clothes for you?" The Librarian asked her. "I can find something similar in your size."

The woman was the most fashionable person Birdie knew, and she always looked amazing. "Duh," she said. "Of course." The prospect of new clothing was foreign to all of them, but now Birdie started getting excited about it. "Maybe something from that one place Tenner and I stumbled into."

"And by stumbled," Tenner said, "she means 'tripped and knocked everything over.' What was it? Bootsie's Boot-i-cue or something."

The Librarian pressed her lips together, trying hard not to smile. "Did you know that many very smart people pronounce unusual words wrong because they've only read them, and haven't ever heard them said aloud? So they might say it wrong until someone corrects them. It's Bootsie's *Boo-TEAK*. Yes, I know that store well. Great choice."

"So that's how you say it," Tenner said, enlightened. "I've been wondering."

"Pro tip—you can look up pronunciations on your phone now that you have one." The Librarian turned back to Lada. "Okay. Sorry—let's get back on track. Please continue telling them all about our first meeting."

"Wait," said Cabot. "When you go shopping for clothes, can you get me a jumpsuit like yours?" She blushed bright red.

"Of course," said The Librarian, pretending not to notice.

"Right." Lada put her empty food container back in the bag and set it on the floor. "So there I was, looking for information on why I was disappearing and reappearing in different locations, and I searched it on the computer in the archives room."

"Aaah," Birdie said as she and Tenner exchanged a knowing glance. "That computer is a trap."

"Apparently," said Lada with a laugh. "She noticed what I was researching, and slipped me a book as I was leaving. Inside the book she'd left a note." Lada touched her throat, and her voice wavered with emotion. "The note said that she was a super, too. And if I ever needed to talk, she was always available. It meant so much to me. I went to my bed and cried for an hour. I hadn't realized how lonely I'd become since everyone shunned me, and how scared I really was deep down to be supernatural, knowing everyone in Estero was against me."

The Librarian reached out and squeezed Lada's hand. "Lada went a whole week without returning, and I thought I'd made a mistake and really messed up my cover—that's not exactly something any of us should be putting in writing. But I took a chance."

"The only reason I didn't return the next day was because of crusty old LaDuca trapping me inside. That's when I started trying harder to teleport, rather than just waiting for it to happen on the verge of falling asleep. I had to figure out how to concentrate and relax my mind so it would work on command. It took me six days to get it right!"

"It was a relief to see you coming back into my library," The Librarian said warmly. "I remember staying behind the desk and not making eye contact because I wanted to make sure you wanted to talk."

"And when I did approach her," Lada said, "and told her where I lived, she told me that she grew up in Sunrise, too. She was seventeen when President Fuerte proclaimed that Estero wouldn't be taking in any more unwanted supernatural children, and those that remained in Sunrise would be banished. She got kicked out of the foster home. Then she reinvented herself as a non-super, and joined the military."

"What do you mean, reinvented yourself?" Cabot asked.

"I returned to Estero City under a false name," said The Librarian, "with fake identification, so I couldn't be tracked as a supernatural person. I spent years in the military and as a spy. Then I got my library science degree, and I've been working undercover at the Estero Public Library ever since, trying to find other people like me so we can fight back against President Fuerte's oppression. And now, with these strange new moves he's making in the middle of the night, we need to figure out what he's doing and stop him."

Cabot gazed at the woman with even more respect than before. "So you already know how to use weapons? And spy on people? And blow things up?"

"I do. Among other useful things."

"And you can do all those things to stop Fuerte?"

"Yes," said The Librarian. "I can."

Cabot nodded slowly. "And will you teach me everything?"

The woman's deep brown eyes sparkled. "Maybe not everything. But a lot of things."

DEFINING NORMAL

They stayed in the lower tunnels for two more days, waiting for the palace guards to give up on finding them and absorbing all the information they could about cell phones, martial arts, and other fighting techniques throughout the vast hallways. Brix taught Cabot and Birdie how to run up the walls and touch the ceiling, though neither of them could do it as well as him. Lada showed the others how she could do wheelies in her chair, and explained that doing them was a necessary skill to maneuver over bumps and had really helped strengthen her upper body. Not to mention it was fun and made her look tough.

They did a fashion show with their new clothing—Tenner showed off his new board shorts and T-shirts. Cabot strutted in her khaki jumpsuit, which even had a patch with the letter *C* on it to match her name. Birdie put on her new skirts and dresses, then chose some boots to replace her worn-out mom sneakers. Later they explored the tunnel system using GPS that actually worked now, which allowed them to figure out where all the doors they'd discovered were located in the city above them. "The only problem is that almost all of them seem to have something impossibly heavy on top of them," Tenner said as the six kids made their way back to home base for dinner. "The doors won't budge. These tunnels would be a lot more useful if we could access them at all the points, not just the two we've found that open."

"I've noted the latitude and longitude points for each door," said Lada, "so we can explore what's covering them once we're free to move around Old Town again. Maybe there are more we can access once we have a chance to check what's resting on top of them."

"There are always explosions," said Cabot. "We could blow up things that are in our way." She rubbed her hands together eagerly. She'd been doing a lot of spy reading lately.

"I'm pretty sure that's one of the things The Librarian *isn't* going to teach you how to do," Seven said.

Cabot wrinkled her nose. "We'll see," she muttered. "I'd be really careful."

When they reached their camp, they found the two adults conversing quietly.

"Cabot wants to learn how to do explosions," Brix announced, bouncing into the room and snatching up Puerco.

"Brix!" Cabot said. "Don't make me sound like a . . . like an explosaholic!"

"I think you mean a kaboominator," Tenner said.

Lada reached up and high-fived Tenner, then said in a refined voice, "An explosion enthusiast."

"Demolitionist?" suggested Seven.

"Definitely a boomomaniac," said Birdie.

"People!" Cabot exclaimed, though she couldn't hold back a laugh. Her cheeks flamed. "I just want to know how explosions work, and then, you know, maybe someday when I'm old enough, use them carefully to help us if we need them." She plastered on a placating smile. "Nothing to worry about."

"I'm not worried," The Librarian said, obviously amused by all the creative word choices. "I think you and I understand each other pretty well. But . . . leave the explosions to me for now until we have a chance to do extensive training. Then maybe I'll let you watch me make some noisemakers."

"I'm not sure you understand what you're doing," Brix warned the woman, jabbing his thumb in Cabot's direction. "Photographic memory, remember?"

Cabot beamed. "Shh, Brixy," she said. "It'll be fine. Noisemakers are virtually harmless."

"If used carefully," The Librarian added with a stern tone that made Cabot's smile fade, but only slightly. Then The Librarian turned to Seven and handed him a small bag. "This is for you if you want it. It might help when you're out in public, but it's up to you."

"What is it?" Seven said uncertainly. There was something about everyone constantly trying to help him with his ability that made him feel uncomfortable. He just wanted things to go back to normal, but that wasn't happening. And it didn't seem like it was going to happen anytime soon.

Elena leaned in. "I remembered that your mom sometimes used makeup to control her shimmering. And I got to thinking that makeup would work on your skin in a similar way to how a face covering defines your facial shape, only makeup wouldn't look suspicious. So I mentioned it to The Librarian."

"And while I was out today," said The Librarian, "I picked up a few different shades."

"Oh," said Seven. He looked inside the bag.

Birdie peered in it alongside him. "Can I try, too?"

"Me too?" asked Tenner.

"I tried makeup at the foster home," Lada offered. "It's kind of a pain. But I can see how it would define the contours of your face, Seven. It would look like skin, I think. Then you wouldn't have to wear the scarf."

Seven looked up. Not having to wear the hot scarf over his face sounded great. "I guess I could try it," he said. He pulled out a few bottles and examined them.

"Which one is closest to the skin color you used to have, Seven?" Lada asked.

Seven studied the bottles. "Um . . ." It had been a long time since he'd seen his old skin. And back then, he'd rarely looked in a mirror—none of the kids did, even though there were a couple of them floating around the cabins. But Seven remembered his arms and legs being light brown. Uncertain, he turned to Birdie. "Do you think this one is about right?" he asked, holding up one of the bottles. "Tawny Fawntastic? Whatever that means."

"That's the one I thought, too," Birdie said. "That's how I remember you."

Seven nodded. "I'll do this one, please," he said, holding it up.

"Great," said The Librarian. "Because I was just telling Elena the good news. The security detail has given up on us, and our path to the monastery is clear. We can sneak over after dinner and get settled there tonight."

As soon as they finished eating, Seven and the others who wanted to try on makeup went to an unoccupied space down the hallway to work on it. Thirty minutes later, all three boys and Birdie had applied slightly uneven coats of foundation on their faces, a dash of color to their lips, and some blush to brighten their cheeks. They used eyeliner and eye shadow to further define Seven's eyes. When they were finished, Tenner and Brix went to show Cabot and Lada, who'd opted out of the makeup experiment.

Birdie stayed behind with Seven. She gently touched his cheek, then booped the tip of his nose. "You look great," she said earnestly. "I love being able to see your face again. But I love it when it's camouflaged, too."

"I look okay?" Seven said with a hint of anxiety. "Like . . . a regular person?"

"What does *regular* mean? I mean, have you met *us*?" Birdie said. "None of us are regular people, and we never will be. Besides, if you looked like a regular person, you wouldn't be Seven. I love your camouflage ability, even if you don't."

"You mean it?" Seven asked softly.

Birdie nodded. "Yeah."

The anxious feeling drained from Seven's chest. He was trying to love his ability, too, but so far he couldn't convince himself it was anything but a big hassle and embarrassment.

"Anyway," Birdie went on, "we couldn't do much with your eyes beyond the eyeliner and eye shadow. But no one will notice you don't have traditional-looking eyes unless they're close-up. You can still wear the sunglasses if you want."

Seven smiled, then gingerly touched the skin on his cheeks where it stretched. "My face feels like that time back home when we put seaweed on it and let it dry in the sun. Like there's something stuck to it."

"There *is* something stuck to it," Birdie said. "Creamy gunk." She couldn't get enough of seeing her best friend after three years of camouflage. His smile! Even though she could usually hear in his voice when he was smiling, she'd missed seeing it. Seven's jaw seemed more pronounced than when she'd seen it last, and the blush made his cheekbones stand out. He looked older than she remembered.

"Your makeup looks good, too," Seven said generously. "Does it feel weird to you? It seems like a lot of trouble to go through for people who do it every day."

"Yes. But it was fun to do it with you." Birdie pulled on his arm. "Let's go pack up our things. And then we can get out of here."

She and Seven started back toward camp. Seven bumped shoulders playfully with her, which made her grin and bump him back.

"It feels good to be all together again," she told him. "Me and you, especially. I missed you a lot when Tenner and I were here alone."

"Let's not do that long separation thing again, okay?" Seven glanced at her. Parts of his eyes were brown like the wall behind his head, still camouflaged. Only the black specks of his pupils stood out, boring into hers. He looked . . . Well, he looked a little creepy with those near-empty eye sockets, and he'd need a hat to cover his invisible hair and help round out the illusion. But he also looked happy.

Birdie nodded and linked arms with him. "Okay."

SAINT GUINEVERE

The eight tunnel dwellers packed up their belongings and ventured out after dark in small groups, the same way they'd arrived: Seven and Lada together, Tenner with Birdie, and The Librarian, Elena, and Cabot with Brix trying not to bounce too much in the middle. Some took the street route, while others meandered through the quiet old cemetery that had the secret entrance to the lower tunnels. Birdie's raven, who'd stayed near the park's wooded area all that time, followed her, squawking excitedly upon seeing her again, and settled on her shoulder. Birdie winced when the bird's claws dug in, but she put up with it because having a raven like you that much was really cool—though she was ready to shoo it away at the first sign of the police or palace guards. Eventually they all met up at the MONASTERIO DE PIEDRA sign next to the entrance to the compound.

A few bald women, wearing small disk-like head coverings and simple tan robes cinched at the waist with black rope belts, were waiting there to greet them, usher them to safety inside, and secure the gate behind them. When a tall bald woman with dark brown skin strode toward them with authority, the other monks bid the newcomers farewell and peeled off in different directions. Cabot noted their baldness, certain they would have a haircutting tool she could use.

"I am the abbess," the tall woman said. "My name is Amanthi. It means 'protector of peace.' Welcome—we're so glad you made it safely."

Birdie relaxed her shoulders and smiled. The raven flew off to somewhere inside the compound. Puerco snuffled around in her backpack. *I'll let you out soon,* Birdie assured him.

"Thank you," said Lada, rolling herself toward the woman. "We're glad, too." As she and the rest introduced themselves, they glanced around curiously. The property spread out so far that it felt like a tiny village, with multiple dormitory-like structures, a dining hall, gardens, and the religious building with a courtyard and a bell tower. There was also a small parking lot with a golf cart, two jeeps, and a corral containing a slew of electric scooters and bicycles.

"The compound is locked at all times," Amanthi said. "You'll be safe here." She beckoned them to follow and pointed out the monks' living quarters and the common mess hall where they could have breakfast with the monks if they wanted to—that was the only meal they ate, because they practiced fasting the rest of the day. "You are welcome to move about anywhere inside our walls. Our monks spend much of the day in silence, but please ask anyone for help if you are in need. We request that you use quiet voices when outside so you don't disturb anyone in meditation."

As Amanthi led them through the well-lit stone courtyard of the Monasterio de Piedra, the bells in the tower above them began to chime. Amanthi noticed a few of the group pause and look up, so she stopped to let them take in the sights and sounds. When the beautiful chiming ended, the bell ringer deftly climbed down from the tower onto a rooftop. She walked along a narrow wall high above them, which made Birdie clutch her stomach. Then the monk stopped, knelt, and appeared to pull a lever. A built-in iron ladder fell open from the wall for her to climb down to the ground.

"A hidden ladder," Cabot murmured, wondering how someone had made such a thing. She imagined the mechanisms that allowed it to move so fluidly and noted how it had been incorporated into the structure, blending perfectly into the stone wall. Through narrowed eyes she scrutinized it from top to bottom. Soon she spied another lever behind some ivy on the wall at shoulder height. It was probably the way to open and close the ladder from the ground level.

The abbess invited them to continue following her. She led them to the other side of the courtyard and through a stone archway with ivy curling around it. There was a smooth sidewalk with grass and flowers on both sides, which led to a two-story fieldstone cottage and then branched off in other directions farther ahead. The cottage had a dark brown roof and large windows overlooking the gardens, and there was a patio out back with two picnic tables and equipment that looked like it was for cooking things.

"Welcome to your new home," Amanthi said, sweeping her hand toward the front door. Her flowing robe hung low from her arm. "It's simple and sparse—no TVs, I'm afraid—but large enough for each of you to have your own tiny room. We normally use the cottage as a retreat for visiting orders or those seeking to learn more about our way of life, but we can accommodate those visitors in our main building as well. So, as I told The Librarian before, you're free to stay as long as you need to."

"I can't thank you enough for taking us in like this, Amanthi," The Librarian said. "It feels very safe here."

"We're grateful for your generous donation," Amanthi said. "And I'm glad the palace guards are standing down. I think you've thoroughly fooled them."

"Did they ever describe to you who they're looking for?" The Librarian asked.

"I spoke with Sabine at the palace," Amanthi said, glancing at Brix. "She mentioned children, but only gave a little description."

Birdie glanced questioningly at her mother.

"Sabine is President Fuerte's daughter," Elena reminded her in a whisper. "She runs the dungeon."

"The one with the diamonds?" Seven asked.

"The one *without* the diamonds," Cabot corrected, then put her finger to her lips to quiet them. She wanted to hear every word.

Amanthi went on. "None of the newspapers or guards seem to know who you are by name—the only photo the guards showed me was Elena's."

"What descriptions did they give you?" Birdie asked, worried.

"They said one child was bouncing around, and another used crutches to attack the guard on duty. And . . . they also said something truly head-scratching about a tiny *pig*. But then they hastened to add that the guard had hit his head, and might have hallucinated that part."

Birdie and Seven bumped shoulders and tried not to laugh. Puerco stayed quiet in Birdie's backpack. "We do have a tiny pig," she admitted, slipping the straps off her shoulders and setting the pack on the ground. She lifted the flap and let Puerco out to roll around on the cool grass.

"Oh my goodness," said Amanthi, reaching down to scratch Puerco's pink-and-gray belly. "So you do. He is very cute. We have some cats on the property, but this is our first pig."

"His name is Puerco," Birdie said. "Is it okay if I keep him inside the cottage? He's trained, and I'll clean up after him outside."

"All in need are welcome here," Amanthi said simply, straightening up again. She turned back to the larger group. "I don't think the guards had much else to go on. They'd been tight-lipped until this afternoon when I went out to ask them about their progress. They speculated that you must have left Estero, and said they were being called off street duty and back to their regular posts."

"That's excellent news," Elena said quietly. "We want them to think we're nowhere near this city." She gazed over the compound. The tall stone wall ran the perimeter of the entire city block. The lawn and gardens were populated with benches and other shaded areas to gather or spend time alone. There were some statues and art sculptures, too, and a peaceful fountain. "This place is so serene. I've never seen inside the walls before. Thank you for your offer of protection. I admit it's surprising to me to find anyone in Estero willing to help people like us."

"That is our way," the woman said. She led them to the far wall, where the compound lighting was dim. "There is a hidden door here that leads to the alley." She pointed to a faint crack in the wall, barely noticeable. "Just step on this pointy rock next to the wall to unlatch it. If you're trying to get in from the alley side, there is a brick that sticks out a half inch—that's the trigger to open it. It was built into the compound a few hundred years ago during the religious wars, to allow the monks to come and go more safely, and to hide those in trouble. There are a few other interesting secrets on the property as well. I'll leave you to find them if you wish to explore." She smiled. "I'm sure you're ready to settle in." As Amanthi turned to go, she paused at a statue alongside the path. There was a plaque at the base of it.

She put her hand on the statue's arm. "This is Saint Guinevere. She was a clever, ruthless woman who fought for the rights of the oppressed. As long as people were in need, she didn't rest. We model our lives after hers. With that in mind, you must all take my cell phone number from The Librarian. If you ever find yourself in need, you may call me, day or night, and I will help you."

"Thank you," Birdie said, and the others echoed their thanks as well. Seconds later, all the kids and Elena received a text message from The Librarian with Amanthi's contact information. The abbess left them, and they moved around to the front of the cottage, which had stairs and a ramp. Lada rolled up the ramp, while the others climbed the three steps, and they entered their new living quarters.

The cottage was a simple setup: There was a wide entryway with a closet for them to put away their shoes and hang up their jackets. The entryway opened up to a large carpeted gathering area with sofas and chairs. On the left wall was a row of doors leading to small, nearly identical bedrooms. Just beyond the living space was a staircase leading up, presumably to more bedrooms. To the right of the stairs was a long dining table with eight chairs around it, and the kitchen spread out beyond that. Sliding glass doors led to the patio they'd seen when they approached. There was ample room in the kitchen for several of them to make meals together, even though the thought of cooking indoors with a flame still seemed dangerous to the forgotten five.

"I like that Saint Guinevere lady," Tenner said, poking his head into one of the tiny bedrooms. "I kind of want to be like her."

"Me too," said Brix. He bounded up the stairs a little too exuberantly and nearly cracked his head on a ceiling beam.

"Amanthi is inspiring," The Librarian said, putting down the things she carried and sinking into a chair with a sigh of relief. It had been a busy few days, especially for her. "Now, let's see which bedrooms inspire you."

THE STASH

The cottage bedrooms were dormitory style—two small rooms connected by a full bathroom. Each had a single bed, a small dresser, and a desk with a chair and a bookshelf. There were four bedrooms on the main floor, which Lada, Tenner, Elena, and The Librarian took. Upstairs were four more, which Seven, Brix, Birdie, and Cabot moved into. Tenner, who was nearly out of the toilet paper he'd taken from The Librarian's bathroom, was glad to see plenty available in the bathroom he shared with Lada. And Lada was relieved to find that her wheelchair fit through all the doors, which made it easier for her to move from room to room.

The group took a few days to settle in, get supplies, wander the property, and continue training so they'd be ready for whatever they might face as they attempted to get to the bottom of what President Fuerte and the criminal parents were doing. With electric hair clippers borrowed from Amanthi, The Librarian clipped Cabot's hair down to a more comfortable three-quarter-inch length on top, tapering it even shorter around her ears and neck. She showed Cabot how to do it herself for the next time—it was so much faster than Cabot's tool back home. Each day The Librarian left and returned to the cottage with mysterious electronics, wires, batteries, and other supplies that she said would prove useful soon enough.

The kids and Elena learned about and practiced forms of combat on the lawn, climbed the walls using their ropes, and maneuvered over, under, and around obstacles. In the courtyard, with the tall buildings to shield Brix from view, they took measurements of how high he could bounce and jump. They also measured how far Lada could teleport, what decibel level Tenner could hear from various distances, and how far he could see. And they started a list of animals Birdie had successfully communicated with. She even managed to pique the interest of one of the monastery cats for about ten seconds before the feline put her nose in the air and chased after a butterfly.

Cabot got a chance to fully examine the workings of the drop-down ladder. She climbed it with the bell-ringing monk, who taught her how to ring the monastery bells. From the belfry, while the last tones hung in the air, Cabot gazed out over the city. As she turned in a slow circle, she could see the park's fountain, the cemetery, the library, the beach where Birdie and Tenner had spent their first days in Estero, and even the president's palace in the distance. Were her parents out there somewhere? Did they ever think about her? Did they know she thought about *them* every day? She stayed awhile in the belfry, alone, missing them. Missing her tree perch back home. Missing the sound of waves lapping the shore. Nothing seemed settled here. They were always on the move. Waiting for something sinister they couldn't quite identify. And most of their own parents had become part of that sinister enemy . . . including hers.

Back at the cottage, The Librarian emphasized the art of creating distractions. "Simple distraction techniques are the key to making big moves," she explained. "They'll help us fight against people who are stronger or smarter than us. And they'll save us if we're in danger of getting caught. Whenever you find yourself in trouble, I want you to immediately think, 'distraction technique.' "

Later, The Librarian brought them out to the hidden door in the wall so they could all practice opening and closing it with the rock and brick triggers.

Lada and Tenner searched the monastery grounds for the location of the door that would connect them to the lower tunnels. Lada had the coordinates, which lined up with an intensely manicured bed of flowers in front of the mess hall. A bird feeder on a pole rose up from the middle of the bed. Birdie's raven friend and a few chickadees perched on it, watching the two and snacking on seeds. The chickadees chided them now and then when they got too close. Birdie had told Tenner that the raven might come to recognize them if they spoke to it in calm tones and looked it in the eyes, so they spent a moment doing that, too.

"What do we do about this flower bed?" asked Tenner,

returning his attention to the petunias. Was there a door beneath them?

Lada shifted on her crutches and studied the coordinates on the app she'd downloaded. She sighed. "As much as I want to find the door, I don't think we should dig up the petunias. We don't want the monks to think we're bad guests."

Tenner examined the things that surrounded the flower patch—the lawn, the mess hall, a statue, and a stone path. None could be moved easily. "Maybe the coordinates are wrong. Didn't you say there was a chance they might be, since we were underground when we took them and things could have gotten wonky?"

Lada shrugged, then nodded. "There's a chance."

Tenner went over to a statue and pushed gently on it. "This seems solid."

"What if it's beneath the stone path?" Lada said. "Or even below the foundation of the mess hall?"

They finally resorted to carefully digging a hole with their hands in the dirt between petunias, then jabbing a pointed stick into it to see if there was any resistance. But it just sank into the earth, and they soon gave up and went back to the cottage.

"OUR FIRST OFFICIAL mission starts today," Elena announced over breakfast on the patio the next morning. "We need to find the stash, which will allow us to do whatever it takes to learn what Fuerte is up to, even if it means chartering our own airplane to track him down. But to get to the stash, we'll have to accomplish some difficult feats. Like getting into the third floor of my old home to search for it without making anyone inside the building or neighborhood suspicious."

"We're too young to pose as workers needing access to the building," Cabot said, methodically moving her fingers over her newly shorn head. She loved the tactile sensation—it calmed her. "So we'll have to find a different way to get inside the house."

Birdie nodded. "Maybe we can draw out all the tenants through a distraction technique, like The Librarian taught us." She took a bite of toast. A glob of jam slid off and landed on her new red dress with white polka dots, which The Librarian had picked out for her. She frowned and wiped it carefully with her napkin, thankful that the jam had dropped onto a red section of the dress, so it blended in.

"First," Elena said, "we need to stake out the neighborhood. Observe what happens around the house. Our goal is to notice everything. Who comes and goes? What time is the mail delivered? When do the tenants leave and arrive home, and is that consistent from day to day? Are they gone for an hour every day at lunchtime, or perhaps they come home for lunch? We'll take photos and learn how many people live in the house and what they look like so we can keep track of them. Surveillance can be tedious, but it's important to know how predictable the tenants are."

"It's a boring job," The Librarian agreed. "But it's crucial. We'll have our devices, so we can do other kinds of learning while we wait for things to happen around the target home." She picked up her plate and stood. "I've already got a big SUV in the parking lot. We should get moving." She started for the sliding door.

Cabot followed, while the others dispersed. "Where do you get these SUVs from?" Cabot asked.

The Librarian set her dishes in the sink. "In the past I've 'borrowed' one . . . from a sort-of friend who is also sometimes . . . not a friend. But I finally broke down and rented this one for a month, because we're going to need it a lot." She paused. "The borrowing thing—that was more than you needed to know. So keep it close."

"I will." Cabot helped her clear the rest of the dishes, then scurried to her room to get ready to go.

Soon The Librarian clapped her hands a few times, rounding up the group. She made sure they all had their devices before proceeding to the vehicle, leaving Puerco at home to finish the breakfast scraps on the patio and nap in the sunshine.

Birdie sat in the front passenger seat again, which seemed to help keep her from throwing up. Elena, from the second row of seats behind Birdie, gave The Librarian the address and guided her through the city toward the apartment where she and Louis used to live.

As The Librarian drove, Elena reminisced about their time there. "We had to hide Louis's hands from the landlord—as you can imagine, no homeowner wants to rent to someone who has a better than average chance of burning the place down. When we signed the lease, I had to tip my glass of water over onto the table to distract the landlord so Louis could quickly sign it without his fingers being seen."

"See, everyone?" said The Librarian. "Tipping the water glass over is a great example of a distraction technique. Humans are so intelligent, yet a simple distraction works incredibly well in so many situations."

"What does the apartment look like, Mom?" asked Brix.

"It's tiny. More like a third-floor studio with a micro kitchen, barely big enough to fit us both."

"Didn't you have the money to get something bigger?" Birdie asked. "You told us that the Palacios and the Cordobas had bought land and stuff like that before you left Estero. But you had money to spend, too, right?"

"Sure," said Elena. "But Louis and I didn't mind being cozy. We didn't need a bigger place. And we were the first ones to talk about leaving Estero for good. So we didn't see any reason to put down roots. We didn't think we'd ever be coming back."

Cabot's eye twitched. She'd forgotten the part about the Cordobas and the Palacios buying land. She blinked a few times, trying to get the twitch to stop. It didn't make sense to her that Tenner's and Seven's parents would invest in property when they were planning to leave for good, too. Or maybe they'd always planned on coming back but never told their children. She turned away from the window. "Do you remember where the land is that the other parents bought?"

Elena shook her head. "I might have known back then, but I can't recall now. All I can remember is that it was somewhere in Estero." She hesitated, then tapped her forefinger to her lips. "I wonder if they've done anything with that property since they've been back."

"That's what I was wondering, too," said Cabot. "Maybe they've built a home base on it. The other day, you said the new names they chose for themselves were clues to help them remember something. Could it have had to do with that land?"

"That's a good theory," said Elena thoughtfully.

Seven shifted in the backseat. He wasn't wearing makeup today, and the tinted windows kept him from having to cover up with the scarf. He glanced at Tenner, who was sliding deeper into his corner of the bench seat. It wasn't easy being the kids of the bad parents. Seven sometimes felt guilty by association for his parents' underhanded sneakiness. Usually Tenner took the brunt of that, but Seven was feeling it today, too. Perhaps because his invisible dad was the only one they knew for sure went with the president on his nighttime flights.

Tenner glanced at Seven and flashed an anxious smile. Then

his expression grew troubled, as if he were trying to put the pieces of information together. "When I was little," Tenner said slowly, "I asked my mom what she would have named me if I'd been a girl. She told me my name would've been Tenner no matter what."

Seven frowned. "What's that supposed to mean?"

Tenner shrugged. "That the name was more important than whether I was a boy or girl, I guess." He narrowed his eyes. "Hey, Bird?"

"Yeah?"

"Aren't the palace and the museum on the same street?"

"Yes," said Birdie. "Remember the sign? When we went up the main street from the beach, the museum was a mile to the right, and the palace was two miles to the left."

"Legacy Avenue," said The Librarian. "That's the name of it."

"That's it!" Cabot shot forward, making her seat belt catch, which abruptly stopped her from moving farther. "Their land," she said. "It's on that street! And I bet the address is either 710, or 107, or something like that!"

"Ooh," Lada said, nodding. "If I owned secret property that I wanted to remember, and I wasn't sure how many years I'd be away, I'd probably remember the street name. But it would be harder to keep in mind where exactly on the street it was."

"Especially if it was merely property, and not a recognizable house," The Librarian added.

"We should search for it after we do the stakeout," said Cabot. She glanced at Tenner with a newfound appreciation. His noticing that the museum and the palace were on the same street was really smart and had directly led to Cabot's theory. Maybe Seven had been right about Tenner after all—he had a lot of common sense. He just got overshadowed and drowned out by everyone else.

"Very clever thinking, kids," Elena said. "We may be onto something big." She glanced out the window as The Librarian turned the corner into the Goldens' old neighborhood. Then she pressed against the door, straining to see. "There's the deli where we'd pick up dinner once in a while. And that house had a very prickly dog on a long chain—he'd come bolting at you, barking his head off. He could nearly reach the sidewalk, but the chain stopped him just short of biting your leg off."

"I bet Birdie could've calmed him down," Brix said.

Birdie smiled. "Maybe."

"Oh, and here's the beginning of our row of houses," Elena said. The homes were all attached to one another. Every now and then, there was a door between two homes with an etching next to it that marked a tunnel entrance. "Almost there—it's just around this curve."

The Librarian rounded the bend and began to slow down. "Oh no," she muttered under her breath.

Then Elena gasped.

"What?" Brix cried, trying to see but not knowing what to look for. "What's wrong?" The others strained to figure out what the adults were looking at.

The Librarian slowly rolled past a huge pile of rubble. "*This* was your house?"

Lada clapped a hand to her mouth. "Wait a minute," she said after a second. "Is this the place that mysteriously exploded a few years ago?"

"Yes," said The Librarian. "Even the tunnel collapsed—so it must've been the one with the dove etching. As far as I remember, the police never figured out who did it, or why." The Librarian pulled the SUV to a stop alongside the curb, and everyone stared. The structures on either side of the rubble had been half torn apart, too, and they stood empty. The Birdie-Brix tunnel entrance had been pulverized.

"Oh my God," Elena murmured, clutching her shirt at the neck. "Do you think . . ." She turned wildly toward the others. "Could *they* have . . ."

"That was my first thought," The Librarian said quietly. "You know them best, Elena. Is it too far-fetched to imagine? If they were angry enough?"

Elena closed her eyes and slumped in her seat. "Not too far-fetched at all," she said, sounding defeated.

"What?" Seven demanded. "What are you saying?"

Cabot's eyes widened. "Wait. Do you mean that . . . when the

Cordobas and the Palacios and . . . and maybe even my parents didn't find the stash in the place they expected it to be, did they guess you and Louis had hidden it here?"

"And once they retrieved it," The Librarian mused, "maybe this explosion was their way of sending a threatening message to you, in case you ever came back for it."

710 LEGACY AVENUE

The eight of them stared at the rubble through the windows of the SUV. It looked as though a machine had come through to level the area, but nothing else had been done to clear the lot or rebuild.

"Is there any sense in searching through it for the stash?" Birdie asked. "What if it *wasn't* the other parents, and it was just a random explosion that happened to be at this house?"

"Is that possible?" Brix said, his eyes fearful. "Do things just explode here?"

"No," Elena said firmly. "Random explosions are not something you should be worried about. If there was anything to find, the police and looters would have gotten to it by now anyway. I'm sure they were all over it."

"I remember when this happened," The Librarian said. "It wasn't considered an accident, like an explosion from a gas leak. The police determined it was intentional. All they had to go on was the type of explosive that was used, which, if I recall correctly, they were able to trace to a foreign entity. But beyond that, the trail ran cold."

"I remember it, too," Lada said, leaning forward earnestly. "Right before it happened, Sunrise Foster Home was raided—we were all forced to go outside while a group of people in bodysuits with their faces covered did a search through the place. They destroyed a room—ripped the ceiling apart and tore the drywall off the walls. We kids weren't told what it was about, and after a few hours we got to go back inside. Someone fixed the damage, and we never really heard anything else about it. But then the explosion happened a couple days later. One witness told a reporter they saw someone wearing a bodysuit and a face covering running away. So I always wondered if it was the same people."

"They raided Sunrise?" Elena said, alarmed. "That's where we originally hid the stash—in Troy's old room! It had a drop ceiling with panels that could be removed. Back when we were students, Troy built a hidden trapdoor in the wall above the drop ceiling. He used it to hide whatever treasures he was stealing back then. Before we decided to attempt our final heist, Martim snuck into Sunrise during an open-house event and hid the stash up there for safekeeping . . . in case we couldn't get to it before fleeing to the hideout." Elena nodded slightly. "Now this is all making sense."

"You never told me about Sunrise being searched," The Librarian said to Lada.

"It was a little bit before we met," replied Lada.

The Librarian's expression hardened. "That Sunrise incident makes it clear what happened. When the supernatural criminals returned to Estero, they went looking for the stash in the wall above the drop ceiling. When they didn't find it, they tore the place up, searching for it. Then they concluded that the Goldens—the only ones not searching for it—had to have moved it and kept the secret from them. They thought logically: Where would the Goldens hide something that would be easy for them to find, but difficult for the others to get to? The Goldens' apartment." She smacked the steering wheel, as if adding an exclamation point to the theory.

"And after they got it, they blew the place up," Tenner whispered. He wiped his hands on his new, non-dad cargo shorts. "They destroyed people's homes. And everything they owned."

Elena bowed her head and covered her face with her hands. "I hope no one was hurt. Or . . ."

"Nobody was home at the time of the explosion," The Librarian said. "Someone in the building next door—I'm not sure which side—had minor injuries. The police said it was lucky timing."

"At least they aren't horrible enough to kill innocent people," Elena muttered, shaking her head. She glanced behind her to the third row of seats and saw the ashen look on Tenner's face. She reached over the seat back and patted his hand. "It's *not* your fault—none of you. And you are not like them. Do you hear me?"

Seven and Tenner glanced at each other, then reluctantly nodded.

But Cabot's face was drawn. She couldn't look at Elena. She knew her parents had given in and joined the bad side just a few days after they'd been captured. But had they been involved in this? It seemed like the opposite of what they'd do. Maybe they'd been the ones to make sure no one was in the house—surely Greta and Jack Stone would've insisted on that. Cabot closed her eyes. Her heart ached, and she yearned to know what had happened to make them leave Elena alone in jail. President Fuerte must have forced them to go along with the bad parents somehow. What kind of deal had he made with them to get them to do such a horrible thing? Or . . . were they really just bad people? She still thought there must be more to the story. But her parents were definitely making it impossible for Cabot to defend them.

After a while, The Librarian started the SUV and pulled into the street, her expression still troubled. Not only had the supernatural criminals done this to threaten or intimidate whoever had moved the stash . . . but now the gang of eight had to figure out how they were going to proceed without having access to the money supply they desperately needed. Suddenly the remaining diamonds were more precious than ever. How long would they sustain eight people? Could they take on the power of the president with limited, dwindling funds?

They drove in dejected silence toward the Cordoba Museum. After a while, even though she was riding in the front seat, Birdie's stomach started gurgling, and The Librarian pulled over so she could throw up on the side of the road. Then they continued past the museum, heading down Legacy Avenue toward the palace, looking at the house numbers on mailboxes along the way.

Lada explained to the others how street addresses worked, and noted that the numbers were going down. "Once you know that, it's a lot easier to find your way around," she said.

Halfway to the palace, The Librarian slowed the vehicle and pulled over to let the cars behind them pass. They went past a large old mansion that sat close to the road, which was labeled number 714. Then they came to a driveway that led into thick woods. There was no house visible. The mailbox at the road was silver and looked new, but it didn't have a house number on it.

They glanced up the road and saw the next driveway's mailbox had the number 706 on it.

"Is this 710?" Seven asked, peering up the winding driveway, but he couldn't see far because of the trees.

"My map app says it is," Lada said, looking at her phone.

"We're going to make sure." The Librarian put the vehicle in park. "Someone go online to the Estero City assessor's office and look up this address," she said. "See who is listed as the owner. And, Seven, will you hop out and check if there's any mail in that box?"

Seven had never gotten mail before, but the process seemed intimidating. "Okay," he said uncertainly. "What do I do if I find something?" He wrapped his scarf around his face and reached for the door handle.

"The name and address of the recipient should be on the center of a piece of mail," Elena explained. "And the return address of the sender is in the upper left-hand corner. Look at both."

"Got it," Seven said, sounding relieved. He went out, ran to the mailbox, and opened it. It was empty. But there was a tiny sticker inside that read 710.

Seven went back to the vehicle and told them what he'd found.

Traffic whizzed by them. The Librarian, not wanting to appear suspicious, began driving again, and the rest of them strained to get a glimpse through the thick trees as they went past. Cabot glanced out the back window. Just as they were about to turn to go around the block, she saw a gleaming silver roadster with tinted windows pulling out of the driveway onto the street, going the opposite way.

"Hey, everybody," Cabot exclaimed. "Look—someone's leaving."

The Librarian slowed the vehicle and watched in her rearview mirror as the car disappeared behind them. Then she sped around the corner. "Let's go check it out while they're gone." She rounded the block and returned to the driveway that had the silver mailbox. This time she pulled into the property. "Stay low," she murmured. "In case someone else is here."

Birdie bent forward, but kept her head just high enough to see over the dashboard. The driveway curved like an *S* through the dense woods.

Lada, who'd been attempting the property search, looked up. "The deed says 710 Legacy Avenue belongs to Cordobio LLC," she said with a smirk. "I think we can all figure that one out."

"*Cordobio?*" Tenner muttered. "I'm embarrassed for whoever thought of that."

Birdie snickered from the front seat. Then she turned thoughtful. "Tenner, this seems like confirmation that your mom stuck with the partnership with Seven's parents," she said. "Even though your dad isn't . . . with them."

Tenner shrugged and turned his gaze out the window. He still didn't know how he was supposed to feel about his father's death. He was pretty sure his mother would stick with the Palacios, though, whether Troy was around or not. Lucy and Magdalia had always been close.

Soon, through the trees, they could make out a sprawling estate. But before they could get close to it, they came upon a hideous industrial-style chain-link fence that zigzagged through the forest around the entire property, even across the driveway.

All along the top of the fence was coiled barbed wire. There were signs warning against trespassers.

"That's not going to be easy to get over," Elena remarked.

Birdie glanced at her. "You sound like you've tried climbing a fence like this before."

Elena sighed, almost as if she missed the old days. "I've tried a lot of things." She measured the height with a glance, then studied the coiled wire. Inch-long barbs were plentiful and would be unavoidable. Her gaze swept over the property and stopped to focus on a large metal box next to the fence in the side yard. "The fence is electrified," she said, shaking her head. "Very dangerous. Deadly, even. They're really not wanting visitors."

Seven spotted several tall trees with large branches that hung over the fence and pointed to them as a possible way in.

"It would be risky," Birdie said. "But we're all getting stronger and better at climbing."

Cabot liked the idea. She was adept at tree climbing—it beat rock climbing any day.

"We should leave before they come back," The Librarian said. "Lucy is clairvoyant, right? We don't want her to sense our presence in the driveway." She skillfully began to turn the large vehicle around, doing it slowly so that she didn't leave any suspicious tire marks.

"We're leaving?" asked Tenner, immediately riled up. "That's it? Aren't we going to . . . I don't know . . . wait for them to come back? Face them? Ask them what they're doing with the president? *Demand* they give you your share of the stash?" He wanted to look his mother in the eye and ask her a lot of questions. He seethed, imagining her flippant answers.

Elena smiled sympathetically as The Librarian drove toward the silver mailbox, then slipped out onto the street and headed for the monastery. Elena understood the desire for answers. But that wasn't the way to go about it. "Not today, Tenner," she said. "Impulsive moves are rarely successful. We're stronger if we plan."

Lada leaned over and patted Tenner on the shoulder. "Don't worry," she said. "I have a feeling we'll be back soon. Surveillance, remember?"

TRAINING AND STAKEOUTS

They surveilled the area around the mansion in shifts, watching for anything that would give them clues about the occupants and their comings and goings. When they were off shift, they trained on the monastery grounds. "I still can't get over Cordobio," Tenner muttered to Lada. They swung by their arms on the T-shaped clothesline pole in the backyard of the cottage. Birdie's raven friend, who had been parked at the bird feeder by the mess hall, took flight and landed on the clothes wire, watching the two curiously.

"Cordobio—it's got kind of a chill vibe to it," Lada said generously. She did a couple of chin-ups, making noises as she strained. Sweat soaked her workout top, and she grunted hard on the last one. She felt her arms stiffen, and knew she needed a break. "Can you help me down?"

"Sure." Tenner dropped to the grass and wrapped his arms around Lada's waist. She let go of the bar, and he set her on the ground so she could reach her crutches, which she'd propped against the pole. "What do you mean, *chill* vibe?"

Lada flexed and stretched her arms and fingers, wincing, feeling her hands stiffen and pulse with dull pain. "*Chill* means kind of like you're calm or content with the situation. Feeling relaxed. Like, we're friends, watching TV, and just chilling on the sofa together." She clipped the crutches to her forearms.

"Oh." Being chilly didn't seem calm or relaxing to Tenner. It seemed stressful and uncomfortable. Which his and Seven's parents definitely were. So maybe Cordobio was chilly. Not chill. Watching TV didn't seem relaxing to Tenner, either. He thought about the big-headed people and the scrolling words on the giant screens that lined the city streets, and trying to listen and read and watch all at the same time. "I don't really like TV."

Lada shook her head and laughed. "You haven't *seen* TV—not the good kind."

As Tenner continued to muse over the etymology of *chill,* The Librarian walked out of the cottage. "Listen up, everybody." She waited until they could focus their attention on her, then continued. "I have newspapers, and there's some juicy stuff inside." She held them up, then laid them on the picnic table. Tenner, who was swinging on the clothesline pole again, hopped down and went to grab the most recent one. The Librarian retreated to the sliding door, then glanced back at Tenner before going inside. "You want to do the next surveillance shift with me?"

"Sure!" said Tenner. He didn't find surveillance boring. He liked looking for clues, even tiny ones. Like the fact that two different cars had gone in and out of the garage—not just the silver roadster, but a red hardtop convertible, too. And another time, a vehicle that looked a lot like it could belong to palace guards drove up and stopped in the driveway. Being quiet in the SUV or stationed in the woods suited him as well. He really missed being alone underwater. That had been his time to think and be with nature and let go of the things that were stressful. There hadn't been any opportunity for ocean time since he and Birdie had left their spot on the Estero beach. And city life was so noisy—especially for a boy with super hearing.

"Read the paper first," The Librarian said. "You're the best at finding the tidbits we need. We'll go in a while."

"I'm on it," said Tenner.

Over by the alleyway wall that had the secret door, Elena went back to coaching Seven and Cabot in the art of scaling a fence or climbing a large obstacle. "If you're in pairs and you don't have a rope to help you get over a tall wall, you can use a sweatshirt or jacket instead," she explained. "Seven, take off your sweatshirt. Then boost Cabot up so she can climb onto the top of the wall. When she's up there, throw one sleeve up to her."

"This won't help us get over that electric fence," Cabot said doubtfully. "We'll be incinerated."

"Correct. We'll try something different for that," Elena said. "But this technique is useful for walls, nonelectric fences, and other obstacles you may need to climb on top of. Like a dumpster, or a truck."

With newfound respect for the variety of things they might

have to climb over, Seven and Cabot carried out the first part of the exercise, and soon Cabot was balanced on top of the wall, while Seven remained on the ground. They each held one arm of the sweatshirt.

"Continue holding the shirt between you. When Cabot drops down the other side of the wall, she'll help pull you up to the top, Seven. Give it a try."

Cabot slid off the wall holding her end of the sweatshirt and disappeared from view. Seven started climbing up, helped along by the sweatshirt and Cabot's weight on the other side of the wall. He lunged for the top and pulled himself up the rest of the way. Then he climbed down the other side.

"Now come back the same way," Elena called. While she waited for them, she turned to Lada and Brix, who were standing nearby in the shade of an avocado tree. "Do you two want to have a go at it?"

"I can just bounce up and over," Brix said, sounding smug. "I don't really need help." He ran toward the wall and bounced, grabbed the top, and hung there as Cabot climbed up, coming back into the property. She slid down the wall holding the sweatshirt, and soon the parts of Seven they could see appeared above her.

"Okay, that's helpful to see, Brix," Elena said, pleased to witness more of what her son was capable of *above*ground, where there wasn't a tunnel ceiling to stop him. "Lada, how about you?"

Lada eyed the wall, then shook her head. "Even an adventurous supernatural hero like me has limits." She held her forearm crutches splayed out to the sides, not touching the ground, to help her balance, like a tightrope walker might use a pole. "I've been working on my upper-body strength, but scaling a wall like that isn't something I can do. Not just getting up there, but also the landing seems like it might be extra uncomfortable and awkward for me." She started moving back to the clothesline pole for another round. "I'll stick to pull-ups and push-ups."

"Perfect. Tenner?"

"No, thanks." Tenner shook the newspaper to get it to open properly, copying what he'd seen The Librarian do the other day. The noise scared Birdie's raven and sent it flying up to the cottage roof. Tenner scanned the headlines and read for a moment, then reported his findings, paraphrasing as he read. "Listen to this: The president went on one of his mysterious night trips again. A reporter caught up to him and asked where he'd been. The president said he was, quote, 'building and strengthening our relationships abroad.' When the reporter tried to follow up by asking who he was meeting with and why he only met sneakily during the night, the president shoved past him and went into his car without comment." Tenner looked up. "That seems like an angry reaction. If he really is building relationships, you'd think he'd want to talk more about it. And welcome the chance to have it mentioned in the newspaper."

"Obviously it's because that's not really what he's doing," Elena said. "We know that he wants to steal things from our neighboring countries and meet other supernatural people there, and that he's using my former cohorts to do it. But we've got to get more information on why. I'm hoping 710 Legacy Avenue will give us some much-needed answers."

THAT EVENING, AFTER several of the kids had taken hot baths to ease their taxed muscles, they gathered in the living room. The Librarian and Tenner returned from their stakeout and joined them. "We learned a bit more information at the criminals' mansion," The Librarian announced, then gestured to Tenner to explain.

"Whoever drives the silver car left for about an hour again," Tenner said. "It was at the exact same time as the past two days. They turn all the lights off right before they leave, too, so we think the place is empty at that time of day."

The Librarian nodded, pleased with their discovery. "The fact that they left at the same time three days in a row means they might go *every* day at the same time. So we hope we'll have an opportunity tomorrow to access the place. Are you ready for this?"

"More than ready," said Cabot. The others agreed, eager to see what secrets they could unearth at the mansion.

The Librarian's expression turned very serious. "There's no time to waste. And remember, safety is key. Let's go over our plans. And then we'll get a good night's sleep. In the morning, we're going to make a bug."

"Why can't we just get one from the backyard?" asked Brix.

"Not that kind of bug," Tenner said. "I read about them in the spy books. You mean a listening device to secretly hide inside the mansion."

"Good!" said The Librarian.

Tenner looked sheepishly at her. "I . . . also overheard you talking about it on the phone with your spy friends," he confessed.

"He does that," Birdie reminded her.

The Librarian let out a rare, warm laugh. "Yes, he does. And we're grateful for it."

"Most of the time," Seven muttered sarcastically. Then he plowed his head into Tenner's shoulder, and the two guys commenced with jostling each other annoyingly on the couch. Brix hopped over and landed on them, making the older two cry out in surprise and pain. Birdie, who'd narrowly missed taking Brix's foot to her chin, rolled her eyes and moved to sit next to Lada across the room.

"Annnd," Elena said, eyeing the pileup of boys falling off the couch, "I think this meeting is adjourned for the night."

"Not quite," The Librarian said, raising her voice over the

din. Her eyes landed on Cabot. "Are you up for building that bug with me? I'll teach you."

"Me?" Cabot's eyes widened, and a grin spread across her face. She would have a hard time sleeping that night. "Noisemakers, too?"

The Librarian narrowed her eyes and studied the girl. "Maybe."

SNEAKING IN

In the morning, with the newly made covert listening device tucked inside The Librarian's skirt pocket and the noisemakers safely secured in her toolbox for future needs, the group set out for the criminals' mansion. They wore camouflage colors—tan, green, and brown—to help them blend in to the forest-like background. Even Seven wore camo-colored clothing, which was . . . well, sort of unnecessary. Nobody mentioned it, though. They all knew how much he hated taking his clothes off. Plus they'd be in the woods and climbing trees, so a layer of protective clothing wasn't a bad idea.

The kids and Elena remained quiet as The Librarian parked the SUV under a tree a few blocks away from 710 Legacy Avenue. Then they headed purposefully down a worn footpath through the wooded area so no one passing by on the street or driveway would be suspicious of what they were doing. Once they were hidden from view, they veered off the path and made their way toward the mansion.

Eventually they neared the side of the house where the

electrical box was. The fence was at least twelve feet high, and they could hear a buzzing sound coming from it, which made them all a bit uneasy. They didn't need the giant WARNING signs to know not to get close to it.

"If our theory is correct," The Librarian whispered, "the silver roadster should be leaving shortly." They stayed hidden in the woods, waiting for the cue that all was clear to proceed.

After a while, the lights in the mansion turned off. Then the garage door opened, and the car drove out. They strained to see who was behind the wheel, but they couldn't tell through the tinted windows. The gate automatically slid open across the driveway to let the roadster out. As the car disappeared behind the trees, the gate moved back into place.

"All right," The Librarian said. "Let's move."

"Even though we think the place is empty for the next hour," Tenner reminded everyone, feeling especially smart after his extra surveillance sessions with The Librarian, "we spies always act as if there might still be someone inside."

"Yes," said Birdie. "That way there are no surprises."

The Librarian and Elena exchanged swift grins. "You've trained them well," Elena said.

"They're quick to catch on." Then The Librarian began directing the operation they'd planned. "Brix and Lada, you're up first."

Seven crouched by his backpack and removed a rope, then handed it to Brix.

Lada looked at the younger boy. "I'll meet you by the transformer once you're on the ground inside the fence. Are you ready?"

Brix nodded and slung the rope over his shoulder. He started up a nearby tree, which had large boughs that spread wide over the fence.

Meanwhile, Lada nervously checked her crutches to make sure she had the tools she needed. She watched Brix for a while as he went up several feet higher than the fence and slid out along a thick branch. A sudden, unexpected pang of grief stabbed her chest—sometimes she longed to be able to move as easily as the others. But she knew they each had struggles, too.

The limb sagged under Brix's weight, and he had to move very carefully so that he didn't come into contact with the fence, because that could electrocute him—or the bough could break or catch fire from the voltage. But he managed to make it. Once he was well inside the fenced area, Brix tied the rope to the end of the branch and let it drop. Then he jumped to the grass and bounced a few times. "Come on, Lada!" he whispered.

"Here goes me," said Lada, glancing at Tenner before she disappeared, because he had the most encouraging smile out of everyone. A moment later she reappeared a few dozen feet away, inside the fence. She stabbed her crutches into the ground to steady herself. Brix ran to her, and together they went to the large metal box that rested on a concrete pad.

Lada chose a cutting tool from her tricked-out crutches

while Brix opened the panel, exposing a network of red, green, and yellow wires. After studying the wires inside and muttering to herself, Lada spotted the ones she needed. She squinted at the faint identifying marks that confirmed her tool was in the right place, then cut the first wire. After a few more swift cuts, the buzzing fence went silent.

Lada sat back. "I think that's it," she whispered to Brix. "Are you ready to test it?"

Brix, who could heal the best of any of them, went up to the fence. He cringed, touched it quickly, and pulled his hand away. Then a smile spread across his face, and he placed his hand fully on the fence. "All clear." He motioned for the others to come.

They'd already started scaling the tree. One by one, they scooted to the end of the thick branch, not having to worry about accidentally touching the deadly fence if the branch brushed against it. Then they slid down the rope into the property.

"All right, now," said The Librarian once everyone had made it safely. "Lada, get us inside."

Lada led them to the back door of the mansion and chose a different tool from her crutches. Cabot watched Lada pick the lock, then noted the name of the security company whose sticker was on the window, while the others peered inside. The Librarian prepared to silence an alarm if necessary. When the lock clicked, Lada opened the door an inch and listened at the opening. "The alarm isn't set," she whispered. "They must feel confident with the fence." She gestured for Brix to come closer. "Cover your face," she reminded him. "Look for cameras and turn them toward the walls."

Brix took Seven's scarf and wrapped it around his face, then crammed the floppy sun hat on his head, pulling it low over his eyes. He set off through the rooms, bouncing to reach the high cameras and hoping that no one would bother to review the security footage. The palace guards already knew about the bouncing boy, but they didn't have good descriptions of the others—and the group wanted to keep it that way.

Once inside, The Librarian did a quick sweep of the house, looking for the best location to plant the bug. The others streamed in and moved swiftly through the place, searching for evidence of their parents and what they were up to. There were no family portraits or photos in frames. No familiar clothing hanging in the closets. No items that had initials engraved on them. No art on the walls to give them a clue of who occupied the rooms. No scents they'd smelled before.

Cabot took photos of the security camera locations, and she looked in all the bedrooms. Most were empty. One had a bed that was neatly made, but there were no personal items in the room. Only two of the bedrooms looked like they'd been used regularly. Men's clothing hung in the closets.

Seven beelined for an office desk that had a stack of mail and some papers strewn over it. Even though he was camouflaged, he still had fingerprints, so he was careful not to touch anything. He scanned the desktop, and his gaze landed on the mail. His eyes widened as he saw his father's name—the *fake* one, Martim Palacio—on one of the letters, right in the center. Had his dad continued using the alias because Estero didn't know him by that name? His real name was associated with being a supernatural criminal. It made sense that he wouldn't go back to it—even The Librarian had reinvented herself to skirt around the issues associated with being a super.

While Cabot checked out the garage, Birdie came over to see what Seven was looking at. "This is their place, all right," Seven said to her. "There's mail for my dad."

"What kind of mail?"

Seven shrugged. He'd only seen a few pieces of mail in his entire life and still didn't really understand how to identify them.

The Librarian appeared. She spied the landline telephone on the desk near Seven and Birdie. "There we go," she murmured, and went to it. She started taking the mouthpiece apart so she could plant the tiny bug inside. "Where's Cabot?"

"In the garage," Birdie said. "Cabot! Get over here!"

Cabot came back in and saw The Librarian at work.

Just then, Tenner came running from the long hallway. "I heard something," he said. He went to one of the front windows and peered out through the curtains. "Someone's coming. We need to get out of here. Abandon the plan!"

At Tenner's announcement, The Librarian turned sharply to look out the window and saw the silver car returning. "They're back already! Tenner's right. Everybody out!" She swore under her breath, then quickly stashed the bug back in her pocket and fumbled to put the telephone receiver together. "Now, kids. Move!" Finally she slammed the phone into its cradle.

Everyone ran toward the door at the back of the house. As Birdie turned, she took one more quick glance at the loose papers on Martim Palacio's desk. There was a small scrap that caught her eye, and she leaned over to read it. The words scrawled on it read *Wed 22:30 Hangar 3*.

"Come on, Bird!" Seven grabbed Birdie's wrist and dragged her with him. They ran out the back door and behind the foliage along the fence to keep from being seen.

Lada took a few quick steps, and then, like when she'd been chased by LaDuca, she and her crutches disappeared. She reappeared on the other side of the fence, then snuck around the property to the tree the others had climbed, waiting to help them once they had a chance to escape.

The rest of them gathered behind some bushes near the rope, ready to climb out as soon as the coast was clear. The car stopped at the fence, which wasn't opening automatically because Lada had cut the power. The car door opened. A tall, broad-shouldered man with medium brown skin and black wavy hair got out. Tenner's eyes widened.

The man closed the car door. Then he turned, allowing the group to see his profile.

Tenner gasped and clapped his hand over his mouth, looking like he'd seen a ghost.

Seven and Birdie gripped him by the arms to keep him from bolting . . . or to catch him in case he fainted.

The man in the silver roadster was Troy Cordoba.

A RISKY PLAN

Troy Cordoba, Tenner's dead father, was definitely not dead. He walked up to the fence and, without touching it, peered up at the top and wrinkled his nose. He studied it for a moment, then went to where it latched and examined the mechanism. He muttered something under his breath.

Tenner, still dazed and in shock, was the only one who could hear what his father had said. "He knows the electricity is out," he mumbled to the others. He shook his head like he still couldn't believe what he was seeing. "He must have some sort of control inside the car that opens the gate, and it's not working." He dropped his head into his hands and groaned.

Birdie gave his shoulders a supportive squeeze. "It's okay," she whispered, not sure what else to say. "Just . . . stay calm." Was Tenner glad? Or . . . not? It was such a shock to see the man they all had thought was dead.

As they watched, Troy tentatively tapped the fence with his finger, much like how Brix had done earlier. When it didn't shock him, he started working the latch. Eventually he heaved and pulled on the gate, forcing it to slide open manually. Then he got back into the car and drove the rest of the way into the garage.

"Now?" asked Seven, eyeing the group and trying to decide what order they should go in to get over the fence.

"Not yet," said The Librarian. "He's got to close the gate."

"He's going to know," Tenner said in a panicked voice. "He's going to know we were in there. Why . . . *how* is he alive?" He started to pace.

Birdie paced with him, trying to get him to be still. "We'll deal with him later," she said. "We need to focus on getting out of here before he sees us."

"They'll figure out we cut the electricity," Tenner said, his voice pitching higher. "He's going to be so mad."

"He doesn't know we're here," Birdie said. "He thinks we're still in the hideout like always, soaking up the sun on the beach and living in our little huts. It wouldn't even occur to him that we'd show up in Estero."

Troy emerged from the garage to close the gate. Then he went back inside, and the garage door closed.

"Quickly now," The Librarian said to the others. "Up the rope and over the fence."

"Should we use the gate since the electricity is still turned off?" Seven suggested.

"Troy would be able to see us from inside the house if we

did that," Cabot said. "Plus there's a camera mounted at the top aimed at the driveway. See?" She pointed to it.

"I still don't understand how cameras work," Brix muttered.

Cabot nudged him. "We'll teach you later. But for now we're better off staying on the side of the house, where the garage obstructs Troy's view from the windows."

"Rope it is," Seven said. He and Brix started toward it.

Brix swiftly ascended and slid along the branch. Soon he jumped to the ground and joined Lada. Seven followed, and then the rest of them, with Tenner and Birdie bringing up the rear. Tenner's hands shook as he climbed. But he made it out. Once Birdie got onto the branch, she untied the rope and pulled it up, then tossed it to Seven on the other side of the fence. She carefully climbed down the tree, and moments later she and Tenner were moving swiftly to catch up with the rest.

They treaded carefully through the woods, then along the footpath, and returned to their SUV.

As soon as everyone was inside with the doors closed, they sank back and let out a collective sigh of relief. "That was close," Birdie said, wiping the sweat off her forehead.

Tenner, in the middle row, wore a stricken look.

Elena put a comforting hand on his arm. "I'm sorry, Tenner," she said.

"Are you okay?" Seven asked him. "That was such a shock."

"I don't know," Tenner mumbled. His emotions were everywhere. There was a tiny sense of relief that his dad was alive after all, but it was overwhelmed by a pounding feeling of despair—because his dad was alive after all.

The Librarian and Lada exchanged a somber glance. They'd recognized Troy from the newspaper photo and had figured out what was going on. They'd heard the way Tenner was freaking out about Troy discovering they'd been inside the mansion—heard the fear in his voice, like Tenner was scared of his father. Knowing Troy Cordoba was alive not only made them feel for Tenner, but it also worried them. Troy was big and strong, and had powerful X-ray vision, which meant the group would have to be extra careful. Their enemy list just got longer . . . and stronger.

The Librarian pulled onto the road and drove them back to the monastery, inside the walls where they were safe.

Tenner breathed easier. But everything still felt really weird. And they hadn't even talked about the worst part yet: If Troy Cordoba was alive, whose bones had Seven, Cabot, and Brix found next to Troy's backpack? Tenner couldn't think about that. Not yet. He knew he wasn't the only one wondering. But he had to process everything about Troy first.

THE TEAM GATHERED inside to debrief and document what they'd learned from the mission. And talk about the mistakes they'd made. "We left the cameras turned to the walls," The Librarian said. "Obviously there wasn't time to fix them. And they'll figure out the electricity was cut, but there was nothing we could have done to repair it safely." She pursed her lips. "Plus, I failed to plant the bug. I should have kept it simple and stuck it under the table." She seemed annoyed with herself. Then she shook it off and sat up straighter. "All of you should remember my mistake and learn from it. Okay? What else do we know?"

"Well," Birdie said, wanting to get it out there, "Troy Cordoba is obviously living there."

"My dad seems to be there, too," Seven said. "There was mail addressed to him on the desk. He's using his fake name, the one we know—Martim Palacio."

"I would assume Troy is using his alias, too," said The Librarian. "To keep a low profile."

The mention of Seven's dad jolted Birdie's mind away from the horror of seeing Troy to the scrap of paper she'd noticed on Martim's desk. She squinched her eyes shut and tried to remember what it said, tried to picture it, like Cabot would do. "Wed, twenty-two thirty, hangar three," she murmured.

"What's that?" Lada asked sharply. "Hangar three? Did you see something about an airplane hangar?"

"Yes," said Birdie, opening her eyes. "I was just trying to remember it. Written on a tiny piece of paper on Martim's desk was a note: *Wed, twenty-two thirty, hangar three*. Today is Wednesday. If that number sequence, twenty-two thirty, is the time, that would be . . ." She worked on converting the military time to the more common way she and the other kids had referred to time in the past. "Ten thirty tonight, right?"

"That sounds like an appointment to go flying with Fuerte," said Cabot, raising an eyebrow and crossing her arms over her chest.

Lada nodded. "It sure does." She took off her glasses and methodically cleaned them with her shirt. "Maybe there's a way we can find out what exactly they're up to on those late-night trips."

"You mean go spy on them in the hangar?" Tenner asked dully.

"Yes," Birdie said slowly. "That, too."

"Too?" said Cabot. Then she caught sight of the other girls as they turned to look at Seven. "Oooh." Cabot's face cleared. "Holy coconuts. Are you serious?"

"What?" said Seven. His face and neck blended with the solid orange drapes behind him. He swallowed hard and shifted in his seat. "Why is everyone looking at *me*?"

"Because," Birdie said with a smile. "We can do more than just spy on them from the hangar. *You* can go along for the ride and get us everything we ever wanted to know. And they'll never know you were there."

A NIGHT VISIT

"No way," Seven said. "I'm not—You can't be—" he sputtered, indignant. "What if they catch me? And, like, my *dad* will be there. It's dangerous, and . . . too *weird*. And not just in a being-naked-in-front-of-your-dad way. In a he-abandoned-me-and-I-haven't-seen-him-in-three-years way."

Seven bent forward and buried his fingers in his hair, perplexed. He'd done the naked thing already. It had gone fine, and no one had made a big deal out of it. But he didn't exactly enjoy it. Why did everyone just expect him to feel okay about running around without clothes on? They surely wouldn't do it. Not at the age they were now, anyway. Maybe when they were little. But things were *changing* for Seven. And nobody needed to be around *that* without at least a layer of clothing between.

Besides, it would be really difficult to see his father. He wasn't sure how he'd react. It was easy for Seven to say he'd be all business and do what he needed to do. But he'd just witnessed Tenner *lose it* back there. "You're not thinking this through," Seven said weakly. "We all have a lot of feelings when it comes to our parents. It's hard to set that aside without dealing with it, and just go in cold and get the job done. Plus, we haven't even mentioned the whole airplane-ride-to-a-different-country thing."

"I know it seems scary," Birdie said, speaking more gently now. "And I can see how this would really mess with you." She hopped up from her chair and went to sit on the sofa next to Seven. "But don't you see? You could find out everything about what our parents are doing with the president. That's valuable information, and we have no other way to get it, since the bug didn't get planted in the mansion. Once we know what they're doing, we can figure out how to stop them."

The Librarian reached into her pocket and pulled out the bug, then rolled it between her fingers thoughtfully. "I'm not sure I want Seven taking such a big risk, being stuck on a plane with people who would blow up a house to send a message."

"I'm not fond of that idea, either," Elena said. "We don't know what Fuerte would do to you if you got discovered."

"But Seven's dad would be there," Brix said. "He wouldn't hurt him, would he?"

"He hasn't in the past," Elena said carefully. "Has he, Seven?"

"He's never hit me, if that's what you mean," Seven said. But his heart hurt a good deal from all the ignoring.

Elena nodded. "But we don't know who is in control of this

operation, or how Martim has changed in the three years since we've seen him. We need to be careful."

"I don't want Seven to go," Brix said anxiously.

"Yeah," Birdie said reluctantly. She sank back and rested her head on Seven's shoulder. "That's a good point. I don't want anything happening to you, Seven."

"I appreciate that," Seven said, but he continued to monitor the group suspiciously.

Then Cabot sat up and raised a finger in the air. "I've got it. He could just sneak aboard ahead of time, before the others arrive. Then plant the bug inside the plane and leave. That would help us a lot."

Seven's shoulders stiffened. "I suppose I could do that," he said gruffly. "If the airplane door is open, I can just stick it somewhere and get out."

"That's a great idea," said The Librarian. She tapped her lips with the eraser end of a pencil, which left traces of her metallic-blue lipstick on it. "But unfortunately, the bug we made is a simple one—it won't transmit if we're more than about five miles away from it. We'd only have a short time to listen before we'd lose the signal. Unless . . ." Her wheels turned. "If I can secure a high-tech covert device, one that has the capability to link to satellites, we'd have ears on them the whole time, no matter where in the world they go." She stood up abruptly, her deep brown eyes flashing, and swished her skirt with an authoritative air. "I'll be back. Be ready after dinner."

THAT EVENING, THE group arrived outside hangar number three at the Estero City Airport, where the president's private plane was being prepped. The Librarian parked in the shadows behind the hangar, near some other vehicles. Lada and Cabot sat together in the middle row with a small laptop computer and their phones, using apps to monitor flight activity. "There's still no record of a private flight scheduled to depart at ten thirty," Lada reported. "President Fuerte must have some way of blocking his activities from the public, or else the journalists would be all over it." As she researched, she taught Cabot about everything she was looking for.

The Librarian climbed nimbly through the SUV over the other passengers to squeeze into the seat next to Seven. She showed him the new high-tech satellite bug she'd procured and explained to him what he should do with it.

At ten fifteen, they heard the huge hangar door rattle as it opened. "That's your cue, Seven," Birdie said. "Be careful." She got out of the vehicle after him, found his hand, and clasped it for a moment, making a silent wish that everything would go smoothly.

But Seven had the jitters. His hands were sweating. And he didn't feel like touching anything at that particular moment. He pulled away and checked his new earpiece, which The Librarian had specially made for him. It was acrylic, which was completely see-through, unlike the old one, which could be seen moving on its own through the air. The wires inside the new acrylic one were so tiny they were hardly noticeable. The earpiece only had a range of about two miles, The Librarian had told him, but that didn't matter now—he was only going a few hundred yards into the hangar.

The Librarian got out and set Seven's earpiece to its own channel tied to Cabot's earpiece, so Seven wouldn't be distracted by the idle chatter of the rest of the team. Cabot and Seven did a sound check to make sure it was working properly—she could hear him, and he could hear her. Then Tenner and Elena slipped out of the vehicle, too, to take their watch positions at the corners of the giant building.

Birdie, undeterred by the earlier rejection, grabbed Seven once more before they separated and pulled him aside. She took him by the shoulders, facing him, searching for those pupils like always. She flashed a grim smile. "Listen to me," she said. "If you don't see a chance to get in and out easily, don't do it. Stay safe."

"I'll be careful," Seven promised, but his stomach churned. He eased out of Birdie's grip but then, feeling bad, slid his hand down her arm reassuringly—she was caring for him, and he usually loved that. But right now it was adding to his anxiety. "I'll see you in a few minutes. Okay?"

Birdie nodded.

Seven trotted to the front corner of the hangar. Before continuing, he glanced all around, waiting for Birdie and the others in view to look away. Then he stripped and dropped his clothing in a pile in the shadow of the building, where he could easily grab it on his way out. He pinched the new, high-tech satellite bug between his fingers, knowing it could be detected, but it was small enough that it might be mistaken for an actual bug zigzagging through the air. The Librarian had applied double-sided tape to it so he could peel the backing off and stick it in the best spot.

He dropped his phone onto the pile of clothes, because it could definitely be detected. But then he hesitated. What if something went wrong and he needed help? What if he wasn't in a spot to speak to Cabot, and could only text? And wouldn't it be a good idea to take pictures of the inside of the plane and document where he hid the bug if he had the opportunity?

Seven glanced inside the hangar. It was dark enough that no one would notice the phone seemingly moving freely through the air unless they were staring right at it. And if he had to ditch the phone to keep it from being seen, so be it. They could always buy another one with the extra diamonds. But there was no one in sight, and it seemed pretty safe. He picked it up and went in.

The airplane hangar was like an enormous warehouse. A row of soft lights was shining overhead, above the plane, but two other rows were unlit. Tools hung on the walls, and there were machines and open-air vehicles with huge iron forks sticking out horizontally at floor level. Seven stuck to the shadows. He had never seen vehicles like that on the streets of Estero. Inside, the hangar smelled faintly of fuel—which he could definitely identify after spending a few days in the city. "I'm moving toward the plane," he whispered to Cabot. "No one in sight, but I can hear some machines."

"Copy that," Cabot said. She'd picked up some lingo from all the spy books she'd read.

The airplane was gleaming white, with six small, rectangular windows on each side and an open door. The presidential seal was stamped near the tail. A woman in a gray mechanic's jumpsuit appeared from the tail end, moving around the outside of the plane with a clipboard, checking it out. Seven froze in place. Another mechanic came around the front end and called out some numbers to the first. Then a third emerged from the open door of the plane and went down the portable stairs to the ground.

Seven started to sweat. He glanced at the front of the hangar, near the giant door, and could barely detect Elena lingering in the shadows, but she couldn't see him like this. He took a few more steps toward the plane and shivered as the night breeze flowed through the space. Were there any more mechanics inside the plane? How many did one small plane need?

He kept going, nearing the steps. Seven didn't know what the airplane would look like inside, though The Librarian had explained that it would probably be fancy, with lush carpet and cushiony seats and tables, so the president and whoever went with him could do their work while in the air. She'd suggested sticking the bug under one of the seats, out of sight, so they wouldn't discover it.

Seven closed his eyes and tried to even out his breath. Even though he knew no one could see him, it still felt scary. And he knew he needed to hurry, but he couldn't seem to convince his body to speed up. What if the stairs creaked when he walked up them? What if someone inside the plane bumped into him? He swallowed hard and continued. As he reached the bottom step, headlights pierced the darkness and bounced off the plane. Seven turned sharply. Whoever it was had turned toward hangar three. Was it his father?

Seven stood uncertainly at the base of the stairs and barely managed to scoot out of the way as the first mechanic brushed past him with her clipboard and went up, then turned left into the cockpit. Seven glanced at the approaching car, knowing his time was limited. Should he bail? No one would blame him. Birdie's words about staying safe rang in his ears.

But this was so important. He was close enough to see the plush chairs and tables inside the door. All he had to do was stick the bug under one and get out. It would be over in an instant. Seven eased up the steps, peering forward to watch for the mechanic in the cockpit and hoping she wouldn't choose this moment to come back out. He reached the aisle and slid to the right, into a space that looked like one of the fancy rooms in the palace. There were eight lounge chairs, with four tables between them. He dropped to the floor and looked for the best, lowest hiding place to stick the bug.

Underneath a table was the easiest option, but it could be visible to anyone sitting in the chairs nearby if they happened to bend down and glance at the underside of the table. The chairs themselves had big, solid, square bases that swiveled. Seven felt around to see if there was room to plant the bug along the base of one of them.

"Seven, where are you?" Cabot's voice whispered in his ear. "More cars arriving. You've got a minute or two to get out of there."

The mechanic in the cockpit reappeared. Seven skittered under a table and froze as she breezed past his bare bum and went inside the bathroom. He needed to get out fast before she came back. The chair base would have to do. Seven hid his phone and fumbled the tiny bug, trying to peel the tape backing off with his sweaty, shaking fingers. Finally he got it. He pressed the bug as far out of sight as he could, but it wouldn't stick. He examined it and realized he was holding it with the sticky side against his thumb. He unstuck it and turned it around, then tried again, hoping there was still some stickiness left. This time it stayed where he pressed it.

"Coming," he whispered, grabbing his phone.

Before he could stand, the mechanic strode past again and turned to go down the stairs. Seven waited until he heard the woman's boots clunk on the steps. Then he crawled into the aisle, got up, and moved swiftly so he could exit, too.

As he neared the boarding door, the mechanic gave a greeting. "Good evening, Mr. President," she said, and sidestepped out of the way.

"We're in a hurry," the president muttered, and started up the stairs.

Seven gasped and panicked, backing up into the cabin and trying to hide his phone—he couldn't throw it or it would make a noise. He slid into a wide space in front of a bulkhead panel, where there was an emergency exit door with nothing in front of it. His eyes darted all around; then he crouched and tucked his phone into a storage panel on the wall that held life preservers. The president blew past him and sat down in the nearest chair a few feet away, dropping his briefcase on the table. He leaned forward and opened it.

"Seven!" Cabot whispered harshly. "Are you coming?"

Seven couldn't respond. He gazed regretfully in the direction of his phone, knowing he'd have to abandon it, and waited until he saw his opportunity to sneak out.

But then another breeze blew his hair back. An invisible one. Seven's heart thudded. He'd felt breezes like that before, back home in their cabin, whenever Martim didn't want to be bothered. Did his dad even know he was detectable in that way? Seven had never told him.

First a closet door next to the bathroom opened, and clothes on hangers moved through the air seemingly on their own. Then the bathroom door opened and closed, the clothing disappearing inside. The person carrying them had to be Martim. Seven glanced at the airplane door, seeing the area was clear and knowing he needed to leave. Knowing this was his chance to get out. But he was frozen. He hadn't seen his dad since the day he and his mom had left. Seven gripped his hair, feeling the strong urge to exit. But part of him insisted he stay to find out for sure. The "stay" part won.

A moment later, Seven's dad emerged, fully visible, tucking his shirt into his trousers, then tying his tie. Looking like a professional businessperson, like so many people on the streets of Estero. Seven gaped. He covered his mouth, trying not to emit a sound. His insides twisted. There was the man who'd left his kid and hadn't returned. The one who'd never seemed to enjoy being a dad. His dark brown hair was slicked back and shiny under the lights. His brown eyes pierced the air, and his nose and chin were as strong and pronounced as Seven remembered. Dressed this way, Martim looked famous and intimidating, like the celebrities they'd seen in the newspaper. Tears stung Seven's eyes, but he couldn't look away.

Martim pulled a suit jacket out of the closet and closed the door. He draped it over the back of the chair that had the bug attached to it—the one across the table from President Fuerte. Then he dropped into the chair. "Evening," he said coolly.

Fuerte nodded but didn't look up. "Martim," he said in greeting.

Seven forgot about escaping and drank in his father. Martim Palacio's flashy gray suit and dark purple tie were a far cry from the T-shirts and shorts he'd worn in the hideout. The man was clean-shaven, not a hair out of place. His usual brown skin seemed a shade lighter than Seven remembered, perhaps because he wasn't spending every day on the beach anymore.

Fuerte handed Martim a packet of papers, and Martim started reading without comment, as if this was something they'd done many times before. Seven sucked in a breath as a jumble of emotions kept him planted, deadweight, in front of the emergency exit. Then Cabot hissed in his ear, bringing him abruptly back to the real-life danger he was in.

"Close call on the way here," Martim said casually as he turned the first page over. "Ran into another journalist outside again. I ditched her."

Seven's eyes widened. Had The Librarian posed as a reporter, or was someone else out there, too? If so, the rest of the team could be in danger. He swallowed hard and inched toward the door, not wanting to stir up a noticeable breeze like Martim had just done.

"You should always arrive invisible," the president said, reprimanding him. "Just assume we're being watched."

"I *did*," Martim said wryly. "But the tether isn't invisible, and the car door still has to open to let me out. I'm not a ghost who can move through solid items, you know. They're going to know it's the same invisible guy as the other times. I'm going to start arriving fully visible and *dressed*. I despise sitting in security vehicles like *that*. If you know what I mean."

"Don't be disgusting, Martim," Fuerte said tiredly.

Seven continued sneaking slowly toward the boarding door, his heart pounding in his ears. Fuerte was just feet away. He took one last look at his father. The man in the suit seemed like a total stranger.

Cabot hissed in his earpiece again. "Seven! Where are you? Do we need to come after you?"

Seven pressed his lips together and let out a careful breath, then took one last look at the storage pocket where his phone was hidden. He kept going without it and hoped no one important would find it. When the men turned toward each other and began discussing the paperwork, Seven moved as quietly as he could to the door and started down the first couple of steps. He leaned back to peer over his shoulder and around the corner to make sure his father and Fuerte hadn't detected him and saw they were intent on their discussion. With a breath of relief, Seven faced forward.

Another vehicle was rolling up planeside.

Seven's knees buckled. He gasped in fear as two people exited the vehicle and started toward him: Troy Cordoba and a woman. In his panic, it took Seven a moment to recognize her. As Troy started up the steps, Seven realized the woman was Cabot's mother, Greta Stone. His heart sank for Cabot at the same time it exploded in fear—he was stuck. There was no way to get past them. He backed up quickly into the plane and darted to the same space in front of the bulkhead to keep them from running into him.

Troy thudded past, shaking the floor with his footsteps. He ducked slightly to keep from bumping his head on the ceiling. When Greta came in through the door, she turned around and pulled it closed behind her with a loud slam. Then she locked it and went into the cockpit.

Seven was trapped inside.

AN UNCOMFORTABLE JOURNEY

Before Seven could even catch his breath, the propellers were turning, and the plane was rolling out of the hangar. Greta Stone's voice came over the loudspeaker. "Buckle up, please, gentlemen," she said in a clinical tone as they started toward the runway. "We're cleared for takeoff." Fuerte and Troy put on their seat belts, while Martim fumbled half-heartedly with his, then left it dangling, unbuckled. Seven scarcely noticed—he was crouched and gripping the lush carpet strands, scared out of his mind.

Cabot was freaking out in his ear. "Are you on the ground somewhere? Or still on the plane? Can't you at least whisper?"

Seven couldn't answer her. He closed his eyes and dipped his head, feeling faint. His legs shook, and not just because of the vibration of the plane. Stuck in the space in front of the bulkhead, with his backside pressed against the cold emergency exit door to stay out of everyone's reach, Seven was going on this flight whether he wanted to or not.

He couldn't risk whispering a single word to Cabot about

what was happening. But then he remembered his phone, and his eyes flew open. He slid over to the wall pocket and pulled out the device, keeping it shielded from view behind the bulkhead.

He pressed his thumb against the button, and the screen lit up. Seven nearly doused it, worried that the light would draw attention to him. But he swiftly glanced around the panel and saw that the three men weren't looking his way. Troy had swiveled his lounge chair around and had his back to him, which was a huge relief because of the man's X-ray vision. Troy could probably see right through the bulkhead if he had a reason to put his supernatural focus there. Seven wasn't about to give him one.

Seven hunted and pecked at the keyboard, still new to the technology, trying to hurriedly type a text message to his group: **Got stuck on plane. Door closed before I could get off. Bug in place. Is it working? I don't dare speak out loud to Cab.**

He sent the message and counted the agonizing seconds, waiting for a reply. His whole body was shaking now. They were still on the ground, traveling fast. The plane sped up even more, and everything inside rattled. Seven tried to grip the panel he was pressed up against. He had never been on a plane before, and he was scared to death that he would go airborne or crash into something when the plane took off.

Then his eyes widened further in a technological panic. He checked his phone's volume button, and melted in relief when he found it still set to silent, just like everyone had done before they started the mission. Technology was stressful.

The plane lifted and tipped. Seven hung on for dear life. They were airborne. Airport lights danced through the windows and grew small and far away. Seven took a few slow breaths.

"Got your t—" Cabot's voice cut off in his ear.

Seven wiggled his earpiece. But all was silent. They must be two miles away already.

His phone didn't make a sound when Lada's text reply came in: **Bug working great! Librarian says stay on board when you land and wait for return. Don't go with them. Also put your phone on airplane mode now or someone on board might detect your hot spot.**

Three dots appeared, and then another message from Lada came quickly. How she could type so fast was beyond comprehension. **Cabot says you're out of range and she's lost contact with your earpiece. Call us when you're alone!**

Seven swallowed hard as he read the messages, not quite understanding the whole "detect your hot spot" part. **OK**, he typed, and sent the reply.

With shaking hands, he stared at the mess of icons on the screen, feeling overwhelmed. Finally he managed to identify the settings app and found airplane mode. He flipped the toggle and let out a breath of relief. So many new words added to his vocabulary in the past few days. So much bumping and rattling as the airplane rose and dipped in the air. He closed his eyes and gave in to the force of speed, which held him against the bulkhead. There was no thrill attached to his first plane ride. He was sick about it. Stuck on this plane with a bunch of bad people. Naked and scared. His clothes in a pile on the ground miles away. Thank goodness the bug was working, because Seven was so unsettled he was having trouble listening to the men's conversation.

Once the turbulence died down and they were flying smoothly, Seven's breath steadied. He built up his courage and peered around the panel again to study his father. His tie was loosened around his neck now, and the top button of his shirt was open. He wasn't wearing socks with his dress shoes, and the outline of a transparent ankle band caught Seven's eye. It had to be the tether that Fuerte forced the criminals to wear. Wires and a silver disk were visible through the band. It was probably acrylic, like Seven's earpiece, made to be as invisible as possible when Martim was using his ability. He tried to look at Troy's ankles, but they were hidden behind the chair.

Seven thought his dad was so lucky. He could turn his invisibility on and off. Right now he didn't appear supernatural at all. He was good-looking, and could be charming when he wanted to be.

A couple of years ago, Louis had told Seven that his dad hadn't been able to control his invisibility when they were younger. That he would randomly disappear at awkward times, leaving just his clothes walking body-less down the street, kind of like how Seven looked all the time. It had put Martim in danger and had also kept him from holding down a job. But Martim had worked on controlling his ability and learned to turn his invisibility on and off on a whim. When he activated it, he went *fully* invisible, unlike Seven, whose outline was barely detectable if you knew what to look for. Because Seven's body didn't disappear; it merely took on the features of his background. His pupils were the only thing that didn't blend in with whatever was behind him.

Seven wondered what full, complete invisibility would be like . . . especially if he could choose to be visible whenever he wanted. Being permanently camouflaged, Seven would never have the same opportunities as his father. He longed to be able to turn his ability off. To blend in with a crowd, like the others. And if he could, he'd probably leave it turned off forever.

But for now, he was glad he didn't accidentally flicker into visibility.

THE FLIGHT CONTINUED without Seven being detected, which allowed him to finally settle down and listen to the men. They said a lot of things about finance, banks, deals, and other things that didn't make much sense to Seven. But then they started talking about a new asset.

At first Seven wasn't sure what an "asset" was. But he deduced from the conversation that they were talking about a person—someone from the country they were going to. Seven peered around the bulkhead, hoping the satellite bug was handling the distance to its receiver better than his earpiece had, because the others needed to hear this. Then his expression brightened with an idea. He reached back and retrieved his phone. Careful to keep it low and mostly out of sight, Seven found the camera app and began video-recording the men.

"You might remember her," Fuerte said to Troy and Martim. "She goes by Cami Leone. She lived at Sunrise Foster Home a number of years behind you. Left Estero when I banished everyone, but wants to come back."

Troy shrugged and shifted in his chair. "Never heard of her. What can she do?"

"She's a chameleon."

"What, like she's camouflaged?" asked Martim with disgust in his voice. He snorted, as if camouflage ability was beneath him.

Seven cringed as his dad's words and tone pierced his heart. Martim had just validated everything Seven had felt about his useless, embarrassing camo ability. His dad thought camouflage was disgusting. Seven dropped his gaze and swallowed hard. He never wanted his father to know what he'd become.

"Not camouflage, thank goodness," Fuerte said, driving the stake further into Seven's heart. Seven's phone wavered as he absorbed the blows. "Much better than that. More of a shapeshifter. She can change her appearance to other human forms and become totally unrecognizable, or at least that's what Sabine tells me. We'll see for ourselves, obviously." He leaned in. "She's at the top of my list of assets, though. Sabine tracked her down, and I'm hoping she's our winning ticket that puts us in *very* good shape after election time."

Election time? Lada had mentioned elections happening next year when they were down in the tunnel, but Seven hadn't paid much attention—his head had been spinning with so many other things to learn. Besides, what did any of this have to do with it?

"Hmm." Martim seemed to perk up. He shifted in his chair and crossed his legs the other way.

"Camouflage has its benefits," Troy commented, sounding almost generous for the first time ever, as far as Seven could remember.

"Please," Martim said with a sneer. "Don't be ridiculous." Seven closed his eyes and lowered his head, but kept filming even as his father continued making him feel worse.

"Whatever." Troy's gaze drifted to the papers Martim was holding. "What's the job tonight, anyway?"

"Sorry." Fuerte pulled an identical set from his briefcase. "Here you go." He tossed it across the aisle to Troy. "There's a painting in an art gallery in Frayzia that I've taken a fancy to," said Fuerte snootily. "We're going to take it home with us."

Troy and Martim exchanged an annoyed glance.

"Don't worry," Fuerte said, catching it. "You'll get paid for your evening, as always."

"It's getting tedious," Troy said.

"We're building an *army*," Fuerte said, immediately defensive.

"Remember? It's going to be tedious until we have all the right people in place. And we need to see Cami's methods when dealing with security guards, and how expertly she uses her ability, before we agree to let her back into Estero. You know this."

Martim sighed in frustration. "It's been a year of these ridiculous jobs. What have we got—twenty new supers in Estero now? How many more do you need?"

"As many as I can get," Fuerte said testily. "And don't forget I'm keeping you both out of jail. That comes with a price. You agreed to do this!"

"How could we possibly forget?" Troy said sarcastically. "You remind us all the time."

"Statute of limitations is coming up," Martim remarked quietly, like a dare.

President Fuerte flashed a condescending smile. "For your old wrongdoings, yes. But don't forget who has protected you ever since you were caught running from the foster home." Fuerte settled back stiffly and lowered his voice. "Anyway, none of that matters, because you've done *so* many more crimes since then. I've got plenty of proof."

"Under duress," Martim shot back.

"*I* certainly didn't make you blow up a house. Or steal from a museum."

That silenced Martim.

So the bad parents *had* raided the foster home and blown up

Elena and Louis's old apartment. And had *they* been the ones who stole the old currency from the Cordoba Museum back before Birdie and Tenner got taken to the police station for trying to use the old currency? Fuerte hadn't been a part of that, but he didn't seem to mind. As for the rest of the conversation, Seven didn't understand much. Statute of limitations? Duress? What was that? Cabot or The Librarian would know.

Just then the plane jolted and rattled. A folder and Fuerte's cell phone slid off the edge of the table and bounced toward Seven, who'd grabbed the bulkhead panel to keep from tumbling to one side. Seven's eyes widened, and he slowly backed up, keeping his phone camera trained on the men, but ready to stash it as soon as Fuerte came for his things.

But instead of getting up to retrieve the items, Fuerte merely held out his hand. He narrowed his eyes as if concentrating. A second later, his phone sprang through the air and landed in his hand with a smack. He set it down on the table and did the same for the folder.

"Ho-lee expletive," Seven whispered silently. Not only had Fuerte just revealed he was building an army of supernatural people to work *with him* in Estero, but he had also just done something extremely unexpected. Seven's hands trembled as he held the phone. He wasn't sure if he could believe his own eyes, so he was glad he'd gotten it on camera. Because President Fuerte had just commanded an inanimate object to come to him. Did that mean *he* was a super, too?

A SUPER ARMY

As they waited for Seven's return to the airport, Birdie, Cabot, Lada, Tenner, Brix, and the two adults in the SUV leaned toward the bug receiver, hanging on to every shocking word of the conversation between President Fuerte, Martim Palacio, and Troy Cordoba.

"Did you hear that?" Cabot whispered. "The president is building an army of supernatural people! He's got twenty of them already!"

The Librarian nodded grimly. She tapped her perfectly manicured fingernails on the leather-padded steering wheel a few times, making a muddled drumroll. "I heard. But I don't understand."

"It makes no sense," Elena said. "He hates us."

"What does statue of eliminations mean?" asked Brix. He imagined a statue of . . . nothing at all. It was such a deep thought it almost made his mind explode.

"*Statute* of *limitations*," Elena said. "It's a law that says if you commit a crime, legal proceedings must begin within a set amount of time, or the charge goes away and you can be free."

"What's the statute of limitations for stealing priceless jewels, gold, and the president's daughter's diamonds?" Lada asked with a sly grin. She tapped her forefinger against her lips.

Elena looked sideways at her with a little glint in her eye. "Fifteen years."

"It's been fifteen since your last heist, hasn't it, Mom?" Birdie asked. "I'm almost fourteen, so it's got to be soon."

"We're coming up on it," said Elena. "I had that in mind when I was being kept prisoner. I knew that eventually—if Fuerte ever let me out—I'd be past the statute of limitations and would be able to walk free and go back to you in the hideout. But, like Fuerte said, Martim, Troy, Greta, and probably Jack have all done other crimes recently, so they could still be punished for those if they get caught."

Cabot paled. "Even if Fuerte is making them do it?"

Elena pressed her lips together. "I'm not sure. Maybe."

Cabot closed her eyes and let out a deep sigh. Her parents were acting so unwisely. She was furious with them. Elena was days away from being free forever, but Cabot's mom, by flying the plane, had started a whole new fifteen-year period where she could be sent to jail. Cabot dropped her face into her hands.

Tenner gave her a quick, supportive side hug—not too long, because she was Cabot and might growl at him. But she allowed it. "Well," he said, "we learned even more things: Troy and Martim definitely got caught after raiding the foster home, but they also blew up the house and stole the money from the museum. And Fuerte is keeping them out of jail no matter what they do. We also know why Fuerte made that unexpected order relaxing the laws against people like us. To keep his new 'soldiers' from getting arrested. So maybe he'll continue protecting our parents, too."

"Ahh," said The Librarian, nodding. "Yes, I think you're right. As long as they keep working for him, of course. That's one mystery solved."

"But why a whole army of supers?" Lada asked. "Fuerte is the leader of the regular military and can send them out if Estero is in danger. But it's not." She paused thoughtfully. "And he keeps saying he's repairing relationships with our neighboring countries, so he wouldn't want to fight them. So who does he think he's going to battle against? And what does this have to do with the election?"

"As far as the election," The Librarian said, "I haven't heard of anyone running in opposition to him. Have you read anything about that in the papers, Tenner? Or seen anything online?"

"Nothing," said Tenner.

"It's because nobody ever opposes Fuerte," The Librarian said. "He's been in power for almost twenty years."

Perplexed, Elena turned in her seat. "I still don't understand. Fuerte hates supernatural people and has been oppressing us for decades. Yet now he's recruiting the same ones he deported years ago. Nothing about this move makes sense. I'm . . . flabbergasted. I didn't think Fuerte could shock me with anything he does. But he just did."

They mulled it over in silence, until the conversation on the plane started up again, clear as day through the satellite bug. Seven had definitely found an excellent place to stick it. They listened as the president talked Troy and Martim through the game plan of stealing the painting with the new super, Cami Leone.

"So," The Librarian said. "Let me try to make sense of this. Fuerte, with Troy, Martim, and Greta, plan to audition the shape-shifting super, Cami Leone, by making her do a heist in her own country, against her own government. And if they succeed, the super gets to come back with Fuerte on the plane and be part of the secret army. Is that it?"

"Sounds like it," said Lada, who was methodically massaging the tight muscles in one of her lower legs while they waited. "Though I'm not sure how that's helping heal relationships with neighboring countries," she added sarcastically. "It seems like Fuerte is doing opposite day."

"Opposite *life*," Brix said. He sat up and wrinkled his nose. "If President Fuerte is trying to get more supernatural people to come here, why isn't he trying to get *us* to join him?"

"Now, there is the question of the day," The Librarian said approvingly. "Obviously he was trying to get your mom to join him for the past three years, but she wouldn't."

"And you see where that left me," said Elena. "In prison. So I don't think he's trying to *force* the supers from other countries to join him—he only wants to work with people who *want* to work with him. He must be finding willing participants. People who want to come to Estero."

"Or," said Cabot, lifting her head, "people who were banished from Estero years ago—kicked out of Sunrise Foster Home. Ones they might have personal records of, right? People who want to return because maybe their families or their future hopes and dreams are here. And maybe this is their ticket back in."

"Oh," said Birdie. "That makes sense. Also, aren't they in danger in their own countries? Hatred against supers is sort of universal, isn't it?"

Lada nodded.

"So maybe Fuerte tells them they'll be protected by him now." Birdie slid sideways in her seat, making a triangle with her leg.

The Librarian nodded. "And Sabine, the president's daughter—"

"The one with no diamonds," Brix added smugly.

"Yes, that one," said The Librarian with a sly side-eye glance. "She must have a database of supers who have passed through Sunrise Foster Home and been subsequently banished over the years. So she knows what their abilities are and where to find them. I vaguely remember having to give them detailed information of my whereabouts when they kicked me out of the country."

"I'm sure they hung on to those records," Elena said. She tapped the corner of her cell phone against her pursed lips, then sat up straight. "You know what else? I bet Fuerte is also appealing to the banished supers' sense of revenge."

"What do you mean?" Tenner asked, tucking a fallen lock of hair behind his ear.

Elena thought for a moment. "Supers have been oppressed for decades. Say Fuerte's people track down someone who has struggled to survive, to find a job, to live a normal life, in a world that hates supernatural people. And he says, 'I can give you an important job with me, the president of Estero. I've changed my ways, and now I'm building an army of supernatural people. This will be your chance to fight back against all the oppression.' Don't you think some people would go for that?"

Lada's expression flickered. "I mean, *I* might be tempted to," she admitted. "If I didn't know how awful he is. And if I didn't already have a group of people like you."

"Exactly," said Elena. "They've been so beaten down that a simple offer to belong somewhere—even from a slimeball like Fuerte—might be better than the life they're currently living."

"He's preying on them." The Librarian's face was troubled. "But we still don't know why Fuerte is building an alternate army when he already has a regular army. And why he's choosing people he despises to be in it. It has to be because they're more powerful than regular people, right? But I'm not sure he'd give up his biases in exchange for that."

"Shh," Tenner said, holding up his hand. "Someone's talking again. Maybe we'll find out."

A MISSTEP

Seven didn't dare check the video to see if he'd captured the president's supernatural move—he didn't want any flash of light or accidental sound to draw attention to him in his little hiding place. And he wasn't confident enough yet on how the phone worked to trust that the volume of the video was really off. Instead he clicked to send the video to the team in a text message.

But the video wouldn't send, and the text message yelled at Seven with an angry red exclamation point. He frowned, feeling personally attacked. Then he remembered he had airplane mode turned on. He'd have to wait.

Greta Stone's familiar voice floating through the speakers startled Seven. "Sorry about that turbulence," she said, not exactly sounding sorry. "We'll be landing soon. Buckle up."

Seven pressed against the emergency door, then returned his phone to the wall pocket space, hiding it behind the floatation devices again. He hung on and tried not to freak out as they tipped and bounced onto the runway. He could only imagine if

Birdie were the camouflaged one and this had been *her* mission. That turbulence and landing would have had her puking left and right. Puke coming out of nowhere? What a surprise that would be for the others on the plane! The thought of it made him grin and kept him from thinking much worse things, like what he would do if any of the criminals discovered him.

But they had other things on their minds, too. Troy, Martim, and President Fuerte took their belongings and deplaned, and soon Greta emerged from the cockpit and followed them, closing the boarding door behind her. Seven breathed a sigh of relief when no mechanics or other people came on board. He flopped on his back and melted into the carpet, exhausted from the stress. But then he sat up just as quickly. He retrieved his phone, turned off airplane mode, and called The Librarian.

He waited, but there was no ringing sound. After a few seconds, a recorded voice came on the line. "Welcome to Frayzia. Your cellular plan is not in service in this area. Please contact your carrier to enable international roaming. Fees may apply." Seconds later, a text message appeared saying the exact same thing.

To Seven, the words were like a foreign language. He ended the call, swiped the message away, and tried calling Birdie, but got the same recording. "Who is my carrier?" he muttered, stabbing the button to end the call. Next he tried sending the video to Cabot and Lada in a text message. But the video failed to go through again. "Augh!" he said too loudly, and had to go peer out the window to make sure no one had heard him. But the hangar they were parked in was empty. He went back to his space. **Hello**, he typed in the text box, and pressed "send." It, too, was rejected by the angry exclamation mark.

Frustrated, Seven tossed the phone to the carpet. He balled up his fists and furiously rubbed his eyes with them. It was late. He was exhausted and anxious and naked and cold. And technology was trying to kill him. He put the phone back into airplane mode and stashed it once more. Then he got up and walked down the aisle, looking around. The men hadn't left anything behind.

Seven wandered into the cockpit and examined the immense control panel covered with levers and gauges and knobs, gaining new respect for Cabot's mom for being able to fly it. Soon the lights in the hangar turned off, making things pitch-dark in the plane except for a few emergency lights running along the aisle that seemed to stay on permanently. Seven felt his way back to his hiding place and sat down on the carpet. Shivering, he curled into a ball, hugging his knees, and closed his eyes. It was after midnight. He decided he might as well get some rest while the criminals were out.

SEVEN DOZED FITFULLY, constantly worried in his dreams that he wouldn't wake up when the adults came aboard again. A few hours later, he awoke with a start. It was still dark. He sat up and checked his phone, seeing that it was past four o'clock in the morning. Would they be back soon?

Seven jiggled his leg. He needed to use the restroom and get a drink—his mouth was as dry as a cork. But was it too risky to do that now? What if they came back? He was disoriented and fuzzy-headed from his nap. It would be a long flight back if he didn't go now. He'd have to risk it. He got up and moved quickly down the aisle to the bathroom where his father had changed clothes.

While he was in there, he heard the boarding door open and muttered a curse word Louis had taught them not to say. He hurried to finish up, slipped through the door as Greta rounded the corner to the cockpit, and bounded swiftly back into his hiding spot as Troy backed into the aisle carrying one end of the stolen painting. Seven's dad carried the other end.

Seven looked curiously at the painting as they walked by. It depicted a woman with her head on sideways, lounging on a bench, surrounded by about fifteen ugly naked babies who all looked as if they had had enough—kind of like how Seven was feeling right now. He couldn't figure out why anyone would want such a thing.

Trying to catch his breath without making a sound, Seven strained to see if Cami Leone had passed the initiation. Fuerte boarded, and then behind him came a woman who appeared to be around the same age as The Librarian—about halfway between the kids and their parents. She looked and dressed like a businessperson, wearing a jacket and pants similar to Martim's. Her white shirt was open at the neck, and she had a necktie loosened so much that she could lift it over her head if she wanted to. She wore gold-rimmed aviator glasses that were lightly tinted. Her skin was olive-toned with a smattering of tiny freckles across her nose and cheeks. Her black hair was long and sleek, straighter and shinier than Birdie's. She wore it in a tight, low ponytail, the end of which grazed the middle of her back and swung as she walked. Seven thought she was beautiful. Then she dropped her duffel bag on his bare toes and left it there.

Seven tried not to make a sound, but his foot throbbed in pain. He carefully slid it out from under the bag and drew his knees up, still wincing.

Fuerte invited Cami to take Martim's seat on the far side of the aisle so he could chat more easily with her on the ride home. Martim sat with his back to Seven, and Troy took the seat across the table from him, giving Seven a chance to study him this time. Troy was huge and muscular. Like Tenner, he had medium brown skin. His hair was black and wavy. His white short-sleeve T-shirt strained to fit around his biceps, and it almost choked his thick neck. He had deep purple circles under his eyes, and he looked worn out. They all did, in fact—maybe these nighttime trips were getting the best of them.

Within minutes Greta was taxiing the plane down the runway again. As they took off, Cami gripped the edge of the table like she was nervous. She made small talk, but Seven could hardly hear her due to the noise from the propellers. He reached behind him for his phone, then leaned forward over the duffel bag and took several photos of Cami's face so he could show the others. It would help them recognize her in the future . . . unless she shape-shifted. Then Seven realized that taking photos of a shape-shifter like Cami would be useless, since she could look like anybody she wanted to. Was this version of Cami the true, original person? He didn't know that, either. He put his phone back into the wall bin, then leaned forward again to listen to the conversation.

Just then, Cami's entire body—face, hair, everything—started morphing into a bearded old man wearing lederhosen with suspenders. Seven's jaw dropped, and he gasped. He'd never seen anything like that before. Cami the businessperson had turned into Cami the . . . yodeler? Mountain climber? Sheepherder? Whatever this version of Cami was, Seven thought they were really cool. He leaned out farther to get a better look, then remembered he was trying to be discreet.

As Seven pulled back into his space behind the bulkhead again, Troy turned sharply, as if his solid-black X-ray eyes had tracked Seven's movement. The man inched forward in his chair, his gaze piercing through the bulkhead. Then he unbuckled his seat belt and got up. He excused himself from the group and took a few steps up the aisle.

Seven peered up, then shrank back in fear as the hulking man got closer. Troy had *always* won at hide-and-seek, except with Martim when he went invisible. Could Seven fool him, too? He cringed, trying and failing to be fully invisible like his dad.

"What's going on, Troy?" the president asked, stopping mid-conversation with Cami. "Did you lose something?"

Troy swept his gaze over the area where Seven was hiding. "I thought I detected some strange movement behind Cami's duffel bag." His hulking body cast a shadow over the space. Seven held his breath, closed his eyes, and turned his head down, knowing his pupils could be seen if a person knew where to look. Sweat beaded on his forehead. Had Troy's X-ray vision detected the faint outlines of Seven's body?

He couldn't hold his breath much longer. After a moment, Troy pivoted back to the others and took a step toward his seat. Seven opened his eyes and let out a breath. Then Troy turned sharply toward him again and kicked the air . . . or what looked like air. He connected hard with Seven's shoulder.

"Oof!" Seven said. He crumpled and lay on his side. Pain seared through him.

"There's someone here!" Troy said gruffly. The man shoved the bag aside and dropped down on top of Seven's curled body, crushing him. "An intruder!"

"Get . . . off . . . me!" Seven gasped, trying to breathe and nurse his sore shoulder and protect his private parts under the deadweight of a huge muscleman.

Troy shifted, pinning Seven on his stomach on the floor of

the plane. He wrested Seven's arms free and held them together at the wrists behind his back. "Somebody give me a zip tie," Troy said to the other criminals.

Martim was already reaching for his suit jacket to get one out of the inside pocket. He handed it to Troy. Seven twisted, unable to free himself and having nowhere to run to even if he could. He frantically wondered what a zip tie was, and what it would do to him. He soon found out, as Troy wrapped his wrists with a strong, narrow band of plastic and secured it. Zip ties did the same job as handcuffs.

Troy pulled Seven to his feet. "Whoever this is, he's a scrawny little man," Troy said to the others. He shoved Seven toward the table, then hung Martim's suit jacket on his head to measure his size, as if he were a coatrack. "See?" Troy scoffed. "I knew I saw something."

"Please remove my very expensive jacket from his potentially disgusting head," Martim said primly.

Troy ignored the request.

Seven wanted to open the emergency exit and jump out. Or sink into the carpet and disappear. Instead his shoulders curled forward. He stared blindly into his father's jacket, unable to do anything.

"Who are you?" Fuerte said coldly to Seven. "And how did you get aboard my plane?"

NO CONTACT

Once the team in the SUV behind hangar number three realized the criminals had landed in Frayzia, they'd waited for Seven to call. And when he didn't do that, they'd hoped he would speak into the bug and tell them what was going on. But he didn't do that, either. Most of them dozed off, knowing it could be a few hours before the plane would make its return trip. Worried and unable to sleep, Birdie and The Librarian had stepped out of the vehicle and debated what was going on with Seven now that the criminals had left to do their heist.

"Maybe he's not alone," Birdie said. "What if one of them stayed with the plane? Or maybe there are mechanics around. Could that be why he's not calling?" She wrung her hands. "I'm so nervous for him."

"I wonder if he's trying to call but forgot to turn off airplane mode," The Librarian guessed. "I've been using a cell phone for years, and I still do that sometimes after getting off a plane. But there's a notification that comes up when you attempt to do anything, so he'd be able to follow the prompts and get it working again."

"Shall I try calling or texting *him*?" Birdie asked anxiously. "Maybe he just fell asleep." She grimaced, knowing Seven would likely be stressing out, not sleeping.

The Librarian pressed her lips together. Her face wore a stern expression as she thought it through. Then she shook her head. "He knows to call us when he can. If we call him, it could give him away to anyone nearby. The best we can do is keep listening to the bug and trusting that he's doing everything he can to stay safe. Since all remains quiet and we haven't heard any signs of a confrontation or struggle, we can assume he's okay for now."

THE SILENCE CONTINUED, and finally even Birdie took a nap. When The Librarian heard the heavy airplane door opening and the criminals boarding the plane through the bug again, she woke her. Elena got up, too, and they went outside to listen in.

"There's a new voice," Birdie said.

"That must be Cami Leone," said Elena.

When The Librarian heard the newcomer over the receiver, she frowned. "She sounds familiar, but I don't know anybody with that name."

"It could be an alias," Birdie said. "Get it? Cami Leone. It sounds like *chameleon*. Isn't that what Fuerte called her?"

"You've got something there," The Librarian said. Her brow

furrowed. "I feel like I should know who she is." She paused, then her lips parted as if she was realizing something for the first time. "I might know some of the other recruits as well." A strange look crossed her face.

"Are you okay?" Birdie asked.

"It's just unsettling thinking that Fuerte might be recruiting some of my childhood friends." The Librarian put her finger to her lips to quiet everyone. They didn't want to miss anything.

As they strained to listen to the subdued conversation, Cabot, Lada, and Tenner woke up and exited the SUV to stretch, get some air, and listen in on the returning flight.

The Librarian's expression changed again, this time to one of concern. "Hang on," she murmured. "I just thought of something." She set the bug receiver on the SUV's rear bumper and pulled out her phone, then wandered to the front end of the SUV and made a call.

Fuerte's voice droned on through the receiver. He asked Cami to show him some of her other personas. But then they heard Troy say he thought he saw something. Birdie and the others froze. They could hear a scuffle, followed by Seven yelping in pain.

"Oh no!" cried Birdie. "They discovered him!" As the others exclaimed their dismay, Birdie paced in the darkness, clenching her fists. "Ugh, Seven. Now what? I hope he's not hurt. What are they going to do to him? This is all my fault. I'm the one who said he should do this."

"Everyone! Shh!" Cabot picked up the receiver and leaned against the vehicle, listening intently. Tenner swiftly opened the tailgate so Cabot and the others could sit together and listen. The Librarian, who was still at the front end of the SUV on the phone, looked over at Birdie to see what had happened.

Fuerte fired questions at Seven, but Seven wasn't answering.

"They don't know who he is," Cabot reported. "They're trying to figure out if he's a spy." She listened again, then slapped her forehead with the palm of her hand and whispered, "This interrogation is painful. Poor Seven!"

After a moment they heard Fuerte raise his voice, demanding again that Seven identify himself. But Seven stayed silent. They heard more shuffling.

"Nobody's screaming or shouting at him, so that seems positive," Cabot said, trying to be upbeat. "It's quiet now." She blew out a worried breath. "What are they going to do with him?"

Brix emerged from the vehicle. "I heard shouts. What's going on?"

Cabot filled him in, then asked fearfully, "Do you think they'll put him in the palace dungeon jail cell where they kept you?"

"They might," said Elena. Her long black hair was disheveled, and the circles under her eyes were visible even in the dim light from the parking lot lamps. "They're not going to let him go, that's for sure."

Birdie stopped pacing. Was Seven captured for good? He'd

have to escape . . . somehow. Her frustration and feelings of helplessness were clear. "I wish he'd called when they were away. We could have coached him—we could have let him know what to do once they got back."

"That doesn't really matter now that he's been found out," said Lada gently. She'd been rolling herself between the group listening to the bug at the back of the SUV and The Librarian talking on the phone at the front, trying to get the gist of both conversations. "Besides, I think The Librarian is figuring something out. She's been talking with the cell phone provider and asking about our international coverage. Sounds like maybe Seven wasn't able to call us because he's in a different country."

"Maybe we should call him," Tenner said. "At least leave a message so he knows we know what's happening."

"Noooo!" said Birdie, Lada, and Cabot together.

Tenner was startled by their vehemence. "Sorry, geez."

"If for some reason they've got his phone," Cabot explained, "they'll listen to the message and know there's a bug on board, and it would blow our cover. And if Seven's phone is hidden, we can't risk it making a noise or the screen lighting up. We have to trust that he's doing the best he can." She hesitated, then added with less conviction, "He's . . . *pretty* smart. Maybe they'll just—I don't know—think he's harmless and surprise us all by letting him go."

Nobody believed that would happen.

The Librarian rejoined the group at the back of the vehicle.

"I figured out why we haven't heard from Seven," she said grimly. "When I bought the new phones, I asked them to set up international roaming on all of them, but apparently they didn't do it. Since our cell provider doesn't automatically allow international usage, I had to call the company to turn on the feature." She grimaced, like she was mad at herself for not double-checking once she knew Seven was heading to a different country. "I took care of it on all our lines for the future, but it sounds like it's too late to help Seven communicate now that he's been captured."

"Too late?" Birdie said, fear in her eyes. "What do you mean? Do you think they'll do something bad to him?"

"I just mean that even if they let him keep his phone, he can't say anything to us in front of them." She glanced up. "It's almost morning. They'll be back soon."

The stars at dawn hung heavy in the murky sky. A cool breeze came up and slipped around the group, reviving them after the rough night. Tenner narrowed his eyes and gazed in the direction the plane had departed. One of the stars looked like it was moving toward them.

Cabot held the bug receiver up as Greta's voice crackled. "Landing soon. Please collect all of your personal belongings and buckle up." Hearing her mom's voice after three years had been twisting Cabot's insides all night long. Why was she participating in this horrible stuff with Fuerte? Did she know about Seven? Had any of them figured out who he was yet? Cabot knew they would soon—there was no way Seven would be able to keep his identity a secret from his own dad. He was probably just stalling for time by not answering them. Trying to figure out how to explain.

"That might be them." Tenner pointed something out, but it was still too far away for the rest of them to see it.

Soon enough the plane was visible to everyone. "Let's all go back inside the SUV to hide," The Librarian said. "I see the president's vehicles kicking up a cloud of dust on their way in."

"Should we try to fight them?" Tenner asked, flexing his hands. "We need to get Seven back."

"We can't take them on," Lada said, getting out of her wheelchair so they could stow it in the back of the SUV. "Have you seen Troy? He could knock us all down like bowling pins. We're getting stronger, but we're not ready for a fight like that yet. Besides, it'll expose that we're here and give them way too much information about us. I prefer they remain in the dark about our identities and our mission for as long as possible." She moved with her crutches to the passenger door of the vehicle as Tenner folded the wheelchair, hoisted it into the back of the SUV, and closed the tailgate.

"But what about Seven?" Birdie exclaimed, following Lada.

"With any luck," The Librarian said, "he can create a distraction and somehow get away from them. Maybe he can hide in the hangar, or get out and run for it. If he does, he'll have enough sense to stay hidden until they're long gone. Then we can find him."

Cabot couldn't stop fidgeting. "So we're just going to stay in the SUV until the president and the . . . the parents . . . are gone?" Now that she knew her mother was there, she longed to at least catch a glimpse of her. "We're not going to spy on them?" She turned around on her knees to watch through the back window as the plane bounced on the runway and moved toward the hangar.

"Not this time," Lada said. "We don't want to make things worse for Seven."

"If it makes you feel better," Elena said, "I don't think they'll hurt him. Especially once he tells them who he is. Martim is a criminal, but I don't think he'd let Fuerte do anything to harm his child. He's not *that* much of a monster."

Tenner frowned. "He might not be. But Troy is."

THEY WAITED. THE Librarian peered through night-vision goggles as the fleet of presidential vehicles arrived. Cabot remembered her short-range earpiece and quickly retrieved it from her pocket. She put it back in her ear so she could talk to Seven. "Can you hear me?" Cabot said softly, adjusting it to make sure it was snugly in place. There was no answer. Of course, being captive, Seven wouldn't be able to talk. "If you are able to break away from them, you could hide in the hangar. We're all still here. We'll get you out."

Birdie heard her and realized what she was doing. "Yes, good," she whispered. "Any response?"

Cabot shook her head. "There never is," she said, frustrated. "Of course he can't talk. He's being held prisoner." After a few moments of dead silence, she took the earpiece out and looked at it. She pressed a tiny indicator button, and it lit up yellow instead of green, like when they'd all first gotten them. "I think yellow means it needs to be charged." She put the earpiece back in her ear and hoped the battery would last a bit longer. She'd have to remember to plug it in later, when they were back at the monastery. There were so many extra things they had to do with all these technological gadgets. It was confusing and hard to remember everything.

"They're walking out of the hangar in a group," The Librarian continued. "I can't tell if they have Seven or not."

"Me either," said Tenner, who was watching closely too. "Seems like they wouldn't just keep walking if he got away, though. Wouldn't they chase him?"

The Librarian put down the goggles, perplexed. "Troy just opened the back door of one of the president's vehicles, and it seemed like he shoved something—or someone—into the backseat. Then he got in, too."

"That could just be my dad making big movements," Tenner said doubtfully, "which is how he moves naturally." He wanted to believe Seven had escaped . . . but nothing indicated that could possibly be true.

When the cars were out of sight and the mechanics had closed up and left, The Librarian let everybody out of the SUV. They ran to the hangar, checking the doors and finding everything locked, as expected. Lada used her lockpick to break into the service door. She pushed it open, and the others rushed inside.

"Seven!" Birdie called out. "Are you here? Everybody's gone. Where are you?"

"Maybe he went back on the plane to hide," Tenner said, grasping at any possibility.

Cabot ran to it and started up the stairs. She wrestled with the handle and finally, putting all her weight into it, unlatched it, then swung the heavy door wide. "Seven?" She went inside with Tenner and Birdie coming after her.

They searched the small cabin, calling Seven's name, knowing deep down he wouldn't respond, because he couldn't possibly be there. They even started feeling around tentatively, in case he'd fallen into a sleep coma or had frozen to unconsciousness from exposure.

"Seven!" Birdie called again, frantically wanting him to be there.

"He's gone," Tenner said forlornly. He went to the plane stairs. "He's not here," he announced to Elena and The Librarian. "He's not anywhere. They've got him."

"They took him prisoner," Birdie said, her voice catching. "What do we do now? Oh, poor Seven! He must be scared. And mortified—he *hates* being without his clothes."

"I have a feeling 'scared' wins out," Lada said, leaning on one of her crutches. "How do you think he's handling facing his father? I feel so bad for him. I'm going to get his clothes before we forget them." She went outside the hangar to the spot where Seven had undressed. Leaning on one crutch, she picked up his clothes. She rolled them up and tucked them under her arm, then continued toward the SUV.

Everyone gathered at the vehicle, silent as they absorbed the shock.

"We'll find him," Elena said grimly. "We'll get him back. Don't worry."

Cabot gave the woman a solemn look as her stomach continued to churn with mixed feelings about everything. Things just got real, and she was angry. Her mother had been a part of kidnapping Seven. And Cabot wasn't about to stand for it. In fact, her wheels were already spinning with ideas.

MORTIFIED AND SCARED

Seven's wheels were turning, too, along with those of the presidential vehicle he was riding in with Troy. He was petrified, and extremely uncomfortable sitting on the cold leather seat with air-conditioning blasting him from all angles—apparently Troy liked the car to be ice-cold. But Seven's fears and chattering teeth didn't stop him from scheming. None of these people knew who he was . . . or even that he was just a boy. He could be a scrawny man. His voice had been changing for months, and it was a lot lower than the last time his father had heard him talk three years ago. Even Elena had remarked that he and Tenner were sounding so grown up now. If Seven spoke, would his dad recognize him? Would Troy or Greta?

Amanthi had told them that the president's guards didn't know the identities of the palace intruders who had busted Elena out of the dungeon cell. The security guard had seen and might be able to identify some of the kids, like Lada and Brix, and possibly Birdie. But not Seven. He'd been fully camouflaged.

The parents hadn't seen any of the kids in three years. They'd all grown up a lot, and none of their supernatural abilities had been revealed before the parents had left. So they wouldn't be able to identify them simply by their powers. Would they even fathom a guess that their sheltered, off-the-grid offspring had been able to travel all the way to Estero, navigate the huge city, and actually find and free Elena Golden? Or would they more likely believe the kids—and specifically Seven at this particular moment—were still enjoying life on the beach with Louis?

Seven had refused to answer any questions on the plane. They'd locked him in the bathroom for the remainder of the flight so they could talk without him overhearing. When they disembarked, Troy had taken him roughly by the arm and marched him to the awaiting vehicle. And despite Cabot's suggestion in his ear that he escape and hide in the hangar, there was no freeing himself from Troy's death grip on his upper arm. Seven had overheard his father filling in Greta on what had happened in the cabin during the flight. And then Troy had tossed him into the backseat of one of the black palace cars. He'd cut Seven's wrists free, giving the boy a moment of hope, only to secure them in front of him instead. Then Troy had used another zip tie to attach his bound wrists to the door handle.

Seven had never felt more exposed and vulnerable in his life. But then Troy had put a burlap sack over his head to keep him from seeing where they were going. It was scary, and the head covering was scratchy against his skin. But at least it helped keep his face warm and his almost-invisible earpiece hidden.

He could hear Troy talking on his cell phone to the people in the other car, first reporting that the intruder couldn't see a thing, and then confirming they were taking him to the mansion, not the palace. Seven felt a wave of relief and even a hint of a smile forming beneath the burlap sack. He thought he knew what mansion they were talking about. They didn't know he already knew where it was. They probably shouldn't have done something so harebrained as naming their children after the address.

The car turned and went slowly up a curvy drive. Then Seven heard the familiar rattle of the gate, confirming in his mind that this was indeed the mansion he expected it to be. They pulled into the garage and parked. As the gate closed, Troy got Seven out of the backseat, took the burlap sack off his head, and shoved him toward the door. Then Troy pushed him to the dining room and zip-tied him to a chair. After the presidential vehicle containing Fuerte, Martim, and Cami arrived, they all stood over Seven intimidatingly and asked him the same questions they'd asked on the plane.

"Tell us who you are," Troy demanded again. "What do you want?"

"How did you know my plane would be in Frayzia?" Fuerte asked. "Did Cami tip you off?" He eyed their new partner with suspicion.

"Me?" Cami, who had morphed back to her businessperson self, recoiled and shook her head. "I don't know anyone besides Martim who can go invisible."

"That one is *not* invisible," Martim said, clipping his words.

"If he were," Troy added, "I wouldn't have detected him. More like he's camouflaged. And . . . I'm pretty sure he's freestyling."

Martim's eyes were like slits, and he looked angry. Did he suspect he was speaking with his own son? If so, he didn't share his suspicions.

"Do you know the bouncing boy?" Troy asked. "The one who helped release a prisoner from the palace, and who broke in *here* yesterday?"

"Of course he wouldn't," Martim said with a sneer. "He's never been here before." He paused, then turned to Seven. "Have you?"

Seven remained silent. He was developing a plan, but he wasn't quite ready to talk. He glanced through the front picture window and saw three armed guards standing around the fence by the driveway. That was new. He hadn't seen them when they drove up because of the sack over his head. He looked up at the corners of the rooms and saw that the cameras were all pointing the proper way, not at the walls like they'd left them. The men must have reviewed the footage and seen Brix. Maybe once Troy and Martim had figured out the electricity to the fence had been cut and intruders had been inside the mansion, they'd decided to beef up security. Seven's heart sank. That would make it difficult to escape—especially if they'd repaired the electricity already. Being mostly undetectable was great, but there was no getting over a fence like that, unless you were Lada and could teleport. And she couldn't come here and take down everyone all by herself. It would be difficult for his team to rescue him. Impossible, even.

Seven was on his own.

HIDING FROM PARENTS

When it became clear Seven wasn't going to answer any questions, President Fuerte and Cami Leone didn't stay. "I need to get Cami processed and settled at the palace with the others," Fuerte said as they started out the door. "The intruder will talk when he gets thirsty and hungry enough. Keep me posted." Seven raised an eyebrow. So all the new recruits were living at the palace? And they weren't going to give him anything to eat or drink, not even water? Seven's mouth was already dry, and the knowledge of what they planned to do made him even thirstier.

With Fuerte and Cami gone, only Martim and Troy remained. Martim disappeared down a wing of the mansion, wanting to have nothing to do with the not-quite-invisible one. Something about the intruder seemed to irk Martim a great deal. He appeared set on believing camouflage was a less valuable ability than full invisibility. And that made Seven's stomach hurt. Now when he imagined telling his dad his true identity, it felt embarrassing and awful. Like a huge disappointment.

How would Martim react? Could Seven keep hiding who he was indefinitely? He had plenty of time to think about it.

Troy left Seven tied to the chair in the dining room. One of the security detail came inside and stationed himself within sight of Seven—or within sight of Seven's chair, anyway. Was he meant to be intimidating? Or did they really think Seven was dangerous? Maybe they just wanted someone to keep an eye on the room to make sure the camo intruder didn't manage to escape the zip ties and sneak away.

Eventually, Seven dozed off. Occasional noises throughout the house startled him awake: A kitchen cupboard bumping closed. The sharp, high-pitched whir of a coffee grinder. Phones ringing. A door closing. And voices: His dad. Troy. A guard. It made him long for the sound of waves lapping on the beach at the hideout—but that seemed like a lifetime ago.

After a while, Greta Stone came in through the front door and past the security guard, carrying a box. Seven jarred awake from the disturbance. He hadn't had a good look at Greta on the plane. Her appearance was almost the same as before, except she seemed shorter . . . or maybe Seven was just taller now. Her tousled brown hair was neatly trimmed to graze her shoulders, and it looked styled, kind of like how Martim's slicked-back hair was different, more professional than his old beachy mop. Greta was athletic, and her light brown skin was more generously freckled than he remembered. He could almost see Cabot in a few of the facial expressions Greta made while she moved through the kitchen, especially around her mouth—they had the same full, pink lips. But other than that, Cabot was almost the spitting image of her father, Jack, with his white-blond hair and pale skin and cheeks that turned ruddy with anger or praise. Seven wondered if he'd be seeing Jack Stone anytime soon.

And what about Lucy? Not to mention his own mom, Magdalia? He'd half expected to find her here, but there was no sign of her. Where was she? She hadn't been on the plane, either. Seven's heart clutched, and his stomach flipped. Did that mean *she* was the one who'd died on the rocks by the bay? The thought gutted him. She hadn't been a great mom, but he didn't wish that on her.

When Greta breezed past Seven with a stack of file folders to put in Martim's office, Seven noticed she was wearing a tracking device around her ankle. It was similar to the one he'd seen around his dad's ankle on the plane, though it was silver, not clear like his dad's was. Troy probably wore one, too—it was the price they paid for not being stuck in jail for their past and current crimes. They were free to come and go, though, so it couldn't be too bad. If Seven was honest with himself, he could understand why Greta and Jack would agree to wear it and help the president if it meant they didn't have to stay in a tiny jail cell like Elena had done. But Martim, Troy, and Greta were *really* helping the president, digging themselves in deep with every crime they committed on his behalf. Something seemed terribly wrong with that. Like, if Greta and Jack Stone of all people had given up on doing the right thing, was there any use in Seven trying to fight for justice?

Seven didn't get the impression that Greta lived here at the mansion, which made sense because it belonged to the Palacios and the Cordobas. But where *did* she live, then? At the palace with the recruited supers? Enjoying her freedom, knowing Elena was in the dungeon below? Not even visiting? Greta was starting to seem . . . *really* terrible.

Greta went back to her box of things, then came over to Seven with a stack of folded clothes and eyed the chair where he sat, seeing basically nothing but zip ties. "Would you like some clothes?" she asked.

Seven saw that up close, she looked a little older and tired around the eyes. He remembered how kind she'd been to the children. She'd been their schoolteacher until Seven was ten years old and had taught them math, science, reading, and writing—all of it. She'd loved being with the kids . . . or at least she'd pretended to. Mixed emotions threatened to spill out of him, as well as confessions of who he was and why he was here. But all he said was a garbled "Sure," trying to make his voice sound lower.

She set the clothes on the dining table in front of him. Then she lifted her jacket to reveal a weapons belt. She chose a knife and pulled it out.

Seven gasped and recoiled.

"Relax," she said gruffly. She cut the zip ties around Seven's wrists. "Don't make me use it on you," she warned, keeping the knife out. "Hurry up with the clothes."

Seven rubbed his sore wrists, then quickly wriggled into the pants, acutely aware that she was poised to drop him to the floor if he tried anything. And he didn't doubt that she could render him motionless with one move. He fumbled with the T-shirt, then slipped that on, too. The clothes were slightly too big, but not Tenner's-dad-shorts big, so that was something. When he was dressed, he sat down obediently.

Greta had pulled out two new zip ties by then, and she attached each of his wrists to a chair arm. Then she went back to the kitchen. A few minutes later she returned with a plate and a glass, and set them in the middle of the long dining table, out of Seven's reach.

"You get this sandwich and water if you give me some info," Greta said quietly. "They're discussing what to do with you." She eyed him coolly, able to see his size for the first time now that he had clothes on. "I suggest you comply, or else they might do something to force you to answer." She hesitated as she continued studying him. "How old are you?"

Seven swallowed hard. It was difficult not to say something to identify himself to Greta. Despite what she was doing now, she'd been such a good parent back when they were little. *And* she was a doctor—didn't doctors have an oath to do good things, or something like that? Perhaps she'd just done a good job fooling the kids into believing she cared about them back in the old days. Maybe she was more like Seven's and Tenner's parents than they'd realized. But even Louis had vouched for her unwaveringly. And Cabot *adored* her—she didn't have a bad word to say about her mother. So what had changed her? Why was she here, doing things to help these bad people?

He was so tempted to answer truthfully . . . tempted to pour out everything to her. Tempted to have her wrap her motherly arms around him like she'd done when he was little, when he'd hurt himself. When he'd needed a hug that his mother or father didn't give.

But Seven knew Greta was the most intelligent of all the criminals—that was her super ability, after all. And she was probably trying to trick him, which hurt his heart more than he wanted to admit, because admitting that might make him start bawling. He turned his head away and swallowed hard. He'd wait until Troy came back to tell his story. Troy . . . wasn't the sharpest. He'd be the least likely to recognize Seven's voice, because he'd barely paid attention to any of the kids back at the hideout, except to ridicule them. And that made him the best one to sell his story to.

Greta waited for an answer. When she didn't get it, she shrugged. "Suit yourself." She left the dining room, picked up her box, and exited the mansion. Seven heard a car roar to life outside, and then it faded away. He closed his eyes, but not to sleep. He needed to be strong if he was going to pull this off.

MAKING THINGS UP

Soon Troy sauntered in looking like he'd just woken up from a nap. He carried a small journal and shoved it into the back pocket of his jeans. He wore the same white T-shirt from the plane, and he didn't smell great. Seven wrinkled up his nose.

Troy glanced at the untouched sandwich and water on the dining table. He took a side chair and sat backward on it a few feet in front of Seven, then crossed his arms over the chair back and leaned forward. His thighs were like tree trunks, and his head was enormous—Seven hadn't really noticed that before, and now he couldn't stop seeing it. And Troy's eyes were like black holes, more unnerving than ever. Seven pressed deeper into his chair.

"So," Troy said, staring him down. "Mr. Fugitive. Let's try this again. Who are you?"

"That's not important," Seven said in his deepest voice. It sounded pretty grown-up to him. And a little bit like his dad, which was weird, and could make people suspicious. He'd have to work on it.

"Oh?" Troy seemed surprised that Seven had spoken. "Well, tell me what *is* important, then."

"Not much, now that I'm here," Seven said, altering his vocal tone and liking it much better. "You guessed it—I'm a fugitive."

"A random supernatural fugitive who just happened upon the plane of the president of Estero?" Troy snorted. "I don't buy it." He pumped his bulging biceps—left, right, left, right—almost like he didn't realize he was doing it.

"Not random," Seven said. He bounced his heel up and down nervously, then stopped it. "I heard a rumor. You know how it is with us. A guy I know told me about President Fuerte's visits to other countries, and the true purpose of them—you're building an army of supernatural people. My friend mentioned you were coming to recruit Cami Leone. And . . . I wanted to be a part of it, too. But you didn't choose me." He clenched one fist awkwardly because of the way his wrists were attached to the chair, and cracked his knuckles one at a time, thinking that would probably seem like a grown-up thing to do. "I'm not blaming you," Seven continued nonchalantly, though he was jittery inside. "You maybe didn't know I existed. But I could think of only one way to show you who I was, so I stowed away on your plane when you were out doing your heist."

"I don't do the choosing of the supers," Troy said, scratching his jaw where gray-and-black stubble lined it. "What *exactly* do you think we're doing?"

"Like I said, you're going to different countries to build an army of supernatural people for Estero. That's all I know. I think I fit the bill. I mean, my camo is . . . pretty . . . great." He failed to muster up the conviction he needed to sell it, thanks to his father, but he plowed onward. "I could do a lot of helpful things for you." *Things my dad thinks he'd be better at,* Seven thought, but didn't say out loud.

Troy narrowed his eyes, trying to find holes in the story. "Why didn't you tell us this on the plane?"

"I was pretty scared to be found out. And afraid of making things bad for Cami. I didn't want to tell you I'd listened in on one of her conversations with President Fuerte right before you came."

"Listened in?" Troy sat back and scratched his head. "How? She said she doesn't know you."

"She's telling the truth. But *look* at me. How hard do you think it is for me to listen to a stranger's phone calls? Once I tracked her down, it wasn't difficult."

"Hmf." Troy's X-ray eyes roamed Seven's faint outline. "You seem pretty young. How old are you?"

Seven was glad Greta had asked him this earlier, because it had given him time to think. And even though Seven thought it sounded preposterous, he knew no one would ever see his face. "Eighteen."

"Eighteen?" Troy seemed to be hesitantly buying the entire conversation. Had he been expecting something else from the fugitive? Hopefully he believed Seven. "So you would have never lived at Sunrise Foster Home—it's been closed to supers for longer than you've been one. Maybe that's why we didn't have you on file. Why won't you tell me your name?"

"I don't want you or anyone else to tell my family I'm here," Seven said. "They don't like Estero politics. And they don't understand me and my . . . desire to work for President Fuerte. But you can call me—" He stopped short. He hadn't thought this part through. Should he pick a common name? Or something flashier like Cami Leone had done, to instill confidence? Or would that just set him up to fail?

"I don't know, kid," Troy said, shifting. He gripped the chair back. On his middle finger he wore a gold ring that could do some serious damage to a face. "You're pretty young. President Fuerte might have something to say about that. Plus everybody goes through an initiation heist to prove themselves. You don't get into the club just for being supernatural. You've got to prove you can handle it."

"I snuck on board the president's plane. Doesn't that prove something?"

"But you got caught. So, no."

Seven grimaced but kept going. "I'm young, but I've been through plenty of ridicule, like you probably have. That ages a kid."

Troy's face darkened, and he nodded thoughtfully.

"Look," Seven said, feeling slightly more confident. "The president wants to build an army of supers. He said on the plane he'll take as many as he can get. I'm here volunteering, and you think he'll turn me away? That seems . . . what's the word?"

"Messed up," Troy mused.

"I was going for 'counterintuitive,' but okay." For a brief moment, Seven appreciated his camouflage, because he could allow a grin to cross his face unhindered—but then he stopped it because he wasn't sure how much of him Troy could see with his X-ray vision. "Big words, am I right?"

Troy almost laughed and nodded. "All right, kid. You seem sincere. I have to admit your ability is extremely useful—*I* think so, anyway. I'll run this by the others."

"This is what I'm trying to say," Seven said. "I'm useful to the cause. I can perform a heist if you need me to prove it. Bring me with you next time. I'll show you." His voice cracked, and he cleared his throat, which ached from trying to sound older.

Troy stood up. "I'm not making any promises." He turned to go back to his living quarters. "Sit tight while I make some phone calls."

"Hey, wait," Seven called, glancing at the sandwich. His mouth instantly started watering. "Can you at least hand me that glass of water and the sandwich?"

Troy smirked. "Sorry. Not my job." He sauntered away.

"Jerk," Seven muttered. He felt repressed anger bubbling up.

For a moment there he'd thought Troy seemed softer than he used to be. Almost likable, on some level. But with a move like that, Seven knew the real Troy hadn't changed much.

But Seven was parched and hungry. When the guard stepped away, talking on some sort of clunky communication device, Seven gripped the arms of his chair and hoisted it off the floor, trying to balance it on his back so he could walk with it. He took a few staggering steps toward the plate. He strained and planted his chest on the surface of the table and slid his body toward the middle. He managed to grasp the edge of the plate between his teeth and pull it toward him. Then he took the top piece of bread into his mouth. After he wolfed down as much of the sandwich as he could get, he tried to bite the cup of water and lift it to drink. But he only managed to get a little in his mouth before it fell over onto the table. As water spilled everywhere, Seven sat down hard in the chair and put his open mouth against the table, catching some of the water and sipping the bit that pooled near the edge. It would have to be enough.

Once he'd wiped his face clean on his shoulder, he peered through the large front picture window. The guards were still there by the driveway. He scooted his chair around and checked the backyard. A few more guards were stationed along the tree line.

The guard who had been near Seven still hadn't returned, and no one had reacted to him thumping around the dining room, so he took a chance, hoping his earpiece was still functional after so many hours. "Cabot," he whispered. "I'm at the mansion. Can you hear me?"

She didn't answer.

He was stuck there with the two bad dads. There was no worse place to be. And he couldn't think of a single way to get himself out of this mess.

HATCHING A PLAN

After searching the hangar, the remaining members of the team had left the airport. On their way back to the monastery, The Librarian rolled to a stop a short distance from the criminals' mansion at 710 Legacy Avenue, wondering if Seven might be there. Birdie, whose stomach was woefully empty, was napping peacefully in the front seat.

Cabot slumped against the car door in the middle row, complaining of a headache after the long night. Wearily, she tried her earpiece again and said Seven's name a few times. But there was nothing—total silence. She took the earpiece out and tested the indicator button like she'd done before, and this time it flashed red—the battery was dead. No wonder it wasn't working. Disgusted, she tossed the earpiece into the seat-back pocket with the bug receiver and closed her eyes, feeling defeated. She hadn't been able to help Seven. And on top of everything else, her mom was a serious criminal, present tense. Cabot had been grappling with the knowledge that Greta was willingly working with *that* group of people. Piloting them around like she wanted to be there. Where had they gone?

Elena, who could run the fastest, slipped out of the vehicle and snuck down the path through the trees to see if she could detect any signs of Seven at the mansion.

She saw two black security sedans in the driveway like the ones the criminals and the president had gotten into. But she also counted eight armed security guards wearing tactical gear. Three of them gathered on the driveway along the gate. Elena crept closer to get a good look at them and memorize their faces, as well as the license plate numbers of the vehicles. The faint buzzing of the electric fence permeated the silence. They'd fixed it already.

Elena returned to the SUV and quickly jotted down the license plate numbers in a note on her phone—she'd started keeping a list in case it would ever become useful. "The place is heavily guarded now," she reported as The Librarian drove off. "And the electric fence is alive again. I can't tell if they've got Seven. My hunch is yes, because we think he went in Troy's car, and there are two of the president's vehicles there. But I can't say for sure because those vehicles all look alike—he could've just as easily been in a different car that went to the palace. They might have put him in my old prison cell."

Lada glanced back as they drove past the mansion driveway. "I'd teleport into the house if I could do it safely," she mused. "If I'm quick enough going in and out, they'd be too startled to capture me before I was gone again. But I can't travel that distance yet, and with guards surrounding the house, I don't think I could get away with teleporting halfway into the yard, and then the rest of the way into the house. It would tip off security. I need more practice first so I can do it in one move from a safe hiding place in the woods."

Birdie, who'd roused when her mother returned, put her elbow on the armrest and propped her chin up with her hand. Lada's idea was great, and it would help them know if Seven was there or not. But it wouldn't bring him back to them. He was probably being interrogated. Were they hurting him? She wouldn't put it past Troy to be rough and mean.

It was almost as if Tenner had read her mind. "If my dad does anything to Seven, I'll . . ." He growled in frustration, trying and failing to come up with something very terrible. "I'll do something *very terrible* to him. I'm not kidding."

Birdie reached behind her and patted Tenner's knee, then said sleepily, "This is your daily reminder that what Troy does is not your fault, so let's just get that out there."

Tenner nodded. "I know. I'm getting better at remembering. Thanks, Bird."

"First thing," The Librarian said as they pulled inside the gate to the monastery, "we rest. We'll think better after we sleep. Then we plan. We have a lot of information to absorb. And there are still some things I'm deeply puzzled about. Maybe sleep will help provide us with some answers."

Cabot nodded, holding her aching head. When they finally all spilled into the cottage, she slipped up to her room, forgetting everything but how miserable and exhausted she felt.

ONCE THEY RESURFACED, they met up on the back patio to eat dinner . . . or breakfast . . . or whatever meal they felt like eating now that their days and nights were getting mixed up. Seven's absence was a constant reminder that they weren't playing games. The president, and their own parents, weren't messing around. The criminals had Seven, and there was no indication that they'd be giving him up anytime soon.

"I wonder how terrible it was for Seven to be face-to-face with his dad," Tenner said glumly as he pushed food around on his plate. "That must have been awkward."

Birdie nodded. "I just feel so bad. I hope he's okay. They probably know by now who he is. And he's stuck facing them without us to help."

"I'm sure he's realized that his safest move is to reveal who he is," Elena said. She leaned across the table toward Birdie and Tenner. "Listen to me. I know how hard this is. You aren't used to this happening. But let me tell you something. What Seven is going through is an example of what it's been like for supers living in Estero. Sneaking around. Hiding out. Supernatural people just trying to stay safe, to live their lives, and being captured and interrogated by the authorities." She touched her napkin to her mouth, then continued. "Now, here's what I know to be true: Seven has a very useful ability, and they will see that for what it is. They're not going to hurt him. They might even find him to be an asset if they think they can trust him. I can imagine Martim trying to talk him into joining the team—just like they wanted me to join them." She paused for a breath. "So while this isn't ideal, I don't think you have to worry about Seven's safety—at least for as long as he does whatever they want him to do."

"Your mom is right, Birdie," Lada said. "It's not great that he's been kidnapped, but at least it's by supernatural people, including his own father, and not, like, the Estero police, who are stuck following Fuerte's orders and have to go after people like us."

"*Were* stuck," Birdie reminded her. "He just changed the law, remember?"

"He changed it to help *himself,*" Lada said, "but okay, it helps us, too, I guess."

"Lada, are you saying it's a good thing Seven got captured?" Cabot interjected. She held a cool washcloth to her head because her headache lingered.

"No," said Lada. "I just said it *wasn't* great. But I think he'll be taken care of better by supers than by non-supers. It would obviously be best if he hadn't been captured at all. But this is our reality now, and we can only plan our future based on where we are at this moment."

"Well, when are we going to go after him?" asked Cabot. "Set him free? Tonight?"

"We shouldn't rush this," The Librarian said. "The palace is heavily guarded, and they have security around the Cordobio mansion now, too. We've got to figure out where Seven is *for sure*, then have a foolproof plan to get past the guards. We'll monitor the locations, and wait to see if they take him anywhere—he'd be easier for us to get to if he was outside of either of those places. I wish we had someone on the inside."

Cabot glanced up. Someone on the inside? Her thoughts churned.

"I could send the raven to look in the windows," Birdie said. "Maybe if I take a scooter, it'll follow me to that neighborhood, and I could direct it from there."

"I'll go with you," Cabot said immediately. It would be another chance to see if her mom was around.

"That's a great idea, Birdie," The Librarian said. She took out her phone and began making a list. "While you two do that, I'll get supplies so we can make our next moves. Surveillance equipment, covert listening devices, maybe a microphonic device, C-4 in case we need to make a new doorway," she muttered. "Maybe Lada can . . . hmm."

Birdie, Lada, and Tenner exchanged a look.

"Make a new doorway?" Tenner asked.

"What's C-4?" Birdie whispered.

Lada shrugged, while Cabot jumped on her phone and

looked it up. Her eyes widened. "Holy coconuts. I'm in." She smirked. "It's an explosive," she said casually.

"Oh, only *that,*" Tenner said, wide-eyed. He glanced at the others. "I think we all need to keep training while we try to figure out the best way to get Seven back with us."

Lada pressed her lips together. "I need to practice teleporting," she said. "The way The Librarian is talking, I have a feeling I'll have to expand my distance before we can accomplish anything."

Before The Librarian could confirm or deny, her phone rang. "Speak to me." She listened for a long moment. Her eyebrows went up, then sank. "Okay. Thanks," she said, and hung up. She turned to face the rest of them. "Birdie and Cabot, take the raven to see if Seven is in the mansion, and hurry back as quickly as you can. The rest of you are going to have a shortened training session. Fuerte's team is on the move again. Tonight."

BIRD WATCH

Birdie and Cabot went to the corral where the bikes and electric scooters were kept. They carried helmets that Elena had found in a closet in the cottage. Elena had seemed more worried about the girls riding scooters for the first time than about them sneaking up to a mansion filled with dangerous criminals—moms were odd sometimes. When she'd offered to teach them how the scooters worked, they'd waved her off and assured her they could figure it out. Tenner had quietly reminded Elena that Birdie had steered more dangerous vehicles in her life . . . like an orca. That seemed to have calmed her.

The girls had watched some of the monks use the scooters before, with their sandaled feet planted firmly on the platform and their flowing tan robes rippling behind them as they went. It looked easy and fun. While Birdie carefully smoothed her hair and placed her helmet gently on her head, Cabot shoved hers down and quickly secured it beneath her chin. She started reading the instructions written on a sticker between the handlebars.

“Okay,” she said, flipping up the kickstand with her foot. “We’ve got to push off and then hop on while revving the right handle.” Cabot pointed the scooter to face the open space. She placed one foot on the wide standing board and gripped the handles. Then she tentatively pushed off with the other foot. When the scooter was in motion, she turned the right handle. The scooter jerked forward, nearly throwing Cabot off, but she hung on and found her balance. Slowly she rode in a wobbly line. She tested the left handle, which was the brake, and came to a stop. Then she pushed off again to get the scooter to drive once more and went faster this time. “I feel like a real kid!” she cried, leaning back, loving the wind on her face.

“You’re doing great!” Birdie exclaimed. She followed Cabot’s instructions and had a bit of trouble at first, like Cabot had. But after some practice in the monastery yard, she got the hang of using the handlebars to speed up and slow down and turn. When they both felt confident, Birdie called to the raven to follow them. The girls and the bird set off out the secret door in the wall and headed toward the mansion.

Riding on the road was scary, but they were getting used to traffic now, and the signs posted said they weren’t allowed to ride scooters on the sidewalk. They soon felt adrenaline surge through their bodies as they sped up along the side of the road with cars and buses just feet away from them.

It wasn’t far to the mansion, and before they knew it, they had reached the winding driveway. The raven flitted up to the trees. The two stashed their scooters and helmets in the brush and crept through the woods toward the house.

When they could see it and all the security guards surrounding it, Birdie summoned the raven, who landed and bounced gently on a low, thin branch. Birdie focused on the bird, speaking to it in her mind. *Go to the windows. Look inside for Seven, the camouflaged one.* She frowned. If Seven was still naked, would the bird be able to see him? She doubted it. *If you can't see him, maybe you could, you know, smell him. Birds do that, right? Of course they do. He smells . . . like . . . a boy . . . Kind of sweaty, but in a nice way, especially now that he uses deodorant, but maybe that doesn't help you. Anyway, he probably hasn't taken a shower in a while, so that might, uh, help make him more noticeable? I guess?* Birdie stopped and lowered her head into her hands. She needed a do-over.

The bird hopped, staring at Birdie without blinking. It tilted its head. Had it understood her rambling, or was it judging her for being weird? Birdie closed her eyes and shook her head slightly, annoyed with herself. She needed to concentrate. To make sure they did this right. Everyone was counting on her. She tried again. *You know who Seven is, don't you?*

The raven sent an affirmation to Birdie's mind. Birdie blew out a breath of relief. "Okay, good," she said, then straightened her shoulders as Cabot watched her curiously. *See if you can detect Seven in the mansion and report back to me. Please.*

The raven hopped again, then flitted to a branch above

their heads. It turned, fanning its tail feathers and stopping to preen. Cabot and Birdie exchanged a nervous glance.

"That . . . took a while," Cabot said, eyebrow raised.

"I might have given it way too many instructions," Birdie murmured.

"Of course you did." Cabot checked the time on her phone. It would be getting dark soon.

Just then the raven took to the air, meandering over to the mansion. It came to rest on the front porch railing and peered into the big picture window.

Birdie felt a negative message coming to her from the raven. "It doesn't see him." The bird took flight again, alighting on the roof and sitting there for a moment. Then it continued to the side yard, where it poked its beak into the grass a few times.

"Take your time, bird," Cabot muttered. "Stop and eat some dirt, why don't you?"

"Be nice," Birdie said.

"Sorry." Cabot closed her eyes as the headache from earlier began to throb again. "My head hurts."

"Did you bump it or something?"

"No, it's just a headache. I've . . . never really had one last this long before."

"Oh. Well, I'm sorry. Did you know there's, like, medicine for that? You don't have to make it out of roots—you can just buy it at the market. I bet The Librarian has some." Then Birdie turned her attention back to the task at hand. "Look—the raven is heading to the backyard." She spoke to it to make sure it didn't forget the mission. It sent her a reassuring message in return.

"I can't see it anymore," said Cabot. Her cell phone vibrated, and she glanced down. Elena was texting them to make sure they'd made it safely on the scooters. It made her heart ping and her mouth turn up at the corners. A mom cared about them. But it wasn't the right mom. Cabot texted back with an update.

"I'm getting something," Birdie said, closing her eyes. She reached over and gripped Cabot's wrist.

Cabot pulled away and searched "medicine for headache" on her phone. "What are you getting? Is the raven's message all garbled because of the dirt?"

Birdie swatted the air in Cabot's direction and concentrated for a long moment. Finally she pressed her lips together in a satisfied smile. "He's there!" she whispered. "Seven's inside."

ON A MISSION

Troy Cordoba shook Seven awake in the chair late that evening. He clipped the boy's zip-tie handcuffs. "Get up," he said gruffly. "You've got five minutes to get ready. I convinced Fuerte to give you a chance to prove yourself."

Seven rubbed his wrists and flexed them. "Okay. Thanks," he said with false enthusiasm. "What do I have to do?"

"You'll find out with the rest of us," Troy said, "once we get on the plane. Let's go." As Seven headed for the bathroom, Troy went down the long hallway that led to the men's bedrooms and offices. "Do you have the old money?" Seven heard Troy ask Martim.

"I'm getting some now," Martim said.

Seven closed the bathroom door with a frown. Were they going shopping in other countries that still used the old money or something? He had no idea what to expect from this trip.

THERE WAS NO special security driver tonight. Greta drove a sedan, and Troy sat in the front passenger seat. Seven rode in the backseat next to his father, who was fully visible and clothed this time, just like he'd told Fuerte he was going to be. He kept throwing suspicious glances Seven's way. Seven's shoulders drew inward from the stares.

Nervously he touched the earpiece, which was still lodged in his ear, then pulled his hand away because he didn't want Martim to notice it. He'd managed to keep it there the entire time he'd been captured, and because it was mostly clear, no one had seen it—not even Troy, who'd apparently stopped using his X-ray vision on him or else he'd have noticed it. Seven had been hoping Cabot would check in again, but maybe they'd abandoned that kind of communication because Seven hadn't been answering them. Or they assumed the earpiece had gotten taken away from him or lost. Or maybe the battery was dead, or he was out of range—those things were entirely possible, too. But he'd wear it just in case Cabot gave it another try.

Seven was proud that none of the adults with him had any idea who he was—if they suspected, they didn't let on. Troy had seemed to buy that he lived in the country they'd visited the previous night and had snuck aboard there. It was a simple enough story to be believable, and Seven got a little thrill from successfully lying to him. Troy had started to call him The Kid, and the nickname stuck, so Seven didn't offer anything more. With all the name manipulation they'd done, Seven refusing to identify himself didn't seem to faze them much. It was a survival technique for supers in a world like this.

They arrived at the airport at around ten thirty p.m., the same time as the night before. Parking lot lamps partially lit the exterior of the hangar, and some low lights streamed out from the open door. There was a row of parked vehicles behind the building, and a few airport workers were driving around in covered carts. This time the plane was being prepped in hangar seven, which seemed potentially lucky to the boy with that number as his name.

Seven took advantage of the fact the others couldn't tell which direction he was looking and turned his head to study the line of vehicles, searching for a familiar one. There was a man in a suit standing outside a beat-up car next to another person setting up a large camera. Seven wondered if he was a newspaper reporter hoping to talk to Fuerte.

Seven didn't really think he'd see Birdie and the others there—they probably didn't expect the president to be going out recruiting two nights in a row. But there was a chance The Librarian would come through for him. Then he caught a glimpse of an SUV driving slowly behind the line of hangars. It looked a lot like the SUV they'd been in yesterday—were they searching for the president's plane? He sat up a little higher and strained to see. But the distance, the darkness, and the vehicle's tinted windows revealed nothing, and soon the SUV disappeared from view.

Seven glanced at the corners of the building as Greta pulled up to hangar seven and parked. They stayed in the car a few moments, waiting for permission to board. Could Tenner possibly be sneaking toward them in the shadows, looking for him with his extra-large pupils? When Seven and the others got out of the vehicle, Troy kept a cautious eye on him as if he might try to run away. Seven stepped around him to make sure he'd be visible to anyone watching.

He hesitated, wondering if he should make a run for it right then and there. Would Troy and Martim go after him? Could he get his clothes off so he could be mostly undetectable? But taking his pants off while running didn't seem advisable. And Troy could see him far better than the average person. It didn't seem safe . . . and what would happen if they caught him? They'd never trust him. And they'd make his life worse—there was no doubt about that. Seven had a chance to prove himself valuable . . . which seemed to be something this group wanted. And maybe if he succeeded, he could find out more about the president's supernatural ability. Was that somehow tied to Fuerte's recent changes to the law and his desire to build a supernatural army? He had to have been hiding this ability for decades, maybe even his whole life. Why embrace it now? Seven needed to know more about everything.

As the reporter and the cameraperson started moving swiftly toward them, Troy grabbed Seven's shoulder and pushed him toward the plane. They followed Martim up the steps and boarded. "Sit there, by that table," Troy said gruffly, pointing to the chair next to the bathroom, which no one had sat in the night before.

"Okay," Seven said loudly in his newly adopted lower voice. He wanted to make sure the others knew he was on board in case they were listening through the bug. But then he worried that they might not know it was him. Seven blew out an anxious breath. He had to stick with the voice, or else Troy would be suspicious.

While they waited for Fuerte to show up, Seven glanced at the chair that had the bug attached to the underside of it. Was it still there? He couldn't see it, which was probably a good sign. And what about his cell phone? With this many people on the flight, Seven didn't think he could get to it without causing suspicion. And the battery had to be pretty low or dead by now, so it wouldn't be useful unless he could charge it. But if he had a chance to take the bug back to the mansion with him, that would be a good move.

Soon President Fuerte arrived. With him was Cabot's dad, Jack Stone. Seven tried to hold in his surprise—he hadn't seen him yet. He wondered again where his mom was, and Tenner's mom, too. After Troy's shocking reappearance, they'd all pondered whose bones he, Cabot, and Brix had found on their journey to Estero. Seven was more and more convinced that the two bad moms were the ones the bones belonged to. Was there a way to learn the truth without giving himself away? It seemed too soon to be asking Troy and Martim personal questions.

"So, this is The Kid?" Jack Stone asked in the same warm, gentle voice Seven remembered. It made Seven's throat ache. Jack made his way to the seat across the table from Martim and looked curiously at Seven's camouflaged face, then politely leaned across the aisle and held out his hand in greeting. "I'm Jack."

"Uh," Seven said, remembering to use his deepest voice. "Yeah, I'm The Kid. That's what they call me." He reached out his clammy hand and shook Jack's. It made him feel like a grown-up. It also made the corners of his eyes prickle with tears. Jack's friendly gesture affected Seven deeply. Memories of his younger days with Jack started pummeling him—horsing around in the water, hiking and fishing, cooking over the fire, listening to stories of Jack's experiences in Estero and his time as an inventor. Jack had been present in Seven's life, unlike his own father, who never thought to play with him. But Seven knew he had to stop thinking like Seven and start thinking like The Kid, because Jack could read snippets of people's minds. Perhaps that was why Fuerte wanted him along—to see if he could glean anything from the new camo super.

Despite that, Seven felt a sudden yearning inside him to tell Jack everything, like he'd felt with Greta earlier. Jack had been an ally for the children—how could this man possibly be a bad person? He'd been a trusted adult. Seven glanced at Martim, overwhelmed with feelings about the old days at the hideout. He longed to ask about his mom. He just . . . he needed to know.

But now was the time to forget Seven's past and focus on The Kid's present and future, and keep Jack Stone from learning anything incriminating.

President Fuerte boarded swiftly and closed the plane door, keeping the reporter from getting any new information other than some photos. As the plane rolled out of the hangar, the president took the seat next to Seven and launched into the details of the heist: They were going to steal a priceless vase to replace the one that had disappeared from the palace after the break-in.

Seven could hardly listen as his nerves took over. He was much more comfortable on this trip, wearing the clothes from Greta and sitting in a luxurious chair. But he would be part of stealing a precious work of art belonging to another country. It wasn't something he'd ever do. Sure, he'd broken into President Fuerte's palace to help free Elena. But this was different—these people were serious professionals. Top criminals. Notorious thieves. And he was being put to the test to prove he could be a part of them . . . even though he didn't want that at all.

Despite his misgivings, he needed to do this for the cause The Librarian had convinced them all to fight for. Seven was undercover, and he needed to keep his identity a secret for as long as possible and get close to these people. Because if the criminals figured out it was him, they'd want to know if the rest of the children were there, too. And then they'd suspect they were the ones who'd freed Elena. In addition to being furious about what Louis had done with the stash. All of that could put them in danger.

With a start, Seven stopped his racing thoughts and noticed Jack was gazing curiously at him. *Frayzia, my home sweet home,* he thought, over and over.

President Fuerte droned on like the small plane's propellers. "And then The Kid and Martim go in and nab the vase."

"Wait just a minute," Martim said, his voice booming, bringing Seven back sharply into the present. "You're sending *him* with me? To do *my* job?"

The air around them prickled. Seven froze, then pressed back in his seat and looked at the floor.

President Fuerte shot Martim a look. "Relax. We need to test him. Plus it's a pretty big vase."

"We don't *need* him at all," Martim said, clipping the words.

Seven glanced up and saw the flash of anger and . . . was that jealousy in his father's eyes? It was startling. He'd never seen his dad act like that before—at least not about *him*. It was as though another person with an invisibility-related trait somehow threatened Martim's career. Could that be what his beef was about? "Look, man," Seven said, trying to smooth things over, but his fake voice was shaky. He slid forward, making his seat belt tight around his hips.

"No, *you* look. If you screw this up . . ." Martim pressed his hands firmly on the arms of his chair and started to get up.

"Stop." Troy leaned over and put his massive hand on Martim's chest. "If he screws up, I'll take care of him. All right?"

Seven slid back in his chair, fearful of both men. *He'll take care of me?* Seven thought. Was that a threat? "I won't mess it up," he said quietly. Then he said it again, louder, so if his friends were listening through the bug, they could hear. "I'm not going to mess up the job." He took in a deep breath and let it out slowly, then looked up. "So, Mr. President, what does this vase look like?"

MISTAKES WERE MADE

"I saw Seven," Tenner said excitedly as he returned to the SUV after the president's plane left the hangar. "It looks like the newspaper people were here. Everyone went quickly inside the plane to avoid them, but I'm sure it was Seven with my dad and Martim—typical headless, armless camo boy in clothes."

"Good work, T," Birdie said. They knew where Seven was right now. And they also knew for sure where he was staying, thanks to the raven peeking in through the mansion windows. Things were progressing.

Cabot pulled the bug receiver out of the seat-back pocket where she'd left it and handed it to The Librarian. Then, with a start, she remembered her earpiece. "Oh no," she muttered, grimacing. She'd completely forgotten about it. She dunked her hand into the pocket again and pulled out the earpiece. As expected, the battery was still dead.

"Oh no, what?" asked Brix from the seat behind her.

"I didn't recharge the earpiece that's paired with Seven's, so I won't be able to hear him if he says anything to us." Her face flushed. “I guess with my headache and staying up all night and still getting used to everything technology requires to work properly . . . I just forgot.” More than anything in the world, Cabot hated making mistakes. Mistakes were for other people to make and for Cabot to feel smug about. It had been her job to communicate with Seven, and she had dropped the ball. She gripped her head.

“He’s never alone to talk, anyway,” Tenner said kindly. “And he’s out of range by now.”

“Do you want me to rub your sore head?” Brix offered.

Cabot frowned and almost said no. But it really ached. And she could sit there and listen to the bug with a throbbing head, or she could sit there and listen to the bug with her head being rubbed. “Okay,” she said gruffly. “Thanks.”

Brix reached over the seat and started rubbing Cabot’s temples.

“That actually feels nice,” Cabot admitted. She settled back in her seat and closed her eyes.

“Do you want medicine for it?” The Librarian asked. “I have a bottle back at the cottage. We can get you some when we get home.”

“Maybe.” Cabot had looked up headache medicine. It came in the form of a giant pill that you were supposed to swallow without chewing. She didn’t like the idea of that. “This is helping, so I think I’ll be okay.”

The Librarian turned up the volume on the bug receiver so everyone could listen to the conversation on the plane.

Despite the relaxing head rub, Cabot strained to hear every word through the airplane engine noises. Then her eyes flew open. "My dad is there," she said anxiously, pulling out of Brix's grasp. She'd known from Elena that Jack Stone had made it to Estero alive, but she hadn't had her own personal proof that he'd remained so until that moment when she'd heard his voice. She blew out a breath of relief, then slid her fingers through her buzz cut and leaned forward, feeling much better. Brix slumped back, exhausted. He squinted and rubbed his own temples for a few moments, then yawned and curled up on the seat, trying to get comfortable.

"Ooh, did you catch that?" Cabot exclaimed. "They're giving Seven a job to steal something."

"Oh no!" Birdie said. "What if he gets caught?"

"He's being forced to do it by the president of Estero," The Librarian said. "He'll be okay. Don't . . . don't worry about that." But she seemed a little worried.

Cabot frowned. "Should we worry about Troy 'taking care of him' if he messes up?"

"Well," said The Librarian, "yes. That is concerning."

"At least Seven is talking now," Elena said with relief in her voice. "Sounds like he picked up a bad cold, poor thing. I hope they're letting him sleep and giving him fluids. Greta will look after him. And I'm glad he's cooperating. Maybe he'll learn something useful while we're figuring out how to get him out of there."

"What do you think he told them about *us*?" Brix asked. He knew the palace dungeon security guard had seen him bouncing around, and that troubled him more than he'd shared with the others. And if Troy and Martim had reviewed the security footage, they'd have seen him, too. Had Seven informed the bad parents that they were all here in Estero City? And had he told them what their abilities were?

"Hopefully he said he came alone," Birdie said. "I wonder if they've pinned him to the palace break-in."

"I think we can safely say no, or they wouldn't be auditioning him with a heist," Elena said.

"You never know with criminals," The Librarian said. "Even enemies will team up together when it's convenient for them."

"That's a good point," Elena said. "Our group wasn't exactly best friends. But we had a common enemy, so that bonded us."

Both groups fell silent—on the plane and on the ground. Brix slept deeply, and Tenner dozed. The others read or worked on their phones.

Cabot rested her eyes, enjoying not having a headache for once, and took a nap as well. She woke up when her mother gave the passengers a turbulence warning. A few minutes later, Greta let her team know they'd be landing at their destination soon, so they should buckle up. There was a sudden small commotion as Martim excused himself to go to the bathroom and change out of his clothes. They could hear the bathroom door shut, but then they heard a loud rustling of papers near the bug. After that there was a muffled thump, as if someone had brushed or bumped against the covert device.

"Whoa," Seven said, much closer to the bug than he'd been the entire trip. "That's some turbulence." There was more rustling of papers, as if he was picking them up. Then they heard the bathroom door again.

"What are you doing?" Martim barked.

"Your papers fell," Seven said. "I picked them up. I guess I should change out of my clothes now?" Then: "Oof! Sorry! I . . . didn't see you, obviously. I dropped—I just need to get my . . . pen. It went flying over there by the emergency exit when the plane jerked."

Martim grunted. "And the president trusts him with a priceless vase?"

"Get over it, Martim," Fuerte said.

A moment later, Seven called out "Found it." They heard the bathroom door once more. Then their ears were assaulted by continuous loud scuffling noises that drowned out everything else.

"What's happening?" Birdie asked. She put her hands over her ears.

"Yikes," The Librarian said. "Someone found the bug." The muffled brushing sound was harsh, and it didn't let up. Finally The Librarian turned down the receiver volume. All they could hear was sheer unpleasant static, like a radio that was stuck between stations.

"What if they suspect Seven of planting it?" Lada said, alarmed.

"He's the only one they *would* suspect," Elena said. "No one else has been on the plane as far as they know. This could be troublesome."

"My dad won't let anybody hurt Seven," Cabot said, though she didn't sound completely certain of that. "But if they think Seven is spying on them, they're going to want to find out exactly why."

Soon, after another long moment of rough static, there was a small thump and some bumps and bangs, and a few muffled voices and a slam. Then everything went quiet.

The Librarian put her head in her hands, then pinched the bridge of her nose. "We didn't hear any raised voices or crying," she said, grasping at positives. "That's a good sign."

Elena looked out the window into the night, her face drawn. She rested her hand on Brix's back as he slept.

"None of this sounds good," Cabot said. "We have to grab him when they get back. Who knows what they'll do to him?"

"That's risky," Birdie said. "If Seven would just keep his clothes off after they finish the heist and all the way home, he could make a break for it while he's fully camouflaged once they land here again . . . That seems like the safest move. I hope he thinks of it."

With the area around hangar seven now empty of workers, and hours to pass while the group on the plane tested Seven in an actual criminal heist, Cabot left the vehicle to get some air. She began pacing in the darkness to help her think. If the bug was discovered and destroyed, they'd have no information coming in. They'd have to do something else—they couldn't just keep coming to the airport and waiting around for Seven to make a break for it, when they had no idea what challenges he was facing. But nobody seemed to know what the right move was.

As Lada, Tenner, and Birdie got out of the SUV, too, Cabot remembered the earpiece and went back to the SUV to confess to the adults that she'd forgotten to charge it. The Librarian waved off her concern and pulled out a cord. "Do you have the earpiece and case? We can charge it right here in the car. There's a port that will work."

"The SUV has electricity?" Cabot asked, incredulous. She fetched the case and handed it over.

"I fear Seven's may be in the same shape as yours, though—no charge left," The Librarian said. "That's if he even still has it. But if he does, we'll be there for him."

"What if someone else took it and is listening in, spying on *us*?" Cabot asked.

"Hmm," said The Librarian. "Well, then we'd be able to listen to whatever they say, and we'd know if it's still in Seven's possession."

Was there a remote chance that Seven still had it . . . and had kept it in his ear? And that it had a charge? And that he would have a chance to let Cabot know he could hear her? Obviously because of the short range, she wouldn't be able to find out until Seven was back at the airport hours from now. And Cabot was fuzzy on how long the batteries could last, because batteries were still such a new concept for her. Just in case, once the plane landed back in Estero, Cabot would listen in.

"Should we text him?" Tenner asked. "Maybe give him some instructions on what to do to get away . . . or something?"

"If Seven had his cell phone, he would have gotten in touch with us by now," Birdie said. "They must have taken it."

"If they took it," Lada said, "they would search his contacts and read his text messages . . . so now they probably know all about what we're doing. It's best not to telegraph our moves. We should wait for the right time to surprise them." She used her crutches to keep steady as she eased to a sitting position on the tailgate. She felt totally deflated but didn't want to let the others know that Seven might not be coming back anytime soon. They were amateurs dealing with professionals, and the odds were against the good guys at the moment. Had the criminals already figured out that this little makeshift group of eight was trying to bring them down? "They probably know that you kids are all here." She closed her eyes and grimaced, feeling physical pain from sitting in the SUV for so long and not getting enough sleep, stretching, or working out her overtaxed muscles. Not to mention the mental pain from imagining all of her and The Librarian's hard work being wasted if the criminals knew what they were doing.

Lada wasn't sure how to proceed. And neither was anyone else. Everything hinged on what Fuerte and the rest had learned about their group. But they had no way of knowing what the criminals knew.

Birdie sat down next to Lada. "This is one of the most frustrating moments in my life." She bent forward, sliding her fingers into her tangled hair and resting her head in her hands. "It's bad, isn't it," she said softly so the others couldn't hear.

"Yeah," Lada said.

All their hopes and dreams for equality and justice seemed like they were about to spiral down the drain. The dissonant scrapings and muffled sounds on the bug receiver had put them all on edge. But the silence was worse. Had someone on the plane destroyed the bug?

"We'll leave the receiver on to see if we get anything," The Librarian said, but she didn't sound hopeful.

Brix lifted his head. His hair stood on end, and one cheek was dark red from lying on it. "Why are we staying here all night again?" he whined. He leaned against his mother, then got up and left the vehicle to join the other kids.

"Should we try to bug the mansion right now while everyone is away?" Cabot said, looking up. She couldn't stop jiggling her leg in nervousness.

"The security guards are still there," The Librarian reminded them. "Until Lada can teleport the distance we need her to go, we won't be able to access it safely."

Lada looked up wearily. So this was on her now.

Birdie and Cabot sighed together. Tenner paced in the parking lot. Brix started bouncing around, trying to wake up.

"Well," Lada said, standing up with her crutches and trying not to groan in pain, "I'm going to do some stretching. Then I may as well practice teleporting while we wait for the plane to return." She ran through several minutes of her usual heel cord and hamstring stretches, pressing against the SUV door frame instead of a wall. Once she was feeling some relief, she looked at the two youngest, who seemed like they needed something to do. "Brix, why don't you go about halfway to the front corner of the hangar. Cabot, you stay here and mark the spot I teleport from. Let's see if I can make it from one of you to the other." She turned to The Librarian. "Do you have your toolbox? We should measure."

Brix seemed relieved to have something else to focus on. He bounced like a rabbit toward the distant point, then turned. "Hey, Lada," he said, "if your crutches teleport with you, does that mean that anything you're touching will go with you? Like, could you teleport *me* with you?"

Lada grinned. "I wish. Sorry, but it doesn't work that way. Things I can comfortably *carry* will go with me, like my crutches. If you were smaller, like a baby I could hold in one arm so I could carry my crutches in the other, I might be able to do it. Though I would never actually teleport with a baby, because there's always a chance I'll lose my balance when I arrive. But anyway, I don't think I can carry you with one arm. So you'd be left behind." Her eyes lit up. "Or maybe just part of you would go with me. Like your head."

Brix stopped moving. "Are you serious?" he asked breathlessly.

Lada pressed her lips together. "Nah. I'm just joking."

"Rats," said Brix, bouncing again toward the spot. "I *really* want to teleport. Even if it's just my head."

"Like I told you," Lada called after him, "it's a lonely ability. You should be happy with your bouncy feet."

Brix ran up the side of the hangar and touched the eaves, then hung there for a second before dropping and bouncing in place. Then he did a series of handsprings and returned to the spot Lada had indicated. Lada beckoned Cabot to stand next to her to mark her starting point.

Tenner sidled up to Birdie, and the two crossed their arms, leaning against the SUV and watching. "Why doesn't Lada just start from the corner of the SUV?" Tenner whispered. "She doesn't need them both for this."

"I think she's trying to give them something to do," Birdie whispered back. "Which is really sweet."

"Yeah," said Tenner. He felt his face heat up, but he wasn't sure why.

Lada disappeared and reappeared next to Brix alongside the building. She moved five or six feet farther away and used Brix as the marker. "Let's try it from here." Then she disappeared and reappeared by Cabot.

Elena joined Birdie and Tenner. "Let's brainstorm a way to get Seven when they return," she said with renewed enthusiasm. The three began to hatch a plan to create a distraction that might give Seven a chance to escape.

Meanwhile, Lada continued lengthening the distance she traveled, sometimes wobbling off-balance when she reappeared, but only falling once when she accidentally left one crutch behind.

The Librarian took the measuring tape out of her toolbox, then went to her bag and pulled out a copy of an appraisal done on the Cordobio LLC property after the mansion was built, which she'd found in the Estero City Hall public records. Along with the appraisal package was a site plan for the mansion property. Setting it on the open hatch of the SUV and using the interior lights to see, she measured the distance from the woods to inside the garage and referred to the key to calculate the distance in feet.

As she worked, the bug receiver started making the same staticky noises again. When they didn't stop, and there was nothing to be gained from continuing to listen, The Librarian turned the receiver off. The bug had helped them tremendously. But now it was dead.

THE HEIST

The plane landed and taxied to a private hangar. Seven and the criminals disembarked and went to a waiting SUV. "We need to make a stop at the far end of the main terminal, Greta," Troy said, leaning forward from the middle seat.

"The money exchange?" Greta asked, glancing sideways at Fuerte in the front passenger seat. "Again?" The president seemed uninterested.

"You guessed it," said Troy. He patted his bulging jacket pocket.

Seven caught Greta's expression in the rearview mirror—her eyes narrowed, and her brow wrinkled. She didn't look pleased. But she drove to a small building attached to the airport terminal. The place was lit up, and two security guards stood outside the door.

"I'll be right back," Troy said. He hopped out of the car, nodded to the guards, and went inside. Moments later he returned carrying an envelope. "Success."

Martim snickered under his breath. Jack and Greta exchanged

a brief, meaningful look as Greta backed the vehicle out of the parking space. Jack shifted uncomfortably. "Leave our share with me once the heist is over," he said quietly.

"*Your* share?" Troy snorted. "I thought you didn't want to stoop to taking any after the whole explosion thing. Are you tossing your conscientious objections out the window? Besides, it's not what you think it is."

"Knock it off, everyone," Fuerte warned. "Or *I'll* take the cash—all of it. It's not yours, anyway, you lousy bunch of crooks."

Seven stared. So *was* it the stash that Martim was pulling old money from, or not? Had the Stones decided not to accept any of the stash because Troy and Martim had blown up the Goldens' old apartment? What would make them change their minds now? He stayed small and quiet, hoping to hear more. But after the president's threat, they all fell silent, and Greta sped to their destination.

SEVEN SHIVERED IN the shadows outside a place called the Museum of Antiquities with the other criminals. By now he knew what the vase looked like and where it was inside the museum. He also knew that it was almost as large as he was, so it would take two of them to carry it—two criminals who couldn't be identified on security cameras. That meant Seven had to do this heist with Martim, while Greta, Jack, Troy, and Fuerte took care of getting them in and out of the building safely. Jack was already working the series of locks on the service entrance as they waited to get inside.

"It's a good thing I'm here," Seven said in a gruff whisper, trying to prove his worth, though he was super nervous. "You wouldn't be able to get that huge vase without me." He was still trying desperately to not accidentally reveal his true self to Jack, the prying mind reader, so he continued being The Kid from Frayzia. "I've never seen a vase that big where I come from. What do you put in it? A tree?" He laughed uneasily. Jack smiled, but no one else did.

"Don't you go to museums?" President Fuerte asked, looking down his nose. "There are several vases like this one in Frayzia. Not as nice, of course. I only want the best."

"Not really," Seven said. "I'm not accepted in public places because of my camouflage. That's why I wanted to go to Estero, because things are changing—*you're* changing them by inviting all these supers to come. I think I could be accepted . . . eventually. With you and the others, at least." He didn't have to fake the forlorn sound to his voice. "I just want to belong," he added.

"Everyone wants that," said Troy. Fuerte and Greta flashed him quizzical glances, as if he'd said something uncharacteristic. Troy grunted and waved them off impatiently. "Tell me it's not true," he challenged. "You all know it."

"We're in," Jack said, stepping back from the open door.

"Now listen up," Greta instructed. "Once that vase so much

as trembles when you touch it, it'll trigger two alarms—a physical one here in the building, which is fairly useless since there is no security presence, and a silent one that alerts the police at the station four blocks away. From that point you'll have three minutes to get it out before the authorities get here. Got it?"

Martim and Seven nodded. Then, realizing Greta couldn't see them, Seven said, "Got it."

"What are you waiting for?" Fuerte said impatiently. "Go!"

Martim and Seven dashed inside. Seven tried not to bump into his father as he ran toward the vase's display case, but he had no idea where the invisible man was.

Meanwhile, Fuerte cased the back room from the open doorway. He didn't want to go inside for fear of being caught on camera. But that didn't stop him from noticing a few precious artifacts on the storage shelves. He held his hand out toward a jewel-encrusted letter opener that looked especially valuable. In seconds, the item was flying through the air and landing in his palm. He did the same with an ancient-looking mandolin and a golden tobacco pipe.

Inside, Seven and Martim collided a few times. "Watch where you're going," Martim growled, shoving Seven away.

"Sorry," said Seven, thrown off-balance and narrowly missing a statue. "I can't see you."

"Figure it out!" barked the man.

Like there was any way to do that. Seven frowned and didn't respond. Once they reached the glass display case and Martim jimmied the lock and flung the door open, Seven reached up. "I've got the mouth of the vase," he whispered. "On three?" The alarm started blaring.

"Just go," shouted Martim, unexpectedly lifting the vase from the bottom end. "The clock's ticking!" Seven bobbled the top of it, nearly sending it crashing to the floor. But he hung on and regained his grip, and then they started back the way they came, with Seven leading the way and picking up speed. He counted seconds in his head as he and his father ran recklessly through the museum with a priceless artifact between them.

It was almost fun for a moment . . . if Martim weren't so horrible to be around. But then, as Seven sailed through the open service door, Martim tripped over the threshold. He shrieked and lost his grip on the bottom of the vase, and his invisible, naked body went bumping and skidding across the pavement. Seven, not sure what had happened, hung on to the mouth of the vase for dear life, but it was too heavy for him to hold alone. Feeling it drop, he crumpled to the ground beneath it to cushion its fall, just barely getting his bare feet below the base before it hit the ground. Seven's backside scraped across the blacktop, and his head thumped the curb. The vase started to roll off him.

Troy dove for it, scooping it up. Seven, dazed, stared at the sky as Jack and Greta ran to help him up. "Did you black out?" Greta asked, putting his arm around her shoulders.

"I don't think so," Seven said as the couple lifted him firmly to his feet. Jack helped him to the car, while Greta went to check on Martim.

"What the—" Fuerte yelled at Martim. "What were you trying to do there? You almost messed up the whole plan."

"No time to chat!" Greta shouted, clapping her hands sharply to get the men's attention. "Get in the car!"

While Troy loaded and secured the vase in the back of the vehicle, Fuerte and Martim joined Jack and Seven in the passenger seats. Greta squealed out of the parking lot, heading back to the plane.

When they were safely far enough away, Fuerte turned to Seven. "You okay, Kid?"

Seven was bleeding—he could feel the slimy blood against the leather seat. His shredded skin burned like it was on fire. A lump had formed on the back of his head. "I'm fine," he said.

"Good job." The president faced forward again, not checking on Martim.

Martim, who was surely just as injured as Seven if not more so, seethed.

Despite the near disaster, the heist was successful. By the time the police could even figure out what was missing, the criminal supers were already bandaged up and in the air with the hideous giant vase, flying back to Estero City.

But there was no definitive word from Fuerte or any of the others as to whether Seven had passed the test.

~

Back at the airport, Tenner spied the approaching plane and alerted Cabot to fetch the partially recharged earpiece—Seven would soon be in range.

"Listen for a little while first," The Librarian instructed her. "But we don't have much time—you'll need to go ahead and speak to him if we're going to get this done right."

"Even if it risks someone else knowing our plans?" Cabot asked.

The Librarian nodded. "They probably already know a lot by now from Seven—not his fault, the poor boy. But we need him, and we can't keep doing this." She waved her arm at the tarmac. "I think it's worth the risk."

Cabot put the earpiece in place and stepped away from the others to make sure she could hear everything transmitting through it.

Meanwhile, Lada was wiped out. She had definitely increased her teleporting distance, but was it enough?

With a few minutes to spare before the plane landed, Birdie worked the measuring tape. "Eighty-nine feet!" she called, running back to the vehicle.

"That's excellent," Lada said, beaming despite her fatigue. "According to this site map, that means I'm within fifteen feet of traveling from a safe location in the woods to inside the mansion."

The Librarian confirmed it. "Another day or two of practice and you should be good. So if we don't get Seven back now, we have hope for the future."

After the kids and Elena packed up their things and stowed them in the SUV, The Librarian gathered them outside the hangar to discuss the distraction plan one more time.

When the plane grew larger and dropped lower in the sky, The Librarian sent everyone to their places. "It's time," she said. "We're going to do our best to help Seven. Let's hope he recognizes what we're doing and has an opportunity to make a break for it."

In seconds, Brix was bouncing up to the hangar roof.

A CRYPTIC MESSAGE

Cabot double-checked her earpiece. The indicator light glowed green. Relieved, she put the device back in. As the plane was about to land, she went to her assigned spot—the service door at the back of the hangar. She listened for a long time in case someone other than Seven was wearing his earpiece. But no one was speaking. There wasn't even any background conversation. Maybe they were all as tired as this group was, or maybe Seven's earpiece was as dead as the surveillance bug.

"Seven," Cabot said calmly when she could wait no longer. "I'm not sure if you can hear me. But we're here at the . . . the place. We're going to create a . . . I mean, do what we've been practicing. So if you see a chance to . . . you know. We can definitely help with that. Can you give me a sign that you can hear me?"

She waited, but didn't hear anything. Nearby, Tenner tossed the last of a tower of rocks up onto the hangar roof, where Brix collected them in a pile. Then Tenner slipped into the shadows, out of sight, while Brix stayed on the roof and flattened so he wouldn't be noticed.

As the plane taxied to the hangar, Cabot repeated her message to Seven. She turned the volume up as high as it would go. Was there any sort of noise or feedback? Other voices that Seven's microphone was picking up? If so, that would mean Seven's earpiece battery hadn't run out yet. But she just couldn't tell if the whooshing sound in her ear was due to the earpiece plugging it—kind of like when she listened to a conch shell—or if it was the sound of the inside of a moving airplane.

"Seven," Cabot said, her voice hitching slightly as nerves set in, "maybe you could just tap your earpiece two times if you can hear me."

A second went by, and then Cabot heard two clicks. She gasped.

"Seven can hear me on the earpiece," she whispered loudly to The Librarian, who was stationed at the front corner of the hangar. The woman gave a triumphant thumbs-up and let the rest of the team know the good news.

"Seven," Cabot said, her voice really starting to shake. What if it wasn't Seven who'd clicked? She continued anyway, desperate to communicate. "When everyone gets off the plane, say you forgot something and go back inside. Strip as fast as you can so you're completely camouflaged, then come running out toward the back service door of the hangar. It's the opposite direction from where the cars pick you up. Birdie and I will be waiting there. While you're doing that, the others will create a distraction near the president's vehicles, so everyone else will be going that way to see what's happening. Okay? Tap twice if you understand what to do."

Cabot held her breath. But Seven didn't tap twice.

"Okay?" she said again. Still no answer. Panic welled up inside her. If Seven's earpiece had been confiscated and someone else was listening, pretending to be him, she'd just given the plan away to the enemy. "Seven, clear your throat or something so I know you understand."

Again there was no response. Cabot was convinced she'd just blown the whole operation.

As the plane rolled into the hangar, Cabot ran over to The Librarian to tell her what had happened. She covered the earpiece so it wouldn't pick up her voice. "I think I blew it!" she whispered. Angry tears stung her eyes.

The woman took Cabot by the shoulders. "Listen, my young friend," she said calmly. "Panic causes us to make mistakes. I think Seven still has the earpiece. But maybe he didn't want to tap or clear his throat because someone was watching him or sitting right next to him. Let's keep going with the plan."

Cabot sucked in a breath and let it out. She nodded profusely. "Okay. Yes. Sorry about that."

"You're doing great work," The Librarian told her. "Now it's time for you and Birdie to get ready to help Seven in case he sees a chance to make a run for it."

Cabot returned to her spot. She and Birdie peered through the window in the service door. "I'm so nervous," Birdie whispered.

"Me too." Cabot tried to catch sight of Seven through the small airplane windows, but if his head was uncovered, he wouldn't be visible. "Seven," she said more calmly, "Birdie and I are at the back door."

Cabot heard a low, disgruntled-sounding sigh in response. She began to second-guess everything again. Why couldn't he make a small, positive-sounding noise? The people with him couldn't see his mouth move—why not just a slight whisper of confirmation? Anything would help.

But if it wasn't actually Seven listening in, and it was a criminal instead, they wouldn't want to give that away by speaking. Cabot's heart pounded. Her eyes were peeled, staring at the airplane door. When it opened, Troy emerged first, single-handedly carrying a huge vase. The president followed with some sort of musical instrument and a few other small items, and then Martim, fully visible. He glanced around to see if any journalists were there before descending. Then came Seven, in the strange clothing. His face and arms blended into the plane and stairs behind him.

Cabot watched to see if he would follow the plan. Just as he reached the bottom of the stairs, two more people came out of the plane. Jack and Greta Stone. Both of Cabot's parents. Jack put his hand on Greta's shoulder, and they laughed together, like they'd done a million times back home on the beach.

At the sight of them, Cabot felt dizzy. She grabbed the door frame to steady herself. "Holy coconuts," she whispered. "It's them. Both of them. Together."

"Are you okay?" Birdie asked.

Cabot shook her head. She sank to her knees. Agony tore through her. She wanted to run to them. To reunite with them, like Birdie had gotten to do with her mom. It wasn't fair that they'd done this to her! She hadn't realized how strongly it would affect her to see them like this. Without her. "You have to help Seven," she whispered. "I can't . . . I can't do this."

Just then, in Cabot's ear, Seven whispered, "Call off your plan. Don't do anything."

Cabot's eyes widened. She looked up at Birdie. Then she shook her head, trying to find words. "Seven just called us off!" she whispered harshly. "You need to stop Brix from creating the distraction!" As she sat next to the doorway, still dazed and disturbed from seeing her parents, she pulled out her phone and quickly texted: **Abort!!! The plan is off!**

Moments later, they watched the line of criminals walk to their awaiting cars. Seven hung back so that he was last. Once Troy and Martim had opened their doors and were getting in, Seven pulled something from his pocket, dipped down low, and casually sent it sliding across the concrete. Then he got into the car and closed the door without looking at any of them. The procession out of the airport began.

UNSETTLED

When the presidential motorcade was gone, Brix got down from the hangar roof while Birdie ran to see what Seven had sent flying across the pavement. "It's his phone!" Birdie called. She tried to wake it up, but the screen stayed black—the battery was dead. She shoved it into her back pocket and returned to the group. They all piled into the SUV, dejected and too tired to think straight. The Librarian headed home.

"Why didn't he keep his phone so he could contact us?" Cabot wondered. Her head began to pound again after all the stress of the night.

"It's dead," Birdie said. "I'll bet he didn't have a way to charge it. Even if they have chargers at the mansion, if Seven tried to use one, they would take his phone away."

"Try this," The Librarian said, pulling a different cord from her bag and handing it back without taking her eyes off the road. "There's a port back there, right?"

This time Cabot knew what to look for. "Yeah." She plugged in the charger, then connected it to Seven's phone. "Still not working."

"Give it a few minutes to get enough juice. Then you'll have to turn it on." The Librarian drove with one hand on the wheel and her other arm bent at the elbow, resting next to her window. She seemed frustrated by the whole experience. "I wonder why he didn't want to come with us."

"He could have known something," Elena said. "Like that they had weapons. That would have put him and us in danger."

"Or maybe they're threatening him," Birdie said glumly.

"Maybe his dad is being cool to him, and he wanted to stay," Cabot said with a frown. She didn't like how that had gone. From the shock of seeing her parents to Seven's refusal to attempt an escape, Cabot felt wary and unsettled about all of it. Something wasn't right. Was Seven in danger? Being threatened, like Birdie said? Or . . . had the criminals somehow managed to convince him to join their cause? They were recruiting supers. Had they recruited him, too?

They knew from their covert listening that the president was building an army of supernatural people. But they still didn't know why, or who he planned to fight. Was there some unique enemy he knew about that would require a specialized supernatural military? Things just weren't adding up.

Back at the cottage, the sun was coming up. Birdie rebooted Seven's phone, but only got to the screen where she had to enter his pass code. "Does anybody know Seven's phone code?" she asked. No one did. Cabot asked Seven through the earpiece, but again there was no answer—no doubt he had people around him.

Birdie made a few half-hearted guesses, but Lada stopped her from trying too many because she was worried they'd get locked out of Seven's phone for good. "Wait until he has a chance to tell us the code," she said.

Birdie set the phone aside. "I can't stand this," she grumbled. "How are we ever going to get Seven back if he's not going to help us?"

Tenner looked wearily at her. "Not now, Bird. Give the guy a break. He's been through a lot more trouble than we have."

Everyone was hungry and tired. Birdie scrounged some cheese and crackers while others grabbed leftovers from the refrigerator to eat.

"Let's get some sleep," Elena suggested after everyone had finished. "We'll figure this out. I promise. But we're all on edge and tired. We'll think better once we've rested."

The group dispersed to their rooms, leaving Cabot and Elena behind to scrape the food scraps into Puerco's bowl. The pig snorted gleefully and shuffled over to eat. Cabot's head pounded with another headache. She couldn't stop replaying the memory of her parents sharing a laugh together in her mind. Like they'd never even had her.

"Birdie told me you had a tough time seeing your parents today," Elena said casually. She put the dishes in the sink. "Do you want to talk about it?"

Cabot stared hard at the table as she wiped up the crumbs, willing herself not to cry. "I just can't believe what they're doing."

"I imagine it was hard to watch them."

"Yeah. They looked perfectly fine. Like . . . like . . ." Cabot couldn't say it.

"Like they were fine without you, when you aren't fine without them," said Elena. "Is that about right?"

Cabot nodded miserably. "I just wonder if things would have been different if they'd . . . if they'd been able to find the stash right away, before getting mixed up in . . . everything. Like maybe they would have been able to get home. To me."

"We never even had a chance to look for it," Elena said. "We hadn't even made it to Estero before we got captured."

"I know. I meant . . ." Cabot sighed, realizing she wasn't thinking straight. Ever since she'd seen the map of flames and known Louis had moved the stash to a place her parents didn't know about, Cabot had been blaming him for her parents not coming back. And it felt *good* to blame him—to have a reason for her parents' behavior. But she knew now it wasn't Louis's fault. "I know it doesn't make sense. I just want to blame Louis, and I feel terrible about it because . . ." She started crying. "Because *he's* dead, and my *parents* turned bad, and *Seven* is captured, and *everything* is just so awful." Once the sobs started coming, they wouldn't stop.

Elena opened her arms for a hug, but Cabot shook her head.

She needed to know the truth. "Why didn't Louis tell my mom and dad where he moved it? Why would he keep that from them? I thought you trusted my parents. Is there something about them you're not . . . telling me? Please—I can take it." Her lip wouldn't stop quivering.

Elena flinched. She dropped her arms to her sides. "Cabot, I trusted your parents fully. They were the only ones Louis and I confided in. I wish I knew what Louis was thinking back then," she said softly. "He didn't tell me, either, you know? There are so many questions we'll never get the answers to now that he's gone. Maybe he was trying to protect us. And maybe he realized his mistake when we didn't return. I don't know. And it's really, really hard not knowing. It eats me up inside, too."

Cabot nodded and swiped at her tears, then got a tissue to blow her nose. "I'm afraid I don't know how to trust anybody anymore," she whispered.

THE TWO OF them made their way to their bedrooms. But after a while of staring at the ceiling, Cabot crept back downstairs to the living area. She put her earpiece in again and tried to talk to Seven, but this time she couldn't hear any whooshing sounds—it seemed like his battery had finally run out. So much for that.

Then, on a whim, she fetched the bug receiver. She turned it on to see if it was still crackling annoyingly and was surprised to hear a quiet conversation in progress. Her eyes widened. For a moment she was confused—had the criminals taken yet another flight? But she didn't hear any of the usual plane hum and vibration in the background. She focused on identifying the voices.

"He did a good job," Troy said. "You gotta give him that."

"I'm not giving him anything," Martim said icily. "And *you* shouldn't have given him a bed to sleep in. He's intruding into my territory."

"There's room for two invisible people," Troy said, sounding shockingly reasonable. "Besides, he's all scraped up and sore."

"He's *not* invisible," Martim muttered. "Besides, I'm not interested in him making me look foolish and vaulting to stardom in the eyes of the president. Who, by the way, hasn't even put an ankle bracelet on The Kid yet. Did you notice that?"

"He doesn't put them on any of the new supers," Troy said. "And it's not like The Kid can go anywhere with the guards around." He yawned loudly. "When do you suppose the news will break?"

Cabot, still unsure of where the men were and how the bug was managing to pick up their conversation, perked up. What news?

"Fuerte thinks he talked her out of revealing it," Martim said, "so maybe it won't happen after all. That monster is asking for some big money to keep quiet, though. She needs it for her silly campaign, I bet."

"It's Fuerte's own fault for turning the country against supers in the first place," Troy grumbled.

Cabot was mystified. Who was "she," and what was that about a campaign? Was it Cami Leone or perhaps Greta they were talking about? Troy and Martim didn't treat either of them like monsters, though. Cabot hoped for more, but only heard the clink of dishes and someone clearing their throat in an icky kind of way. Could they be at the mansion? Then she heard them talking from farther away. "Landscapers are here. Open the gate."

Cabot sucked in a breath. They *were* at the mansion. Somehow, Seven had managed to take the bug with him to the criminals' hideout and plant it there. The awful feedback they'd heard overnight must've been because Seven had put the bug in his pocket before he changed out of his clothing.

"Who's a clever boy now?" Cabot murmured, pleased with Seven's sneaky ways. But then her mind turned back to the last thing she'd heard. The criminals had landscapers coming into the property. And the gate was open.

Now was her chance to get this job done once and for all.

SNEAKING IN

With everyone else asleep, Cabot dressed in the khaki jumpsuit The Librarian had bought her. It was similar to the one The Librarian owned, and it made Cabot feel special. The jumpsuit also reminded her of a uniform, the concept of which boggled her mind—she'd noticed people wearing identical clothing in various types of jobs, and not because it was cool. Lada had told her that was the policy for some companies. It made their workers easy to recognize, so customers would know who to ask for help. Cabot was skeptical. Customers automatically trusted a person in a uniform, with no basis for it other than what they wore. That was trust Cabot thought they didn't deserve.

People could take advantage of that trust—people like Cabot.

Cabot had observed landscapers before. They wore khaki or light-colored clothing—coveralls, or long pants with matching shirts, and hats to protect them from the elements. Perhaps a casual observer might think Cabot in her khaki jumpsuit was a small member of a landscaping team if they didn't look too closely.

She left the cottage carrying her phone, a helmet, and a few specialty items from The Librarian's toolbox tucked in her jumpsuit pocket, and headed for the monastery scooter and bike corral. She chose a scooter and snuck out the secret alley door with it. Before she started riding, she pulled the earpiece from her ear and turned it off. She didn't want anyone trying to convince her not to do this. Then she headed straight to 710 Legacy Avenue.

About halfway there, she began to second-guess herself. Was this a mistake, going alone? But she knew if she'd told anyone, they'd have talked her out of it, or begged to go with her, and that would have wasted precious time. This job was better left to a single, small, sneaky person—one who paid attention to little things. Cabot had noticed a few details about the house the last time they'd been inside, like the fact that the side door to the garage wasn't locked, so that might be a great way to get in. And there were a number of rooms that didn't appear to be occupied by anyone. They could certainly come in handy.

Cabot was sure Seven was scared. His dad wasn't being very nice to him. And her team really couldn't live without him any longer. He had the best ability of them all, except for maybe Lada—that was just a fact. Cabot was envious of it. That was a fact, too. If only she could spy on people while camouflaged! But she wasn't overly jealous. Just enough to keep her wanting an ability of her own, though she'd all but given up on that by now.

She pulled up next to the gleaming silver mailbox on Legacy Avenue and watched the traffic for a moment. Then she started down the curvy driveway through the woods on her scooter, ready to jump into the brush at the first sign of life. She made it halfway to the fence before she caught sight of the guards and the landscapers and had to ditch her scooter in a bush.

The gate was wide open. A landscaping truck was parked just inside with plants and sod in the back. Two guards patrolled the area around the open gate. Three landscapers, wearing khaki-colored uniforms and floppy sun hats with a company logo on them, were working with rakes, leaf blowers, and noisy trimming tools in various parts of the yard.

Cabot smiled to herself. She'd made a good choice with her clothing, but she was missing a key element of her disguise. If only she'd brought The Librarian's floppy sun hat, she might have blended in even more. She studied the landscaping truck, noticing the landscapers' personal items on the back of the open truck bed. Three water bottles, a big ring of keys . . . and a company hat with a brim and a protective neck flap hanging down.

She studied the guards and their movements, kind of like how she used to study Birdie, Brix, Tenner, and Seven back home from her tree perch. The guards seemed fairly nonchalant about their duties to protect the driveway from intruders. They were more intent on watching the landscapers, as if they were suspicious of them.

Cabot climbed up a tree to get a better look. As she hung

there, she searched the property for weaknesses and opportunities. What was the best way to get through the maze of people in order to reach Seven?

The criminals were likely asleep after being up all night, just like the rest of Cabot's team. So once she got inside the house, she'd be fine. She spied a section of lawn on the opposite side of the property from the garage service door. It didn't have anyone near it—no landscapers, no guards, no criminals. She plotted her moves, then closed her eyes and played them out in her mind.

As she did so, the dull ache in her head grew, just like the headaches of the past few days. But this time, what felt like a flash of hot lightning shot through her pupils, making her wince and press her eyelids. Perhaps it was the pollution from the big city that affected her, or the drastic change in sleep patterns that was causing the unusual discomfort. It was definitely throwing Cabot off her game.

But she needed to concentrate. This wasn't going to be an easy move, but it was a simple, straightforward plan. If it worked and she got Seven out of there, she would pretty much be a hero. Like usual.

Before she could enter the property, she had to put her distraction technique in play. Her mouth salivated at the thought. This would be the most exciting part of the rescue. She climbed down the tree and moved stealthily through the woods so she was closer to the open section of lawn she'd identified earlier. Then she reached into her pocket and pulled out the flashing noisemaker she and The Librarian had made together, back when they'd made the first bug. It was perfect—oblong, with a pin at one end. She turned the rough, makeshift creation in her hand, and rubbed her thumb across the ridges of tape that held it together. Then, with her heart beating fast, she pulled out the pin and sent the noisemaker sailing over the fence.

Cabot didn't wait to watch what happened. She took off running toward the gate. The noisemaker made three explosive sounds, and out of the corner of her eye, Cabot could see the lights flashing from it. The guards turned sharply, then left their posts and ran to see what was happening. With their backs to her, Cabot darted inside the gate. She grabbed the landscaping hat from the back of the truck and set it on her head. She pulled a rake off the truck, too, and started purposefully toward the side door to the garage.

It was open, just as she'd expected. She slipped inside the dark garage, seeing Troy's silver roadster and the red convertible parked there, and listened for signs of people. Hearing none, she slithered around the vehicles to the entrance to the house. That door was locked.

Using the screwdriver she'd brought along, Cabot pried the decorative base of the handle loose from the door, revealing four screws. She unscrewed them and quietly pulled the door handle loose. The inside handle fell with a thud to the floor. Cabot flinched at the noise, hoping it wasn't loud enough to wake anyone, then slowly opened the door.

Once inside, Cabot looked around, getting her bearings, then methodically began her search for Seven. Based on what Troy and Martim had said about giving the kid a bed to sleep in, Cabot assumed she'd find Seven in one of the bedrooms that had been unoccupied before. She stayed away from the long hallway where she remembered Troy and Martim had bedrooms and offices, and checked an open door off the kitchen. But that room was more like a walk-in closet, empty except for some boxes. Then she tried a door off the dining room and found what appeared to be a headless body under the covers on a bed. Definitely Seven. She ran in and shook him awake. "Seven!" she hissed. "Wake up!"

Seven rolled over and groaned in pain from his scraped-up back. "Huh?" He rubbed his eyes, then sat up as if he'd seen a ghost. "Cabot!" he said in a loud whisper. "What the heck are you doing here?"

"I'm getting you out. The coast is clear, but we need to hurry!"

Seven got out of bed, flustered. "I . . . but . . ." He turned stiffly, like he was looking for something but wasn't sure what. "I . . ." he said again. "I'm making progress!"

They heard the two men moving down the long hallway. "Did you hear an explosion?" Troy said.

"I heard *something,*" replied Martim, his voice gravelly with sleep.

"Explosion?" Seven whispered, even more befuddled.

Cabot whirled around. "Come on!" she said. "Strip!" She ran to the doorway and peered out. "We need to go now before the guards return to their stations. Hurry *up,* Seven! The gate's wide open!" She made a frustrated noise. It almost seemed like Seven wanted to stay there.

"I'm just . . . confused," Seven said. "I've had, like, three hours of sleep in the past three days. It's been a little difficult. Why are you wearing that weird hat?"

"Holy coconuts, Seven," Cabot said, trying to breathe without exploding. "Take your bleeping pants off now, or we're not going to make it!"

"Well, turn around, then!" Seven finally did what Cabot told him to do.

After a moment, Cabot peeked at him. Seeing the large bandage on his back, she lunged at him and ripped it off.

"Yow!" Seven whispered harshly. "A little warning next time?"

"Shh!"

They heard the front door open as the men went outside to see what was going on.

Cabot returned to the bedroom door and peeked out into the dining room. She could see part of the hallway and a sliver of the kitchen. Beyond that was the exit to the garage, where she'd come in. The dads hadn't noticed the broken door handle yet. "We're going out through the garage. I want you to run for the open gate," Cabot whispered. "Head for the road. You go first, and make a noise to warn me if you see anybody."

"Okay. Got it," Seven said, blowing out a breath. He was still befuddled from the abrupt rousing, but he crept out and emerged into the dining room.

Cabot, unable to detect Seven, realized too late that she didn't know how fast he was walking or where he was. She also realized it wasn't exactly good that he didn't have a quiet way to warn her if he did see someone—she wouldn't be able to see him wave or make a signal. Even though she knew he was there, she felt like she was in this alone.

They were running out of time. Cabot moved recklessly through the house. When she saw the door to the garage opening, she breathed a sigh of relief. Seven was right in front of her. She ran to catch up.

"Oof!" Seven said.

Cabot froze as she heard Seven grunt again and fall down the steps into the garage. She ran to help him. As she reached the doorway, a hand closed tightly around her shoulder. At the same time, Seven let out a whimper.

Cabot gasped and looked up. There was no one in sight.

Martim Palacio.

TROUBLE BREWING

Cabot and Seven writhed and kicked in the Cordobio mansion garage, connecting with the invisible man, but Martim held them fast. He hauled both kids back into the house and zip-tied them to dining room chairs. Then he called to Troy outside. "I found an intruder!"

Cabot yanked on her zip-tied arm, but it was stuck fast to the chair. She wouldn't get far dragging it. She slumped and pulled the brim of her landscaping hat down over her eyes.

Troy came running from the side yard after discovering the source of the explosive noises and thundered into the dining room. "What the—" His eyes landed on Seven's chair first, seeing only the zip tie until his X-ray vision caught the outline of Seven's body. Then he looked at the other chair. "I thought you vetted these landscapers," he muttered under his breath.

Martim, who had apparently left the room after securing the kids to the chairs, returned in sweatpants, looking like his normal self as he tied the strings at his waist. "Look closer, Troy," he said wryly.

Troy bent down, trying to see Cabot's face. She squirmed in the chair and bent forward so he couldn't.

Annoyed, Troy pulled the cap off Cabot's head and gripped her chin, lifting her face to the light.

"Let go of me!" Cabot kicked him hard in the shin. "Give me that!"

"Ouch!" Troy hollered. "You little twerp!" He looked closer. Then his eyes widened. "Cabot Stone?" He swore under his breath. "What are you doing here?"

Cabot glanced at Seven, but she couldn't see any part of him. And he wasn't talking. What should she say? Tell the truth?

"I came to rescue Seven from you," she said. "You abandoned us, and you can't hold us hostage. Let me go!"

Next to her, Seven crumpled forward and put his face in his hands.

"Seven?" Martim said, getting in Cabot's face. "What are you talking about? Is he in Estero, too? Is *Louis* here with you?" He sneered, and in that moment Cabot hated him more than she'd ever hated anyone.

"Yeah, where's Louis?" Troy demanded. "I'd like to have a word with *that* dude."

Cabot was confused. She glanced at Seven, still seeing nothing. Hadn't the criminals figured out who he was by now? Not even his own father? How was that possible? The realization that Seven had been playing this incredible game with them—and that she had just messed it up royally—filled her with admiration and a lot of dread. "I, uh—" She sat back, her eyes darting about, wide with fear. She tried to find Seven's pupils, but she'd never been good at that.

"Why do you keep looking at *him*?" Martim said, suddenly suspicious. "Do you *know* him?" And then his face went through a rapid transformation, from suspicion to doubt to trepidation to realization and finally to anger at being bamboozled. "Oooh." He stepped back and let out a sharp breath and another swear word. "Geez. Are you serious?" He moved in front of Seven and stared coldly at the boy. *"Seven?"*

Seven let out a deep sigh. "Thanks a lot, Cabot." He sounded incredibly disappointed.

"I'm so sorry," Cabot whispered as remorse filled her chest. "I didn't know."

After a moment, Seven reached over with his free hand and touched Cabot's. Her eyes filled. She took his hand and held it tightly.

"It's okay," Seven told her softly.

"Wait a dang minute," Troy said, his face still a mess of confusion. "This kid is eighteen. He's from a different country. Now you're trying to tell me . . ."

"It's Seven, you brain fart," Martim muttered, shaking his head at Troy. "My own son, spying on us. He's not eighteen, he's . . . How old are you?"

Seven recoiled. "You . . . don't know?" he asked faintly.

Martim didn't wait for an answer. "I can't *believe* I went along with this, Troy." His eyes became slits, and he sent a steely, withering glance at the children. "I should have gone with my gut when we discovered him on the plane. I knew he wasn't to be trusted. But I never expected my own son would deceive me. *Lie* to me." Abruptly he left and went into the room Seven had been sleeping in. Troy remained, standing uncertainly, still trying to piece it all together. Martim returned shortly with Seven's clothes and threw them at the boy.

Seven absorbed the thrown clothing as if it were a blow from Martim's fist. Tears brimmed and spilled over. He stared at his father, trying to figure out why he was so hostile. So explosively angry at him. Sure, he'd misled the men. But once they realized who he was, he thought there might be at least a hint of warmth or pleasure at seeing him again. But this was no reunion moment. There was no joy or thrill in his dad's eyes to know his son, who he hadn't seen in years, was sitting three feet away from him. Only disgust and anger.

"Yeah, Dad," Seven said quietly, this time without altering his voice. "It's me. The child you abandoned. I'm pretty sure I'm the one who should be angry, not you."

Martim lunged toward the camouflaged boy, pinning his shoulders to the chair and almost tipping him over. Seven shrieked as his wounds scraped against the chair back. "You listen to me," Martim seethed. "We protected you kids all this time. We didn't tell Fuerte that any of you existed. You should be thanking me, not spying on me."

"You left us and never came back!" Seven said, exploding back at the man. "I'm not going to thank you for that! I'm not going to thank you for treating me like an annoyance my whole childhood. And I'm not going to thank you for your superior attitude—how you think being camouflaged is not as good as being invisible. *You* did this to me! This is who I am now because of *you*! So you can just shut up. Forever!" He shoved his father out of his face with his free hand, and his chair went slamming back down onto all four legs. Seven stood up awkwardly and moved the chair around, putting it between him and his father. "What the heck is wrong with you?" Seven seethed. "Were you going to hit me? Like Troy hit Tenner?"

"Hey, knock it off!" Troy roared, coming toward him. "Who do you think you are?"

"Both of you better stay out of my personal space!" Seven warned, pushing the chair toward Troy. His heart pounded, and tears continued streaming down his cheeks. One landed on the chair and splattered.

"Leave him alone!" Cabot screamed, infuriated that these men were upsetting Seven so much. She kicked her feet and connected with Martim's knee.

Martim jumped back and glared at Seven and Cabot. He worked his jaw. Finally he turned and strode toward the front door, then swung it open. "Lock down the mansion and the property," he said to the nearest security guard standing outside. "Don't let anyone in or out until we clear up this mess."

After a moment of uncertainty, Troy followed Martim, leaving the kids shaking.

When the two were alone, Seven sat down heavily. "That was intense."

"I'm really sorry," Cabot said again.

"I know." Seven's voice sounded like normal. Not like he had a bad cold.

"So you disguised your voice? Is that how you kept your identity a secret?" Cabot glanced sidelong at him, wondering how furious he really was. She hated making mistakes, and this had been her second one in twenty-four hours. She also hated when Seven was upset, especially when it was with her.

"Yeah. They had no idea." Seven rubbed his eyes. They could hear the men moving around the house. "Are you all right?" he asked, turning to her.

"Yeah." Cabot scooted her chair next to Seven's. She rested her head on his shoulder. "I'm just scared," she whispered, hoping Seven would reassure her.

"I'm scared, too," he said. He reached over and patted her bristly head. "But at least I'm not alone."

MESSAGE RECEIVED

Lada awoke to shouts outside her bedroom. She got up, scrambled for her crutches, and went to the door. Tenner had already emerged from his room next to hers, as the noise had been especially loud for him. He'd jumped out of bed before he was fully awake.

"Who's yelling?" Lada asked, disoriented. "What time is it?"

"It sounded like Seven and Cabot," Tenner said, confused. They moved into the cottage's gathering place. The satellite bug receiver was on the table, turned on, and it was picking up a conversation loud and clear.

"Cabot?" Lada called softly, looking around. "Where are you?" Had Cabot been reacting to something she'd heard through the receiver? Lada was so confused. She looked at Tenner. "Why are we hearing anything at all? Are they on the plane again? I thought the bug was destroyed. Where's Cabot?"

"I know I heard her," Tenner said. He started listening intently as the conversation quieted. "Wherever the bug is, Cabot is there. And so is Seven—they're talking to each other."

"Cabot . . . is *there*?" Lada's face wore an incredulous expression. "She just . . . went there on her own?"

Tenner scratched his head and wiped the sleep from his eyes with his T-shirt. "I don't hear any airport noises. Seven must have taken the bug to the mansion." He turned to Lada. "Cabot's kind of a loner," he said. "And she's so smart. I'm not really surprised that she tried to do . . . whatever this is. But it doesn't sound like she succeeded, does it?" He started up the stairs, taking them two at a time. "Let's wake up the others. We have a serious situation."

Lada and Tenner roused the rest of the group, and they all gathered in the living room to hear what was going on. A new conversation began, this time with Troy, Martim, Seven, and Cabot.

"All right," said Martim icily. "I need some information, and you're going to give it to me."

"We don't owe you anything," Seven said.

Martim continued as though he hadn't heard Seven. "Who is with you here in Estero?"

Seven rushed to answer. "It's just Cabot and me."

After a split second, Cabot chimed in. "Just us two."

"Where's Louis Golden?" Martim demanded. "Did he send you to do this? Is he using our own children against us?"

Several listeners at the cottage gasped at the accusation against Louis. But Cabot and Seven were silent. Finally Seven said quietly, "Louis is dead."

Elena, in a nightshirt, hair disheveled, flinched and closed her eyes. Birdie squeezed her hand.

"Dead?" said Troy, incredulous. "Are you lying?"

"He's not lying," Cabot said. "Louis is dead. He got sick . . . and died. A few weeks ago."

"Where are the other kids?" Troy demanded. "Where's Tenner?"

"Cabot and I came alone," Seven said. "We're the best climbers. The others wouldn't have made it."

Birdie glanced around the cottage. "He's so smooth with those lies," she whispered. "How smart of him to plant the bug in the mansion."

Tenner nodded, then put a finger to his lips.

"How did you find us?" Martim demanded, at the same time Troy asked, "Why didn't you tell me who you were when I discovered you on the plane?"

"I read the newspaper," Seven said to his dad. "It didn't take much to figure out who the invisible person accompanying the president was. I stowed away on the plane because . . . I wanted to see you." Seven paused. "I was going to leave before the plane took off, but then Greta arrived and closed the door, and I was stuck. I panicked and didn't know what to do. So I made up that story. And it felt cool that you guys wanted to include me. Then . . . it got harder and harder to explain who I really was." He paused. "It was a mistake."

"And I didn't know what happened to him," Cabot said,

sounding small. "I waited all night for you to come back. I found my way here by following your car from the airport."

"You followed our car . . . on foot? All the way here?" Martim looked suspiciously at her. "Impossible. She's lying."

"Not on foot," Cabot said slowly as she scrambled for an explanation. "I found an electric rental scooter on the sidewalk that had time left on it. I was able to keep up just enough to see you turn by the Cordoba Museum onto Legacy Avenue. And by then I'd figured out your little trick, naming your sons after the address of the property you owned." She paused. "Brilliant idea, by the way," she added sarcastically. "Super clever."

Everyone at the cottage exchanged glances. Cabot and Seven were killing it. Had they planned it out? It wasn't like Cabot had been gone long enough for them to do that. They had to be winging it.

During the stunned silence, Birdie tugged The Librarian's sleeve to get her attention. "How does Cabot know about *rental* scooters?" Birdie whispered.

The Librarian shrugged. "I just assume she knows *everything*. It's easier that way."

"No," Lada said, "I explained them to all of you days ago in the tunnels. But there was a lot of information being given around that time—I'm not surprised you forgot." She started cleaning her glasses nervously as the conversation continued. "I'm also not surprised Cabot remembered."

"Well," said Martim through the bug receiver, sounding like

he'd had enough of an eleven-year-old embarrassing him. "And what do you know about the break-in at the palace?"

Cabot and Seven didn't answer at first. Then Cabot said, "What break-in?"

"I don't know what you're talking about," Seven said.

"Do you know who the bouncing boy is?"

"The *what*?" Cabot exclaimed.

"You already asked me about him," Seven said, "and I still don't have a clue who you're talking about."

Brix squirmed on the sofa, gleeful yet terrified that they'd mentioned him.

There was an extended pause, and Birdie imagined Martim giving the kids a long, hard look. But he asked no more questions, and the two men left the kids alone.

When the men's voices and footsteps faded, Cabot whispered, "I bet that was loud enough to wake the rest of the team. I left the receiver on full volume at the cottage. They need your pass code to open your phone."

"Good move," Seven said. "Bird, or anyone, if you can hear me, I gave you my phone for a reason. Have a look at my text messages and videos. My pass code is seven one five one seven."

"And if you can hear *me*," said Cabot, "I'm sorry I ran off without telling anyone. I had a great plan, and it almost worked. I didn't have time to explain."

The two continued to whisper together as Birdie fetched Seven's recharged phone. She used his pass code to unlock it, and opened his text messages. There she discovered the texts with the angry red exclamation points, which had failed to send when Seven was in Frayzia. Including a video.

Everyone gathered around Birdie as she played it. And then they all saw what Seven had witnessed the other night: President Fuerte summoning his phone and the folder he'd dropped to come to him. The items flying through the air, into his hand.

"Holy expletive," Birdie said. She replayed it so everyone could see it again, then looked up and caught The Librarian's shocked expression.

"My God. He's telekinetic." The Librarian put her palm to her forehead. "The president of Estero, who hates supernatural people, is a supernatural person." She blinked. "This . . . changes everything."

TELEKIWHATNOW?

"Seven is a genius," Lada said as they watched the video of President Fuerte again. "Everything is starting to make sense. Fuerte is a supernatural person, yet he hid his abilities from the general public and instigated oppressive laws for people like us—like him. He's also building an army of supernatural people. And why? My guess is it's because of his huge secret. He fears he's going to be exposed, outed as a super, and the people of Estero will turn on him. Because that's exactly what he taught them to do." Lada looked triumphantly at the others. "Do you think he'll realize what it means when we reveal that we have evidence of this?"

Brix frowned from his spot on the sofa. Puerco snorted and readjusted his position on the boy's lap, and Brix put his hand on the pig's warm hairy back to soothe him. "What *does* it mean?"

"It means," Lada said, "that we can hold this over his head. We can be the ones who threaten to expose him. It *means*," she said again, with even more emphasis this time, "that we can get Seven and Cabot back."

"How?" asked Brix. "I still don't get it."

Tenner looked up. "If we give this video exposing Fuerte's secret to *Estero City News,* it'll make Estero explode because of how terrible he has been to people like us. But we can also just tell Fuerte we have proof, and only threaten to give it to the newspaper. And we can promise him we won't do it if he hands over Seven and Cabot."

"Oh," said Brix. "But do you think he'll believe us?"

"He won't have much of a choice," Lada said. "I doubt he'll risk thinking we're bluffing. Just telling him we know what his ability is will scare the pants off him."

"We can send the video to him," Birdie said.

"But that would put Seven in danger, and it could expose us," Elena said, "since it was obviously filmed aboard the plane. They'll know it had to be Seven who filmed it. And they can guess the few people in the world Seven might know who he could send it to. I think just telling Fuerte that we have obtained proof of him using his telekinetic ability will be enough to scare him."

"Oh—right. That makes sense." Birdie reached over and picked up Puerco, then gently scratched his snout. The pig closed his eyes blissfully. "We don't want to pile on more trouble for Seven. So how do we tell Fuerte that we know about his big secret?"

"We need to think this through carefully," The Librarian said. "It's only a matter of time before they realize we are organizing against them. But for now, according to what we just heard from Seven and Cabot, they still don't know we're the ones who sprang Elena from the palace. And they don't know the rest of you kids are here in Estero. In fact, they probably think there's a different group out there working against them. And it's fine to let them think that. That gives us cover for a bit longer."

Everyone was quiet for a moment, thinking. Lada looked around the small group. "Well, I feel like I should be the one to confront President Fuerte. It's too dangerous for any of you three," she said to Birdie, Brix, and Tenner. "Because if Fuerte brings along any of the bad parents, they'll recognize you, and we don't want them to know you're here. He obviously knows who Elena is, and we also don't want to compromise The Librarian because of her contacts, so they should stay out of sight."

"I won't compromise you, either," The Librarian said. "We need to do this without anyone seeing our faces or knowing our names." She got up and paced the length of the room. "Hmm." She continued pacing, then stopped abruptly in front of the group. "Is there any chance Cabot thought to put in her earpiece before she left? I think we're within two miles of the mansion as the crow flies."

"What crow?" asked Brix.

"I think there's an excellent chance of that," Birdie said to The Librarian as Elena explained to Brix that "as the crow flies" was an expression about direct distance.

The Librarian went to get her earpiece from where it was recharging. She returned with it in her ear. "Cabot? Seven? Can either of you hear me?"

She waited a moment, then clicked through different channels, unable to remember which was the one Cabot and Seven had been using for the past few days, repeating what she'd just said. Then she touched the earpiece, and her lips parted.

"Cabot's listening!" she announced to the others. They—especially Tenner—could just barely hear Cabot whispering too, through the bug, though it was difficult to understand her—it sounded like she'd turned or moved away from the listening device. The Librarian asked Cabot, "Are you okay? We heard a lot of that conversation through the bug." The Librarian listened for a long moment, then filled in what the rest of the group wasn't able to understand. "She says she's fine. Seven's earpiece battery is dead, and hers is back to having a yellow indicator. Cabot, tell Seven we found the video of President Fuerte using his supernatural telekinesis. And we're going to use it to threaten Fuerte to make him let you both go. Okay?"

They all waited as Cabot responded to The Librarian.

"Okay," The Librarian said to her. "I'm still figuring out the plan, but stay calm and keep doing what you've been doing while we figure this out. And see what other information you can gather about why they're building this army. Is it because of Fuerte's secret supernatural status? Does he fear backlash from the people of Estero if they find out? If so, that'll help us." She hesitated, listening. Then her eyes widened. She turned to the others. "Cabot said she overheard Troy and Martim talking this morning about news breaking, and the president fearing exposure from someone they called a monster. And . . . something about a campaign? So we're on the right track."

"A campaign?" Elena asked quietly. "A campaign for what?"

The Librarian shrugged, then addressed Cabot once more. "We'll be listening to the bug nonstop until we have you both back safely. Keep playing innocent like you have been. See if you can figure out if there are any strains or cracks in the relationships. And talk about how you just want to go home, back to the hideout. Say that's what you plan to do when they let you go. You want to be the most nonthreatening people ever. Also . . . be annoying so they get tired of having you around. We're going to make them happy to let you go."

She listened for a moment, then smiled. "Good job, Cabot. Save your earpiece battery by turning it off, since we don't know how long you'll be there and we want it to last in case they take you somewhere away from the bug. But tune in again whenever you need to. I'll keep mine in all day. Take care, now."

After a moment, The Librarian looked up. "I'm feeling so much better about all of this," she said with a breath of relief. "The kids are okay. And with this revelation about the president, things are finally turning around. We'll all be back together before you know it."

FINDING THE WEAK SPOTS

Seven and Cabot dragged the chairs they were attached to over to a sofa so they could lie down and sleep, and no one seemed to mind. They stayed in close proximity to the bug Seven had planted. After long naps and laborious trips to the bathroom dragging their chairs with them, they tried to give the people back at the cottage as much information as they could.

"So, it seems like only Troy and Martim live here," Cabot said quietly. "We haven't seen anyone else."

"I saw Cabot's mom here once," Seven said. "She stopped over when I first got here to deliver files to Martim. But she hasn't been here since then."

Cabot turned to look at Seven. "Do you think Martim and Troy will tell my parents I'm here?"

"Probably. I think they talk to each other throughout the day."

Cabot let her head fall back on the sofa cushion. "I'm so conflicted," she said. "I want to see them. I want to . . . I don't know. Yell at them for what they did. But I miss them so much. You know?"

Seven felt tears stinging his tired eyes. "Yeah, well, I guess I was hoping my dad would have at least a small amount of . . . whatever. Kindness or warmth toward me once he figured out who I was. But he's pretty mad."

"I'm really sorry, Seven," Cabot said. "When I heard them talking through the bug, he seemed worried that President Fuerte would think you're the new favorite or something like that. Like, he sounded jealous."

"Of me?" Seven snorted. "Whatever. He's mad because he almost messed up the heist. Mad because I saved the vase after he dropped his end."

After a while, Cabot ventured a new question. "Do you know if your mom is . . . here?" *Or alive,* she thought, but she didn't want to say it.

"I don't know." Seven closed his eyes. "I'll ask next time he comes over to give us a hard time."

"They don't seem very organized," Cabot mused. "Troy and Martim, I mean. I don't think they know what to do with us. They're only half-heartedly keeping us prisoner. They have these guards outside who won't let us escape, yet they've only secured us to these chairs with one wrist. So we could just, you know, carry our chairs over to the kitchen and cut ourselves free if we want. It's as if they're still parental types deep down, and they sort of trust us."

"Which I'm fine with," said Seven. "I'm tired of wearing these zip ties, but at least they don't mind us moving around."

"Yeah." Cabot lifted her head. "Hey, do you think they'll even notice if we cut these things off?"

"They might," said Seven. "But we can just say the other adult took them off. It's not like we can escape. They locked down the whole place."

Cabot got up. She dragged her dining chair with her so she could peer down the long hallway. "I don't see anybody around. I'm going for it. Be right back."

She picked up the heavy chair and held it in front of her, carrying it all the way to the kitchen, bumping her shins repeatedly in the process. Then she set it down and searched the drawers. She pulled out a pair of kitchen shears and clipped her zip tie, then threw it in the trash.

"Well," she called softly. "That was easy. Do you want anything while I'm over here?" She opened the refrigerator and peered in, then frowned. "Not a great selection." She found a wedge of cheese and a can of some sort of beverage, and brought them and the scissors to the sofa. Then she went back to the kitchen to fetch the dining chair and put it next to the sofa where she sat, so to a casual glance, it might look like she was still attached to it.

Seven clipped his zip tie, too, and then they sampled the cheese.

"Tangy," Cabot said, not quite sure if she liked it. She wrinkled her nose. "Smells like feet."

"They should put that on the packaging," Seven said. "Everyone would buy it."

Cabot laughed. She picked up the canned beverage. "*Craft root beer,*" she read. "I am familiar with roots."

"Just don't shake it—isn't that what Birdie did? Be careful."

"Right! Thanks for reminding me." Cabot read the instructions on the top of the can and wondered idly how someone had managed to indent such perfectly formed words in the aluminum. Then she cringed and opened the tab like she'd ripped off Seven's bandage—swiftly and with lots of energy. The can hissed, but nothing came out. She sniffed the opening and sucked in a breath when tiny bubbles exploded and made her nose wet. She took a tentative sip. Her eyes popped. "Yikes!" she said. "It's alive on my tongue!"

Seven held out his hand for a taste. "Sharp!" he exclaimed. "It feels like when your foot falls asleep. Tiny pinpricks." He took another sip. "I like it."

Cabot sipped again, bigger this time, and swallowed, making her eyes water. "Beer of roots, my one true love," she murmured. "Wow, it's so sweet, though." She took one more swallow. "I think I've had enough for now." She handed the can to Seven. "Birdie doesn't know what she's missing." She let out a huge belch.

Seven laughed appreciatively. "Where do you think the dads are?"

"They're looming," Cabot said. "I hear some sort of machine going in the wing where they sleep."

Seven ate the rest of the cheese. "We should explore the next time they go to sleep. Yesterday, before we did the heist, I overheard them talking about taking some 'old money' along. They ended up exchanging it at the airport for the new Estero money." He told her—and the others listening through the bug—about the awkward conversation in the car on the way to steal the vase. And that Jack and Greta seemed to have not been taking any of the stash on principle after Troy and Martim blew up the apartment . . . but now they wanted their share. Then Troy had indicated they didn't know what they were talking about, which was confusing. "But anyway, the rest of the stash is probably here somewhere." He yawned loudly. "I'm so mixed up on what time it is. Not used to being up all night and sleeping when it's light outside. It's backward."

They heard Troy cough and clear his throat, then his footsteps in the hallway. They both sat up and pretended like their arms were still attached to the chairs, and soon the man entered the room.

"Hey, Troy," Seven said, sounding remorseful. "I'm sorry I didn't tell you who I was."

Troy narrowed his eyes. "All right."

"And I really appreciate you trying to make me part of the team early on."

Troy emitted a rumbling growl of uncertainty.

Seven hesitated, then added, cringing as he said it, "You've been nicer to me than my dad, actually."

Troy glanced over his shoulder down the hallway, then came toward the two. "You figured out that your dad isn't thrilled about your ability," he said quietly. "He won't admit it, but it's because he's threatened by it. He thinks Fuerte might want to keep using you in our heists, which means Martim is less important. Plus you're smaller. You could get into a house through the dog door, you know?"

"Dog door?" Cabot asked, mystified.

"Oh," said Seven, sitting up straighter. "I wouldn't want to make my dad feel like that. Not at all. And . . ." He leaned toward Troy conspiratorially. "All we really want is to go back home to the hideout. You know? Cabot and I just don't think Estero life is for us. We miss the other kids. But . . . do you happen to know where my mom is?" As he said the words, he could feel his chest tighten and his throat constrict. He wasn't sure he was ready for the answer.

Troy's eyes widened, and his mouth fell open. He glanced over his shoulder again, as if worried Martim was listening. "Um . . . your mom . . ." Just then, Martim's footsteps could be heard coming down the hallway. "You better ask your dad about that." He shifted, then said softly, "Is Tenner . . . doing okay?"

Cabot stared at the man. She'd always thought him to be incurious and unfeeling. Uncaring. And really mean. So it surprised her greatly that he even asked. "He's fine," she said coolly.

"Any abilities for him? Probably not, right?"

Seven and Cabot both cringed. From his tone, it sounded like Troy didn't think Tenner was capable of having supernatural abilities. No wonder Tenner had been so low in the self-confidence area. "No," Seven lied. "Not yet."

"What about the rest? Birdie and . . . the little one."

"Brix?" Cabot prompted. Did he really forget one of their names?

"Yeah."

Cabot just shook her head in disgust. Troy took it as a no.

Martim strolled into the kitchen wearing another sleek suit and tie, and carrying a thick envelope that Seven identified as the fat wad of cash from the previous night's exchange. His hair was slicked back again, like it had been on the plane. He poured some coffee into a travel mug. "I'm heading to the bank to make the deposit," he said without looking at any of them. He wore earbuds and pulled his phone from his jacket pocket, then texted someone with his thumbs. "We'll deal with you kids later."

"We just want to go home," Cabot said in a quickly generated tearful voice.

"Yeah . . . I don't think so," said Martim, sneering. "Seven, maybe you should have kept your nosy self out of the president's plane, and out of our official business. I'm not sure you're going anywhere." He deigned to glance at the kids finally. "Especially not looking like that."

"Dad," Seven said. He could feel a sense of hurt and panic welling up, and the panic was winning. "Just don't tell Fuerte who I am. You guys can let us go, and we'll get out of here for good. Tell him we escaped."

Martim snorted.

"Martim," Troy said, "the kid was wondering about his mother. Maybe you should tell him."

Martim's shoulders stiffened. He turned with a glare toward Troy. "No, that's okay," he said icily. "I've got to go now. You can tell him."

"Wait," said Seven, his voice pitching. "Is she dead? Just tell me!"

Troy took a step back. "Whoa. What makes you ask that?"

Martim let out a slow breath. He flung his jacket over his shoulder. "No. She's not dead. She's just . . . not to be trusted. I don't think you should look for her. Nothing good will come of it anyway. Especially for an ungrateful boy like you." He grabbed his coffee and stomped to the door. Finding the handle on the floor, he seethed, "Somebody better fix this before I get home." He went out the door to the garage without another word. A moment later, a car roared to life, then faded away.

Cabot looked from Seven to Troy. She was tired of the mind scramble caused by the parental-life-and-death guessing game. And if Elena Golden, Troy Cordoba, Cabot's parents, and Seven's parents were all alive, there was only one person left who could have been the skeleton dashed on the rocks. Careful to be sensitive to anyone listening from the cottage, Cabot said softly, "So is Tenner's mom still alive, too?"

THINGS CHANGE

Troy Cordoba gave Cabot a long hard look. Then his stern face crumpled. He pulled her chair over to him, not even noticing that she wasn't zip-tied to it anymore, and sat down on it, facing the two. "No," he said. "Lucy died on our journey. She fell while climbing down a cliff."

"Oh no!" Cabot exclaimed. Even though she'd figured out Lucy was likely dead, it still hit hard to get confirmation. "I'm . . . sorry. I'm sure Tenner will be really sad to hear that."

"That's really horrible news. We had no idea." Seven, reeling from finding out his mother was alive, pressed his invisible finger against Cabot's arm to warn her not to say anything about finding the remains and the backpack. He didn't want anyone asking them about the diamonds and their whereabouts.

But Cabot had already thought of that. And she was more interested in the way Troy was behaving. In the short time she'd been here, she'd noticed a difference in him. He wasn't the belligerent bully she remembered. Sure, he was still loud, and he wasn't a good person. But his demeanor had changed, even if only slightly. "Are you okay?" she asked him.

Troy's solid-black X-ray eyes were emotionless and gave nothing away, but his mouth turned down at the corners. He didn't answer at first. And then he leaned forward and put his hands over his face. "I thought I was until you asked about her," he said through his hands.

Seven froze. He'd never seen Tenner's dad let his guard down like this. Sure, Troy had been suspiciously supportive when Seven had first arrived, compared to what he'd been expecting. And there were definitely still shades of the old Troy, like when he'd refused to give Seven the food and water on the first day. But Troy had gone to bat for The Kid with President Fuerte, and he'd even given Seven a bedroom—for a few hours, anyway, until they found out who he really was. Now Seven was almost feeling sorry for the man.

"We'll be sure to let Tenner know when we go back home," Cabot said. "You want us to do that, right? Since it doesn't seem like you're ever going back to tell him?"

Troy lifted his foot and pulled up the leg of his jeans, showing a thin metal ankle bracelet. "I couldn't even if I wanted to. It's the price of freedom. Fuerte tracks all of us, and if we so much as go near the border, his team will come after us. And, like Martim said, we never want anyone to follow us back to you kids in the hideout."

"Seems like a good reason not to tell Fuerte that we're your kids, then," Seven remarked. "He'd put trackers on us, too, or have us followed when we go back home. You don't want him to know where your hideout is, in case you need it in the future. Right?"

Troy's brow furrowed. "I'll . . . see what I can do," he mumbled.

"About those tracking bracelets," Cabot said, laser focused on finding out more information directly from Troy's own lips and getting it transmitted to The Librarian and the monastery team. "Does everyone wear one? Seven's mom, too? Even though she doesn't seem to be working with you?"

"I don't think Magdalia has one. She's not in prison—I know that much. But I haven't seen her since shortly after we got here. She abandoned us, and has been, well, a bit *threatening* to Fuerte." He frowned. "I shouldn't talk about that. Pretend I didn't say it."

"Okaaay," said Cabot. "What about my parents?"

Troy snorted. "Yes, they've got ankle tethers, too."

"Why are you laughing?" Cabot asked, feeling her face grow hot.

"Because out of all of us, they've turned out to be the ones deepest inside Fuerte's pocket. Imagine that."

Cabot's breath caught, and her chest caved in. "How do you mean?" she asked faintly.

"They're like the teacher's pets. They'll do anything Fuerte says. Really surprising, considering how loud they were about never committing crimes again, let me tell you. They're hypocrites."

Cabot's mind reeled. "Oh," she said. She felt like she was in a backward world. Troy was sitting and chatting with them, and Cabot's parents were the worst of the criminals. What was going on? What had happened in the three years the parents had all been away? Cabot's disgust for her parents grew exponentially. She almost didn't want to talk to them or even see them again—at least not until she had time to process this disturbing nugget of information. "Do they know I'm here?" she asked weakly.

"Not yet," Troy said. He frowned. "You said you two were the only ones who could get here, huh?"

Seven cleared his throat. "Yes," he said. "As you know, the trek is pretty difficult."

The man cringed and nodded. "Well, if Fuerte ever says we can let you leave, tell Tenner . . . tell Tenner that I . . ."

Seven leaned in, as if straining to help Troy say something that would give Tenner some hope, especially after hearing definitively that his mother had died.

But then Troy's phone rang. He pulled it out of his pocket and swiftly got up. "I've got to take this," he said gruffly, and strode quickly out of the room, leaving Seven and Cabot trying to figure out what to make of it all.

Seven twisted on the sofa and studied Cabot's face. It was always so hard to tell what she was thinking. She didn't express her emotions very often. But Seven knew the news about her parents would bother her. She'd already been so conflicted about their involvement with President Fuerte. But now she had confirmation that they weren't just helping because they were forced to. Jack and Greta Stone were actually really into it.

"Nothing makes sense," he said.

Cabot nodded, dazed. "Nothing." She sank against the wall, feeling icky.

A few minutes later, Troy walked through the room with a fresh shirt and dress pants on, carrying a laptop bag. "I've got to head out for a few. Don't try escaping—you won't make it. We beefed up security outside, and that fence will fry your eyebrows off."

"Okay," Seven called. "We'll stay here. Is it all right if we drag our chairs into the kitchen to eat something?"

"Knock yourselves out," Troy said, picking up the door handle and setting it on the countertop. He headed into the garage without bothering to check their wrist ties.

WHEN TROY WAS gone, Cabot got up. "It's time to explore," she said softly, eyeing the security guard outside the front door. She headed down the long hallway, looking for Troy and Martim's office.

Seven followed. "At least they didn't bring a guard inside today like they did before they knew who I was."

"Maybe Troy and Martim think we're just innocent kids who wouldn't know how to do anything," Cabot whispered.

Seven grinned. "Maybe. But they would be wrong."

TAKING IT IN

When the truth came out through the listening device that Seven's mother was alive and Tenner's mother had died, Tenner flopped onto the sofa and curled up, covering his head with his arms. Birdie jumped up from her chair and went to him, wrapping her arms around him. "I'm so sorry, T," she said. "You've been taking blow after blow."

Tenner felt numb all over again. He'd been through so much in the past few weeks. It was a relief to know for certain who was dead and who was alive. But what a terrible ride he'd been on.

He hadn't been close with his mother. She'd been clairvoyant—seeing flashes of near-future events before they happened. Tenner had always thought it was too bad she didn't foresee and stop Troy from being a jerk to him, like that time Troy had hit him. Or maybe she *had* envisioned it but hadn't cared to stop it.

As he lay on the sofa, with Birdie hovering over him to make sure he was okay, he half listened to what his father was telling

Cabot about her parents. And then, when they started talking about Tenner, he heard something in his father's voice that he'd never heard before. A softening. A hint of warmth and emotion. He seemed sad about Lucy being gone. And he almost said something about Tenner . . . but then he didn't.

Why did that seem so typical? What a letdown.

"All right, everyone," The Librarian said once Cabot and Seven's conversation ended. She held up her cell phone, indicating she'd been conversing with someone via text. "It took an entire diamond in negotiations, but I've just managed to get Fuerte's personal cell phone number. I'm going to use an unidentifiable burner phone to tell him what we know, and demand he let the kids go, or we'll go public with the proof of his supernatural ability." She picked up a cheap, throwaway phone from her stash of supplies and started typing. When she finished, she read the text aloud for approval before sending: "President Fuerte, I know your secret. Let the two people out of the mansion where they're being held prisoner, or I'll alert the newspapers about your supernatural status."

"Hmm," said Elena. "You're not going to tell him everything we know? That he's telekinetic?"

"I decided to make him ask. He'll be worried about some stranger getting his personal phone number. He might think we're bluffing, and then we hit him with it hard and knock the cockiness right out of him. Sound okay?"

"I like it," said Birdie.

"Good plan," said Lada. Elena and Brix agreed. Tenner, still on the sofa, grunted, which they all took as agreement, too.

The Librarian tapped the "send" key, and everyone waited breathlessly to see what President Fuerte would say in response.

As they waited, they could hear thumping noises through the listening device. It sounded like someone was moving boxes around. Then there was a brief conversation between Seven and Cabot that was so far away from the bug that even Tenner couldn't make out the words. "They sound excited about something," Tenner said listlessly. "That's all I can tell."

The Librarian received a text alert on the burner phone. "He says, 'Who is this?' I'm going to tell him, 'I'm someone who knows you've kidnapped two young people.' Okay? I'm trying to be vague about their ages since Fuerte still doesn't know they're the supernatural criminals' children, and we don't want him to ever find out."

Everyone nodded emphatically. The Librarian sent the message. They waited again.

From the listening device they could hear more bumping and exclamations.

"What's happening at the mansion?" Brix asked. "Are they tearing down the place or what?" He bounced around the cottage, filled with nervous energy. "I miss Cabot. When are we going to be able to get them back with us?"

"Soon, I hope," Elena said.

The Librarian's burner phone chimed once more. "He's saying

the only new person he knows about is there willingly." She grimaced, but then another text came in. "He's asking what we know." The Librarian started typing and then read aloud her response: "Willingly handcuffed? Nice try. I know you're a telekinetic super. I have evidence. You have thirty minutes to release the two outside the electric fence, into my awaiting vehicle, or I'll contact *Estero City News.*"

The group approved. The Librarian pressed "send." Then she looked at the others and touched her hand to her wildly beating heart. "This is scary."

"What if he says no?" Brix asked.

"Then we do what we said we'd do." The Librarian stood up and put on a determined face. "But I guarantee this will work. I'm going to get ready to pick them up." As The Librarian adjusted her earpiece and collected her car keys, the phone chimed.

The text message from President Fuerte read **I'm sending someone now to release them.**

A SURPRISE VISIT

The Librarian paused at the door. "Cabot, can you hear me?" she asked, using her earpiece. She waited a moment, then looked at the group and shook her head. "She doesn't have it turned on."

"Why not just call her if neither of the dads are there?" asked Brix. "She has her phone, right?"

The Librarian frowned. "I'm tempted to do that," she said. "But if they took her phone, they might check to see who's calling, and if it comes up 'The Librarian,' that could tip them off to my identity. Or at least narrow it down to a few dozen library workers. I can't expose myself, and neither can any of you."

"We should change each other's names in our contacts," Lada noted. "Make them unidentifiable or use code names so we don't have this problem in the future." She set a reminder on her phone to do it.

"Can you call or text her from the burner phone?" Tenner mumbled from the sofa.

The Librarian paused. "Hmm."

"No," Elena said, firmly shaking her head. "Not worth the risk—Fuerte has that number now. He could discover that whoever threatened him also knows the kids' numbers . . . and since the kids have few contacts, that might get them suspecting it's me and that the kids were part of my escape."

"Oooh," said Brix. "You think of everything."

"It's a team effort," said Elena. "A very good team."

The Librarian turned to address them all. "Seven and Cabot will find out soon enough that they'll be freed. I'm going to park near the mansion so when they let them out, I can pick them up. It's possible they'll have security looking for us, so, Elena, you should stay here—you're too recognizable."

"I'll stay with you, Mom," Brix said. He hopped over to her.

"I'll go with you," Lada said to The Librarian.

"Me too," said Birdie.

"I'm going to stay here," said Tenner dully. He was still processing the news about his mother.

And so Lada, Birdie, and The Librarian headed out and made their way to Legacy Avenue.

TENNER, ELENA, AND Brix stayed near the listening device, waiting for Seven and Cabot to come back and explain what all the bumping around was from.

"Hey," came Cabot's voice in a breathless whisper, as if she'd been exerting a lot of energy. "You're not going to believe what we—" She stopped short and didn't finish her sentence.

Tenner sat up, trying to identify what the background noise was.

Cabot abandoned her narrating. They heard pounding footsteps, then something garbled.

Tenner understood it. "She said, 'Seven! Someone's coming up the driveway. Get out of there! Hurry!'" Tenner glanced worriedly at the others.

Soon there was a slam, like a door closing hard. Then more pounding footsteps growing louder. "Someone's here," Cabot whispered near the bug. "I hope the bug is picking this up. Seven and I had to get back to our spots where we were tied up. But we found—"

"Shh!" Seven said. "Don't say anything!"

The three listening from the cottage could hear the faint sound of a door opening.

"They're there to set you free!" Brix yelled at the device, though of course Cabot and Seven had no way of hearing him.

Things were quiet for a long, tenuous moment. Elena, Brix, and Tenner all squeezed each other's hands. Then came a gasp. And Greta Stone's trembling voice. "Cabot?"

The room was filled with breath that rushed from lungs, and guttural noises trying to land on the right emotion. But there was no right one. "Mom!" Cabot cried. "Dad!" Her voice grew deeper and more ragged with each word.

There was a commotion, like a chair being knocked over. Then more exclamations and sobs. Tenner gripped his face, peeking between his fingers, and Brix clung to his mother as they listened to Cabot's reunion with her parents, who she'd missed so much—and who she'd felt so conflicted about. Tears ran down Elena's face.

Finally Seven whispered for the sake of those listening in, "Well. Jack and Greta are supposedly in President Fuerte's pocket—the worst of the worst. But watching them reunite with Cabot . . . I've never seen anything more beautiful."

ALL THE FEELINGS

Tears of joy and longing poured down Seven's face as he witnessed Cabot's reunion with her parents. It was so intense he had to look away. It was everything he'd ever wanted from his dad, only he'd gotten none of it. Everything they'd all wanted from their parents, but especially Cabot. And she deserved it. Something broke loose inside Seven, and he couldn't hold back his sobs. He couldn't narrate it for the others, either. His voice wasn't to be trusted. No doubt they heard him and understood.

Cabot had been so angry. And Greta and Jack were still very much criminals. But it seemed like they put all those things aside for a few blissful moments to cry together and pretend like everything was okay. How long would it be before Cabot called them out on their actions? Because Seven was sure she would. It wasn't going to happen right then, though.

As soon as the three broke apart and wiped their eyes, Greta, still clasping Cabot's hand, sought out Seven. "Seven—I never guessed it was you. We need to get you two out of here right now. President Fuerte is releasing you from the property, and he gave us a deadline of thirty minutes. So grab your things and let's go. I'm . . . not sure why he's letting you go. Or what your plans . . . are . . . from here on out."

Cabot stared up at her, her eyes welling anew. Her heart ached. Even her skin ached. She knew what their plans were. She and Seven were going back to be with their group . . . and fight against her parents.

That's when the anger boiled up. "Why did you have to align yourselves with *him*?" Cabot blurted out before her tears had a chance to dry. "I can't believe you'd go along with such a horrible person! What's wrong with you? What happened to your promise that you were done with crime? And why the heck didn't you come back to me?" Rage tore through her, banging into the love and warmth and confusion. "I'm so mad at you!" she screamed. Then she started pummeling her dad in the stomach.

Jack staggered back but didn't stop her.

"Cabot, it's complicated," Greta said weakly. It sounded like she was grasping for an excuse but didn't have one. "Please stop. Let's talk about this."

Seven had never seen Cabot like this before, and he could tell she'd lost control and needed help. He went up to Cabot and touched her shoulder to let her know he was there. But she couldn't stop fighting the dad who'd left her. Finally Seven pulled her off her father and reached out to her for a hug. "Come 'ere, Cab," he said as she turned into him and buried her face in his shirt. "There. I've got you. We've got each other."

He motioned impatiently for Greta and Jack to start moving toward the door, but they could only see his shirt sleeve moving. Luckily, they did it anyway.

Seven patted Cabot's back as she clung to him. "Hey, Cab. Let's get out of here before Fuerte changes his mind, okay? And then we'll figure this out."

Cabot wiped her nose on his shoulder and nodded, exhausted. "I don't like having all these feelings," she muttered. "This stinks."

Seven laughed, then pulled away. "It's hard when all the emotions hit at the same time," he said. "You ready?" He took her hand, like he'd done when she was little and they'd walked along the beach together.

Seven and Cabot followed Jack and Greta out the front door, past the guard, and down the driveway. The entire security detail appeared to have already been alerted to the president's order, and they opened the electric fence and let the four pass through it.

They continued down the winding driveway, with Cabot walking glumly and her parents still not doing a very good job of explaining themselves.

"Cabot," Jack said when they reached the end of the driveway, where Greta's car sat. "We're so sorry we didn't come back. We can only imagine how terrible it was for you—it breaks our hearts. But . . . we got captured. We hadn't planned on that. We've got these tethers on our ankles now, see?" He lifted his trouser leg and showed her. "They're GPS trackers. We can't go anywhere outside of Estero unless Fuerte is with us—if we tried, Fuerte would send his teams to hunt us down. And we didn't want to lead him to you children."

Their story corroborated what Troy had said. But Cabot wasn't satisfied. "Troy told us that you two are the worst of the criminals now," she said, her tears dried and her eyes flashing in anger. "He said that you're in President Fuerte's pocket. You're the teacher's pets."

Greta and Jack exchanged an uneasy glance. "That's true," Greta admitted.

"How could you? And *why*?"

Greta put her hand up to smooth her hair. "I . . . we . . . can't explain that. It just . . . happened. And then we were stuck. And . . ." She reached for Jack's hand as tears streamed down her face. "And we missed you *so* much, Cabot. It nearly broke us. But we're trying to do what we need to do to get through this."

"What happens if you walk away?" Seven asked. "Or don't you want to?"

Jack swallowed hard and lifted his chin. "We . . . can't. And we won't."

"I don't get it." Cabot felt dizzy. She looked at Seven and found his pupils. "I feel sick," she whispered.

"You can throw up anywhere on this property for all I care," Seven assured her. "Do you need me to hold your hand?"

Cabot nodded and moved toward some bushes along the driveway.

Greta and Jack watched as their daughter naturally turned to Seven when she was in need. They stared at the two interacting like siblings who cared for each other. It was beautiful to see, but . . . Jack shook his head and covered his eyes with his hand, as if he hated himself.

The kids didn't witness that, though. While Cabot threw up, Seven rubbed her back. Eventually she stood up and stared at the brown pool of vomit. "It tasted like root beer," she said.

"Could be worse," Seven said. "Could've been that feet cheese." He smiled and used his shirttail to dab the tears at the corners of her eyes. Then he rested his hands on her shoulders. "You okay now?"

Cabot nodded.

"We should probably get moving," he said gently, spying the familiar black SUV through the trees about a block up the road.

"Where are you going?" Jack asked, sounding anxious. "Will you be staying in Estero?"

Cabot closed her eyes, knowing they were the enemy and she had to lie. "Back home."

"Is that what you want to do?" Greta asked, sounding desperate. She seemed like she was having a hard time keeping herself from grabbing her daughter and taking her away. "It's . . . probably the safest place for you." She choked on a sob and covered her mouth with a shaky hand.

Cabot's bottom lip jutted out, and her face crumpled. She shook her head. "I want you to come with me wherever I go. I want things to be like they used to be."

Jack got down on his haunches and held out his arms.

Cabot glanced up.

"Go ahead," Seven said softly as he felt himself choking up again, too. "It's okay to love them. It's okay to say goodbye."

Cabot ran to her father and embraced him, all of her feelings fighting against each other. "Why did you have to do this?" Cabot said again, her voice ragged in Jack's ear. She pulled back, then turned to her mother and embraced her, too. Then she used the line that she'd always dreaded hearing when she was little. "I love you. But I'm so disappointed in you."

It hit her parents hard. "I hope one day we can make it up to you," Greta said, her voice cracking. "We'll strive to get there. I'm devastated it has to be this way."

Finally Cabot let her parents go. She turned and went to Seven, who slung a protective arm around her shoulders. "You're amazing," Seven told her. "I'm so proud of you." The two started walking along the street. They took six steps. Ten. Twelve. Cabot slowed down.

When she heard her mom's car door slam, she whirled around and stared. Then she ran back toward her parents, leaving Seven standing alone.

"Wait!" she screamed, waving them down. "Wait! I want to go with you!"

GOODBYE

Seven's heart dropped. He watched helplessly from the side of the road as Cabot climbed into the backseat of Greta's car. Was he supposed to try to change Cabot's mind? How could he possibly do that? Cabot had been longing for her parents for three years, and now she had them. What kind of heartless person would try to break them up? Cabot knew things would never be the same as before. She was smart enough to make her own decisions. Seven had nothing more to say, other than to keep showing her that he cared about her, no matter what happened.

Greta drove up alongside Seven. Tears stained her cheeks. "Seven," she said. "What a lovely young man you turned out to be. Thank you for bringing Cabot here. And . . . I'm sorry I didn't give you the sandwich and water—I wanted to."

Seven looked down at the ground. "It's fine."

"Are you going to be okay? Can you make the trek home alone?"

"Oh. I—" Seven swallowed hard as the reality of losing Cabot began to sink in. His team needed her desperately, but he couldn't tell the enemy that. Cabot was choosing to go with criminals, but they were her parents. And despite their mistakes, they obviously loved her and wanted her . . . unlike how Martim had acted with him. "Yeah," Seven said weakly, searching Cabot's face. The girl wouldn't look his way—he was sure she was feeling terrible for him. "I'll be fine. I might stick around Estero for a few days just to see if I can find my mother."

Concern flickered across the Stones' faces at the mention of Magdalia. "Oh," Greta said, glancing at Jack and then back at Seven. "Be careful there."

Seven shrugged. "Trust me, my expectations couldn't be lower." Troy and Martim had warned him about her, too. But he had no truthful intentions of finding her, so it didn't matter. He plowed on. "Anyway . . . Cabot." He dipped his head, trying to get her to look at him. "You know where to find me if you change your mind, right?"

Cabot lifted her gaze and nodded. Her eyes were bloodshot, and her cheeks were red. She held her head as it pounded even harder than before, because of all the crying.

Seven kept going as if the words were forcing their way out. "The others—they're going to be really sad when you don't come back, Cab. You're . . . our walking dictionary. You're the swing vote. You're the one who cares when everyone else forgets to. And we all love you *a lot*. So yeah, this will be hard. But you need to do what you need to do. And I get that you're a kid with parents who love you. So . . . I only want you to be happy."

Cabot pressed her lips together. She stuck her arm out the window and reached for Seven's hand. She had a tiny bit of dried vomit at the corner of her mouth. "This is what I've wanted for three years," she said. "You all know it. I thought my parents were dead, and they're not. And I need to be with them. Tell the others . . ."

Cabot grimaced as she thought about how they would all take the news. Brix would be devastated—he counted on her. And Birdie and Tenner and Elena would be sad, too. But so would their new friends, Lada and Cabot's precious Librarian. Cabot suddenly questioned whether she could she really do this. There were so many conflicting thoughts going on in her head. Cabot's logical thinking had left her.

But her heart was telling her to be with her parents. So she was going to follow it. She blew out a breath. "Tell the others I love them. And I'm so sorry." Her headache intensified. Lightning struck through her pupils and flashed behind her eyelids when she blinked.

Seven swallowed hard, then clasped Cabot's hand between his. "I'm so glad you found them," he said. "Maybe having you around will help the smartest people I've ever known figure out a way to change their lives."

"Maybe," Cabot said, glancing at her parents in the front seat. They sat rigid, hearing every condescending word and taking it, as if they knew they deserved it.

"All I know is that they'd better not put you in any danger," Seven warned.

"We won't," Jack said through gritted teeth. "We'd *never* do that to her. We're not monsters."

"We'll see about that," Seven said coolly.

Cabot pulled her hand away. "Bye, Seven," she said tearfully. "Thanks for being the best brother I've ever had. And thanks for helping me get to Estero. I love you so much."

Seven choked and had to look away. "I love you, too, Cab. Don't forget what Louis taught us—tell yourself the story every now and then. And think of us all sitting around the fire together, sharing it. Okay?"

Cabot nodded. "You know I won't forget it. I have a photographic memory, remember?"

Seven laughed through his tears. "I remember."

And then Greta slowly pulled the car into the road and headed away. Cabot turned around in her seat and waved to Seven through the back window until they were out of sight.

As Seven stood there, waving back for no one to see, he thought about the story Louis had made them tell, and in his grief, he began to recite it. "How did our parents get here?" he whispered as he turned the other way and started trudging, heavyhearted, toward the SUV a few hundred yards away. "Fifteen years ago, after decades of being oppressed . . ." The words caught in his throat.

The SUV pulled toward him. The window rolled down, revealing The Librarian at the wheel. "Seven!" she said, alarmed.

"Are you okay? Where's Cabot?" She had the earpiece in her ear, but Cabot had never turned hers on again.

Seven's face crumpled. Had he done the right thing? Should he have argued more to get Cabot to come with him? He climbed into the backseat of the vehicle, bent forward, and started sobbing into his hands. "She's gone."

GOOD NEWS AND BAD NEWS

The Librarian made a hasty retreat to the monastery compound while Birdie held Seven in the backseat and stroked his hair and tried not to throw up on him. Once they were back in the cottage and everyone had assembled and given Seven a warm greeting, Seven told the whole story. He filled them in on everything from the moment he stepped onto Fuerte's plane, to the heist and the money exchange he'd been a part of, to his dad's negative reaction after finding out who he really was, to Troy's surprising moment of compassion, to Cabot's reunion with her parents . . . to the part where she'd said goodbye.

"And now I don't know what to think," he said, feeling empty. "Is she gone from our lives forever?"

"No way," said Brix, whose lip was quivering. "She'll come back. She has to."

"She knows where to find us," Birdie said, trying to comfort them both. "Maybe she just needs to spend a day or two with them." But Birdie understood what Cabot was going through.

Just a couple of weeks ago, Birdie had been convinced she was going to leave Estero with her mother. She would have followed her anywhere. And she was so glad to have her—she wouldn't let her go for anything now. Deep down, Birdie didn't think Cabot would ever come back. "Why not send her a text message, Brix? Does she still have her phone, Seven?"

"Yes. I'm not sure how she's going to explain it to her parents, but that's on her now, I guess. She'll come up with something." Seven felt deflated, but he desperately wanted to feel better. He sat up. "At least we know more now about what they're doing. They've recruited about twenty supers, who are living at the palace. They're training them somewhere in Estero City. And now we know why President Fuerte needs a whole different kind of army. It sounds like he was expecting to be exposed as a supernatural person eventually. And he wants to stay in power, because I guess there's an election coming. So when the people of Estero turn against him, he's going to use the supernatural army to fight to stay in power, and turn Estero into a dictatorship." Seven took a deep breath and looked at Birdie. "He's never leaving. Anybody running against him would never succeed—he'll do absolutely anything to stop them."

The Librarian, who seemed preoccupied and out of sorts now that she'd lost her new sidekick, tapped her phone on the chair's armrest a few times. "You did great work, Seven. And I'm so sorry for the trauma you went through, and are still going through, as a result of this. Thanks for taking one for the team." She thought for a long moment, then mused, "Maybe our best move now is to catch Fuerte off guard. And make it clear to him that he doesn't control everything. He doesn't have a free ride to the finish line. We know he's going to play dirty. Well," she said, looking up with a gleam in her eye, "we can play dirty, too."

Seven frowned. "What are you saying?"

She started typing on her phone. "I've got a contact at *Estero City News*. I think now's a great time to break a front-page story, don't you?" She paused and looked up. "Catch him off guard and stop him in his tracks, at least for a minute."

"But he gave back the children," Elena said, worried. "We gave our word."

"Not technically," The Librarian said. "He didn't deliver both children to my awaiting car, as promised. So perhaps we're going to leak the story after all."

"One hundred percent yes," Seven said, sliding to the edge of the sofa. He felt his sorrowful heart lift a little. "Send that video in. These supernatural people are planning to destroy Estero, and if they do, the whole world will turn their hatred for us into something much stronger—full-out war." He sat up straighter. "We need to stop Fuerte. I don't care if he figures out I took the video. He doesn't know who I really am—not yet, anyway. And I bet our crappy parents will keep our identities a secret, if not for our sakes, then for the sake of protecting the hideout location."

The others rallied in support. The Librarian attached the video that Seven had taken and sent it to the newspaper contact.

As they waited for a reply, Seven realized he'd neglected to tell them the one good piece of news, which lifted his spirits even more. "With all the Cabot stuff, I forgot to tell you that I have good news and bad news." He grinned as the others turned to listen. "Right before her parents showed up, Cabot and I found something really important."

"What was it?" asked Tenner.

"We found . . . the stash." Seven clasped his hands together.

"What?" Birdie exclaimed.

"The stash!" Seven exclaimed. "We found it!"

Brix started bouncing around the room. Birdie jumped up in joy, then stopped. "What's the bad news?"

"Well," said Seven, "the bad news is that it's stuck in the attic of a criminal-owned mansion that's surrounded by guards and a deadly electric fence."

"Oh, is that all?" Lada said, waving him off. "Something tells me we'll be having a little look around for that sooner rather than later."

The Librarian's phone rang. "It's my journalist friend." She bit her bottom lip, then answered. After a brief conversation, she hung up and looked at the others. "She's working on another breaking news story at the moment," The Librarian told them, "but she's going to run this story in tomorrow's print newspaper and online with the video. The city of Estero will react hard—I'm warning you. And we need to be ready for anything. We're basically declaring war on the president." She closed her eyes briefly and tapped her fist against her chest. "I desperately wish we had Cabot. I miss her brain already."

THE NEXT DAY

Tenner awoke to the sound of someone dropping a rolled-up newspaper on their back patio. He sprang up and brought the newspaper inside. "It's here!" he called. The others came out of their bedrooms to see what it said.

Tenner spread the newspaper out on the dining table as everyone gathered around. The headline, in huge letters, read:

PRESIDENT FUERTE SECRETLY SUPERNATURAL!

It was accompanied by a screenshot of Fuerte's outstretched hand and the phone in the air, taken from Seven's video.

"Wow!" said Brix. "This is amazing. I know your name isn't in here, but you're kind of famous now, Seven."

"It's okay," said Seven. "I don't need to be famous. I'd rather be . . ." He tilted his head and stopped as he was about to say *invisible*. With a start, he realized that he didn't hate his camouflage quite as much as he used to. Maybe his father hated it enough for them both.

But Seven didn't have time to reflect more, because Tenner spoke up, sounding scared. "Everybody, check out the article *below* the fold."

MAGDALIA PALACIO, POLITICAL NEWCOMER,
ANNOUNCES CANDIDACY FOR PRESIDENT;
HOPES TO OUST FUERTE.

Seven's jaw dropped. "Um," he said, pointing to it. "What's going on?"

Tenner quickly scanned the article and studied the photo that went with it. "Your mom is using her hideout name to run for president. Does she think people won't know she's a supernatural criminal?"

"To be fair, Fuerte is a supernatural criminal, too," Lada said.

"And," The Librarian said, "let's not forget that as of today, the statute of limitations on their earlier crimes is up. And as far as we know, she hasn't committed any more. So she's free to do whatever she wants." She paused. "I wonder if that's why she chose today to announce."

"That means you're free, too, Mom," Brix said, relief in his voice.

Elena nodded. "It's a big day." But the news before them was even bigger.

The group took it in, wondering what it all meant. And wondering how this development was going to affect them.

As Seven read the article, he scratched his head and dropped into a chair, overwhelmed. His father worked for President Fuerte, who had an army of supernatural people preparing to fight. And his mother was about to run against the guy. No wonder they weren't together anymore.

After a while, they heard people shouting outside the monastery walls. Seven laboriously and half-heartedly put on his disguise while the others patiently waited. Then they went outside through the secret wall exit to see what was happening. The people of Estero were gathering in the streets with their neighbors, holding newspapers and cell phones, and lifting their voices in anger.

Seven, Lada, Tenner, Birdie, and Brix stood together, leaving a small space in the middle in honor of Cabot. They put their arms around each other as they watched their neighbors scream terrible things about the president and about supernatural people. Seven, nervous about the way he looked, nevertheless stood tall, and took in the hatred that was being spewed about people like them.

Soon Amanthi and the monks from the monastery filtered over to them, nonchalantly surrounding them. Protecting them, just in case. It was a gift to know the monks would help them if they ever needed it. It gave all of them the courage to go on.

After a while, Seven's nerves calmed. He lifted his chin and removed his sunglasses. Then he took off his gloves, slipped off the floppy hat, unwound his scarf, and stood proudly as a camo boy in the midst of people who thought they hated him.

"I've had enough hiding," he said to his friends, sounding more like a grown-up than he'd ever sounded before—without having to disguise his voice. "We don't need to absorb this hatred anymore. Besides, we have plenty of work to do." He turned to go toward the monastery, leading the others. Ignoring the strangers beginning to point at him and Brix because they looked different.

The group thanked the monks, then returned to safety inside the grounds and retreated to their cottage. Seven tossed his disguise into the front closet. He shivered, then smiled grimly at his own bold, unexpected actions. And he wondered what the future held, now that everything was changing. Now that Cabot was gone. Now that they were in a war with President Fuerte . . . and their own parents.

He had a feeling things were about to get *really* complicated.

ACKNOWLEDGMENTS

MANY THANKS TO my editor, Stephanie Pitts, and the Putnam/ Penguin Young Readers team for your support, guidance, and cleverness, and to my agent, Michael Bourret, for excellence as usual with book number twenty-nine.

Thanks to Stacy McNeely for your thoughtful, careful reading and notes as we strive to tell Lada's story.

Huge thanks to the Nancy Drew community on social media for their overwhelming support of my books, and to Kennedy McMann, who brought us together (and agreed to film a hundred thank-you videos). McMum loves you! And thanks also to Book Posse and Book Allies for their help in telling the world about kids' books. You are the greatest.

Thanks to Kilian McMann for the amazing design work for my school presentation slides. You made me look like a pro.

Thank you, Leo, for the cool supernatural trait ideas—I can't wait to implement them.

Joanne Levy, you are amazing and I'm so grateful for all your help. And Nicole Caliro—you knocked it out of the park.

Deepest thanks for all of your publicity and school scheduling so we could get the word out about these books during difficult times.

Special thanks to all the readers for sharing your love of this series with your friends, teachers, and librarians, and to teachers and librarians for sharing your love of reading with your students.

Booksellers, you rock. Thanks for everything—I mean it.

Finally, to my husband, Matt: I couldn't have pulled this off without you. Thank you for always being there. P.S. You're next.

PHOTO CREDIT: RYAN NICHOLSON

LISA McMANN is the *New York Times* and *USA Today* bestselling author of dozens of books, including the first book in The Forgotten Five series, *Map of Flames*; The Unwanteds series; the Wake trilogy; and *Clarice the Brave*. She is married to fellow writer Matt McMann, and they have two adult children—her son is artist Kilian McMann, and her daughter is actor Kennedy McMann. Lisa spends most of her time in Arizona, California, and Vancouver, British Columbia, and loves to cook, read, and watch reality TV.

You can visit Lisa at
lisamcmann.com

Follow her on Twitter, Instagram, and TikTok
@lisa_mcmann